Special Thanks to:

James and Susan Nohelty

Victoria Nohelty

Paul Jarman

Scott and Victoria Kent

Thomas J Fortunato

Monique

Cordell Falk

Sorry for Existing

By:

Russell Nohelty

Edited by:
Melissa Van Natta

Proofread by:
Katrina Roets

Cover by:
Serenay Daphn

Dedicated to my Pop, our complicated relationship was the basis for this entire book and he died while it was in editing. Thank you to my mother, who somehow had the courage to read this book even while she was grieving. This was the hardest, most personal book I have ever written.

First Edition, May, 2019
Printed in the USA.

www.wannabepress.com

ONE

It started with a bang and a whimper.

Well it wasn't really a bang.

It was more like a slap. Well, exactly like a slap.

Actually, it wasn't really a slap either. It was – what's the sound a fist makes when it connects with a woman's jaw? Like a woomp, or a thud, or a thwonk.

Well, that was the sound. The sound of my mother being punched across the jaw by my father; her hair, her body, suspended motionless for a second, then falling gracefully in slow motion, as I watched horrified and petrified, nestled in the corner behind her.

He'd aimed for me, but Mom jumped between us so that I wouldn't face his assault. She always did that.

She told me that the initial blow was always the worst; that she became numb after the third or fourth hit.

At least that's what she told me. I never believed her. I too often saw the pain on her face when he kicked her ribs for the eighth and ninth times. I watched helpless as the tears welled in her eyes. It was complete and utter misery.

Dad screamed the vilest things imaginable while he beat her. I blocked out the worst of it through years of willful self-delusion. But a few burrowed deep into my memory. I used to wake at night, drenched in cold sweat. His screams jolted me out of my daydreams. They snapped me back to reality.

"You vile, worthless WHORE!"

"Lying sack of shit!"

"Dumb Bitch!"

Those were his favorites. She would cry and cry, for hours it seemed, until giant snot bubbles came out of her nose. He punched, kicked, screamed, and stomped my mother within inches of her life on more than a dozen occasions.

She spent weeks in the hospital, battling to breathe, hoping to die. Punctured lungs, broken noses, and cracked rib cages became the norm; police reports and flimsy denials, standard operating procedure. He didn't like lies, but truths only made him madder and the beatings more vicious. After a spell we kept our mouth shut and did our bid –hoping to one day get paroled.

*

Mom wouldn't let him take out his anger on me. Not on her twelve-year old baby with an oxygen tank; not to the little kid whose simple existence was a miracle. Not to the kid that she made this way.

And I don't mean in the way her egg and his sperm did the freaky-deeky so I could eventually be popped out nine months later.

Though of course that's 100% accurate in the most literal sense. I mean you could interpret it that way for sure. But more so my condition was brought on by their negligence.

I have a condition called pulmonary fibrosis. There's a couple of causes from genetics to environmental factors. It basically meant my lungs were all messed up, scarred over, and didn't work right. If they worked worse, I'd be on a lung transplant list, but they work just well enough that I'll just have crappy lung disease for the rest of my shortened life.

Now, one of the causes of pulmonary fibrosis could have been my mother smoking during pregnancy. As much as I'd love to blame her for that, she took impeccable care while I baked inside her. She didn't smoke, took prenatal vitamins, listened to classical music, and stayed away from fish. She didn't even drink. Not one drop. It wasn't until after my diagnosis that the pills and booze took hold.

No, the cause of my condition comes from being poor; really, really poor; so poor that we couldn't afford adequate housing. Poor enough to squat anyplace that accepted our meager cash, even if it meant buildings riddled with asbestos.

As a child I was susceptible to all sorts of things that my parents' immune system could withstand.

I'm 18 now.

I was 12 during this story.

I was 8 when they diagnosed me.

That's the worst part. My condition wasn't some genetic defect. It wasn't some moment-of-birth botch. It wasn't something I'd lived with my entire life.

I remember being a normal kid; playing sports, running, jumping, living outside a protective cocoon. I remember biting into a fresh apple without tasting sand. I remember breathing without pins and needles stabbing my lungs. I remember a life where my parents didn't blame themselves for my existence, where even for a moment we were blissfully happy.

I mean blissfully happy. Over the moon, laugh every night, Norman Rockwell, Kodak stock portrait happy. The kind of happy we would nauseatingly shake our heads at today. The kind of happy that breaks my heart to think about, because I can never have it again.

Seven though, that was a magical year. Dad came home every night to a warm cooked meal. He regaled Mom with stories of his day as she sat enthralled on the edge of her seat. We made pillow forts and watched old movies that went way over my head, all cuddled up around the tiny CRT Dad found at a yard sale. We were dirt poor. We didn't care though. We didn't need things to be happy. We just needed to be together.

It wasn't meant to last though. I started getting winded at soccer practice, then I could barely make it home from school. My chest began to burn and ache throughout the day and into the night. Then, the wretched coughing started, followed by the blood.

We went to doctor after doctor after doctor and our meager finances ran dry, but Mom and Dad were vigilant. They endured any cost, no matter how high, to ensure that my health was sound.

Specialist after specialist shook their head and confirmed my parents' worst fears. By my eighth birthday it was a foregone conclusion. They didn't get me toys, or video games, or even books. They got me two shiny oxygen tanks. I still use them to this day. Happy Birthday to me, right?

*

As you can imagine, having a kid that lived off oxygen tanks, with hardly any immune system, all because you couldn't afford a nicer place, puts a strain on a marriage financially, emotionally, and physically; even to the most well-adjusted, intelligent, and/or thoughtful among us.

My father was none of the above. Seeing a constant reminder of his shortcomings was too much for him to handle. He, who was supposed to protect me, instead created a feeble monster – kept alive by tubes and machines.

It pissed him off. It pissed him off more every time he looked at me. He was too simple, too stupid, and too cowardly to look inside himself – to beat himself, so he redirected it out onto everybody around him. He was once a gentle giant, now he was consumed by rage.

My mother's love, on the other hand, collapsed upon itself like a neutron star. She grew numb and callused. She gave freely and unrepentantly to my father, who for decades fed off that love to make it through the day. When his rage boiled over, she loved harder and harder. Surely her love could bring him back from the brink. Surely, they could get through this together. Surely, she would not have to go it alone.

No matter how much she gave, it fell into a black hole of rage and bitterness. He shunned her, ignored her, berated her, and eventually beat her when she tried to reason with him. It's very hard to love a man that changed so violently and so quickly. She gave everything of herself away to him and she had nothing left for the child that needed it.

All she could do was use her numb, powerless body to take a beating for me. She had no other way to show her love. She'd given it all away, and my disease overloaded her circuits. It overloaded both of their circuits. I was the surge that fried their marriage.

What an awful place for an eight-year old to be.

*

Mom was a night owl by necessity if not by choice. She hated sleep. More so, she hated dreaming. Once she dreamed of nice homes, butterflies, and fairy tales; that her life would be better, hopeful, possibly, even kind.

Those dreams soured in my ninth year and curdled in my twelfth. By then she hated dreams, not for the nightmares, which showed her the true horrors of her mind, but for the dreams, which filled her with the hope of a better life. There was no better life for Mom, and she hated the flutter in her stomach that accompanied that moment of wakening where she believed her dreams were realities.

Cheap wine helped. Lots of cheap wine. She wasn't picky. It never filled her with restful sleep, but it blocked her dreams from invading her reality. Five, six, some nights eight glasses of wine would be the only thing that allowed her to sleep. When we couldn't afford wine, she skimmed my pills. She skimmed a lot of pills. I learned to live in pain to numb hers.

*

The night after her vicious beating she wandered up to bed early, nursing her wounds. I begged her to call an ambulance, but she refused.

"I know my own body, Sammy. I'm fine," she assured me. One day those words will be emblazoned on her tombstone. "You can get to bed yourself tonight."

Mom never let me get myself to bed. Something was amiss. Every night she tucked me in, kissed me on the cheek, and pulled the oxygen mask over my face.

Oxygen masks are uncomfortable to sleep in. The plastic tube tickled my fingers or wrapped around my turning body, waking me abruptly and unkindly.

I stopped wearing them most nights. Lying in bed never did much to aggravate my condition. My heart calmed, my breathing slowed, and my body stopped shaking profusely. Only my mind raced faster in the darkness.

*

I never slept well. I tossed and turned. I twitched and fidgeted. I sighed and harrumphed. I jerked awake and laid silently for hours. I peeked into hallways and listened for fights, whether arguments or bare-knuckle brawls. I stared at the ceiling or out the window toward the stars, wishing I could get lost in them forever. I waited patiently for an ambulance or a weekly run to the emergency room.

In those rare instances when I slept early and deeply – when the stars aligned, and the sleep fairies released me from their dance between awake and sleep – those were undoubtedly the nights when I woke gasping for air.

Those nights worried me the most – ironically, they kept me up more than any other. I hated choking and gasping for every molecule of air. But more than that, I feared an oxygen tank exploding in the night and killing me in my sleep – or worse, leaving me disfigured and even more crippled. I feared I would never wake up and I feared I would.

*

I enjoyed dreams though, when they came. My imagination was the only place I could become normal again. My dreams weren't filled with the knights, Dark Knights, spaceships, fantasies, or wild pursuits that accompanied most peoples' dreams. They were filled with the simple moments, the lost moments, the hopeful moments that were never meant to be.

I dreamed of my fourth birthday, when my Father built a swing set out of discarded lumber. The stupid thing wouldn't sit straight, and after a week it crumbled to the ground. "But I built it, Sammy. You have to give me credit for that."

I did, of course. It did little to offset the brutality of his later years, but he did get credit for being a good father eight years of my life. I dreamt often of him carrying me around the house in his arms when I was just a tiny poop machine. He sang to me; terribly, of course, but he sang to me. The look of love in his eyes in those dreams, I tried to hold onto that, remember that there used to be a warm-hearted man where now a cold, brutal monster lurked.

Dreams never filled me with the pain and suffering they elicited in my mom. Dreams were what my life should have been, could have been, might have been, and one day might be again. I know it was a stupid thing to hope, but hope is all somebody sickly has most days, most moments of most days. Pills, injections, doctors, abuses, and constant pain drove you insane, something had to pull you back from the edge. For me, it was those dreams.

*

It was well past midnight when her frail hands jostled me awake. I'd been deep in a dream about my father teaching me how to grip a baseball bat. Mom clamped my lips tight. "Get up. And be quiet about it."

"But—"

"Don't question me! Just do it!" I hadn't heard my mother stern in a long time.

Her frail desperation masked the fire of a warrior; a determined, stoic yeoman. Most people, places, things, and even ideas would have petered and died when faced with the living nightmare she dealt with on a daily basis.

"Stay quiet," she said. "Grab your oxygen tanks."

"Where are we—?"

"Just grab them, alright?"

I scooped up my two tanks into their ripped backpack case and squeezed her hand. Her pulse thumped loudly through her cadaverous fingers.

"Careful," she whispered over her shoulders. "Only step where I step."

I mimicked her pointed feet as we tiptoed down the hallway and down the stairs toward the front lawn. It was slow going. My mother calculated every move carefully, tiptoeing over the cracks and loose floorboards of the landlord's shoddy, ramshackle house.

Every move she made was masterful, a stroke of genius. It was as if a ballerina replaced my mother. She knew which floorboard wouldn't creak and where the safest landings were. She slid ever so carefully down the banister so that the middle three stairs wouldn't squeak – and jumped off centimeters before it swayed and cracked.

We eventually reached the front door. She swung it open just enough to avoid tipping off the rusty hinges and slid me outside. Her face peeked out of the door, then disappeared back inside.

"Run!" she screamed through the partially closed door. I stood frozen for seconds that felt like years. I heard Mom's ragdoll body crash against the door with a heavy thump.

My feet separated from my brain and rushed forward on their own. They slammed into the door once, twice, three times. My brain knew it was a bad idea, but the rest of my body didn't care. My tiny, frail body reared back a fourth time and finally crashed through the door.

The force knocked Dad over. He stumbled backward against the staircase.

"You little shit!" he screamed.

Mom stuffed her keys in my hand and shoved me back out the door. "Go! Start the car!"

I'd never done anything like that before, but I obeyed. My chest burned with a fire I hadn't felt in a long time; panic, excitement, my lungs collapsing. I had to fight through it. My mom's life depended on it. I saw the fire in my dad's eyes. Rage overtook him completely. There was no semblance of humanity in him, nothing could hold back his fury. If I didn't get Mom out tonight, she'd be dead by morning.

I heard her scream again and again as I fumbled with the keys. I managed to open the door and slide into the driver's seat. Mom's belabored breath struggling out a whimper through the door. "Hurry."

The neighborhood's normally darkened porches suddenly illuminated. I didn't care. My father didn't care. Even the neighbors didn't care. They just wanted to make sure that their cars weren't being robbed or vandalized.

I stuck the key in the ignition and turned until the car puttered to life. Mom sprinted out the front door. "It's on," I shouted. "Hurry up!!!"

"Move over!" she yelled.

I scooted myself into the passenger seat just as she jumped inside; her nose bled; her eye swelled. She wheezed in pain as she threw the car into reverse and tore out of the driveway, taking the mailbox with her and barely missing a neighbor's cat.

My father leapt out of the front door and flung himself on the car as my mother shifted the car into drive.

"Whore! You dumb, freaking whore," he screamed. "Stop this car right now or I'm gonna kill you!!!"

Mom clenched her eyes closed and floored the gas pedal. Dad lost his balance and crashed into the windshield. He bounced as we sped up and hit the roof, caving it under his massive weight.

He rolled off the trunk, limp and motionless. The last thing I remember was watching my father lay on the ground, blood pooling around him.

I hoped he was dead.

TWO

We spent the next week praying that Dad was dead. We wished on shooting stars, threw pennies in wells, held our breath, prayed, and crossed our fingers, hoping he was dead. We dreamt of a life without him. We fantasized of a world where our every move wasn't scrutinized or brutalized.

Those fantasies quickly faded into reality, though. Our hopes and dreams became horrifying truths when we realized just how screwed Mom would be if Dad died. She'd at least be convicted of manslaughter or vehicular homicide, if not premeditated murder and kidnapping for what she did. Those happy thoughts we held in our mind's eye quickly replaced themselves with dread and panic after the first week.

He would have killed us if we hadn't left. We knew that, but what would the neighbors say? Would they back us up when the cops came? Would did they think when they saw us driving off in the night leaving my dad to die in the middle of the street like a dog?

*

It haunted us in every new town we passed through. I kept my head on a swivel with every officer we passed. Mom kept the TV off and played the same Carole King record on repeat to avoid the radio. She was sure police blotters would tell news channels, which would tell radios, which would send out an Amber alert for me and make Mom America's Most Wanted.

"What's your name, ma'am?" a clerk asked our first night out of town.

"Underhill," my mother replied without hesitation. "Gloria Underhill."

It happened night after night in dump after dump. She always used a different name. She slipped extra ten-dollar bills into the clerks' hands and we never heard another word about it.

They handed us keys to dirt-infested hovels and we kept to ourselves. Ironically, they were probably filled with asbestos.

Every week she dyed her hair, cut her bangs, bought a wig, or changed her appearance in some way or another. Once, she took a marker and drew a nasty mole on her cheek. Nobody looked at her then.

She loved that. She loved the freedom to blend. She loved that nobody looked over her shoulder. She hadn't had that in half a decade or more. It just sucked what she had to do to get it.

*

Over time, the pieces of my mother's plan crystalized into sharp focus. This wasn't some fly by night operation. She planned every piece meticulously over years.

The second and sixteenth of every month, when my father's paycheck cleared, she stopped at the grocery store, bought two weeks of groceries, and asked for $20 in cash from the register. She tossed the receipt before she left the store. All Dad ever saw was the credit card charge.

"Jesus Christ," Dad always said. "When did groceries get so expensive?!"

"That's the cost of taxes," Mom responded. It deflected blame seamlessly off her and onto the government. My father hated the government, even though half of our family's household income came from welfare and food stamps. Even though without the government, we would be on the street. Even though without Medicaid, I would be dead.

"Stealing all our money, shipping jobs off to China, insert other Fox News buzzword," he spewed over whatever government subsided meal my mother cobbled together. He blamed the government for his terrible job, his crappy salary, and his awful life, instead of realizing he was just the worst.

Mom ran a perfect scam. After all, what was $20 on a $200 bill? But for my mother is meant $40 a month, every month. Over a year that's $480. After a half a decade it's nearly $2,500; enough to run for a bit, as long as you were careful.

She'd tried to muster up the courage to leave for six months, before she finally pulled the trigger. That last beating left her no choice. She wouldn't survive another one. Her will to live waned with each passing day. Another hit and she wouldn't be able to fight the sweet release of death. And she couldn't leave me alone with a monster.

She grabbed a suitcase she kept packed, her keys, and me. As long as she had those three things, she would be fine.

Except she forgot my father passed out on the couch. He was a light sleeper. Even the flap of a butterfly's wings roused him. Mom was careful, oh so careful, but she wasn't perfect. A slight creak of a beam or the whinny of the front door or even a gust of cold wind woke him. His drowsy eyes focused on my mother scuttling out the door. The rest you know.

*

We lived well in those first days, content and even momentarily happy from time to time. Smiles flickered across our world-weary faces on more than one occasion, and I even heard my mother laugh once. I hadn't heard her laugh in half a decade.

But living well came with a price; a literal price. We watched our meager fortunes dwindle, wane, and vanish. To continue running, we had to work.

In town after town we struggled. Even though being a mother was 20 full time jobs, employers didn't care. They saw an out of work loser with no job skills, not a cook, psychologist, bodyguard, chauffeur, rock god, et al.

We had no social security cards, driver's license, bank card, or anything to tie us to a past, so that made filling out an I-9 or proving we were US citizens difficult at best, which meant only the shadiest of the shady companies, ones that paid cash and didn't ask questions, would look our way; companies that didn't live up to the high standards of cleanliness that a rural hut in Somalia upheld.

What work she found didn't last long. Mom was perpetually skittish, which forced us to uproot our lives every two weeks; just long enough to get paid.

*

While she worked, I panhandled on the street. I made up signs to alleviate the boredom and kept track of which ones worked best. My best-seller was "BORED, SICK, HUNGRY, AND BROKE. ENTERTAIN ME, MEDICATE ME, FEED ME, OR PAY ME. DON'T CARE WHICH."

One time an old man propositioned me; $20 to follow him into a back alley for five minutes. It was a bad idea no doubt, but $20 was more than my mom made most days, so I went.

I turned the corner and caught a full-frontal shot of his tiny penis. I chuckled.

"Wanna touch it?" he asked.

I didn't. I didn't even like touching my own tiny penis. We sat in silence for five minutes, him naked as a jay bird, me averting my eyes. Then, as promised, he handed me $20, and bought me dinner as a bonus. I never told anybody about that.

Stuff like that happened from time to time. But most days, things were so mundane it almost hurt. Mom worked. I panhandled outside. We scraped together every measly penny we could. Some days it was enough for a nice dinner and a hotel room, sometimes it was tacos and a motel, others it was stale bread and the back seat of our car.

*

People ask me all the time, "What's the worst part of being homeless?" which is kind of like asking, "What's the worst part of getting your testicles ripped off?" It's all bad.

I always felt guilty giving my answer, because I was homeless for such a short time in the grand scheme of things. I'd met people who'd been homeless for fifty years, with no hotel, motel, or Holiday Inn; people so far gone from the system that they couldn't work.

I met those with jobs, for sure; real jobs, honest jobs, and yet still they couldn't make enough to break the cycle. Some of them even had two jobs, but they were paid so little at each job, that they couldn't have gotten by if they worked seven.

But for the most part, the people I met weren't one hot meal away from turning it around. They couldn't just shower, shave, and pull themselves up by the bootstraps. They had serious, real, debilitating mental and physical problems. They'd been left to rot by their families—or lost their families and became unwelcome wards of the state. They ran away from abusive homes and never ran back, and lost every chance they ever got, either from their own carelessness or the fickle hand of fate.

They'd fallen to drugs, or apathy, and as the years went on, they lost all hope. I met them at every stage, and I knew all kinds. I'd met the ones just starting out after getting a bad beat, the ones who couldn't panhandle because they "looked too clean". I met those living in shelters and those unfortunate enough to be turned away.

I hung out with homeless people. After a couple years in, the hope faded from their eyes. They wanted, needed to believe for so long that their situation was temporary; that they were good people fallen on hard times and things would turn around for them. But they knew the reality in the back of their minds. Their skid wasn't turning around.

The long time homeless scared me; not because of their disabilities or "craziness" either. It was because of how easy their slide happened. Their stories were equally horrific and amazing. Captains of industries struck down by car accidents and heart attacks, men and women who'd birthed children and taught and gave back to society, forced to eat garbage. Teachers and bureaucrats felled by a chemical imbalance. Middle class legacies bankrupted by medical bills.

True, some were lazy. Okay, many were lazy. More than I'd like to admit were just lazy. But it wasn't the majority, not even close.

That was the worst part. The fear, the driving fear, every day that I would become them; that we would become them.

I feared every minute that even if we ended up in a better state, I'd turn into them some day. It took so little, it seemed.

The pain of withheld or rationed medications, of unfilled oxygen tanks, of skipping meals, were nothing compared to that fear, which haunted me every day of my life. Still does.

*

It went on like that for a time, driving from town to town, sleeping in our car, scraping just enough to get by if we were lucky, but it couldn't last. I hadn't been to the doctor in months and I felt my body shutting down.

I hated doctors, but they were essential to keep my condition in check. I hung out in a lot of waiting rooms. I smiled politely at thousands of terrible doctor jokes. Some weeks I visited doctors more than I attended school. I was on more medications than a geriatric octogenarian with cancer.

And therein laid the CATCH 22.

My mother stashed enough excess medication to last for a spell, but not forever, especially not the pain killers. Of all the drugs and cocktails prescribed to me, the pain killers helped the most. They were the only drugs that made life bearable. The others only kept me upright, wheezing in misery.

We ran out of the painkillers faster than anything else, and my pain was becoming more and more unbearable. Mom's blatant skimming didn't help matters either. She didn't take much at first, just enough for me to notice. The longer we ran, the more she took.

We couldn't just go to the doctor either; not without them figuring out my real name. There were only so many kids with my condition in the entire country. You could run an exhaustive search in the time it takes to cook and eat a

Lean Cuisine. Plus, they always ran blood tests to check for problems, and my DNA is on file with EVERYBODY.

On top of that, when you don't exist, you don't qualify for Medicaid. Without Medicaid, we couldn't afford the doctor bills.

Frankly, we were really stuck. Even at the discounted rates given to us by pitying clinics, the charge was double what we'd cleared from months on the run. I told my mom to leave me, to keep going, but she refused.

"I've kept you alive this long, I'm not leaving you now," she said to me, over and over. I could see it in her face and hear it in her voice though, she was running out of options.

Then, one day she came home from work. We were staying at a rundown motel at the outskirts of town. My mother had "splurged" on it. We'd been living out of our car for the last week. I was too sick to panhandle by then.

"Pack your stuff," she said. And that was all she said. She wouldn't answer my questions. She didn't say one more word. So, I packed in silence.

THREE

We drove straight through the endless night. I nodded off for a couple minutes at a time between rotations of smooth jazz, classic rock, and Kesha (without the dollar sign). I forced Mom to buy some different tapes during our travels. Carole King made me want to kill myself more than I already did, which was a lot.

At some point early the next morning, I woke up to a familiar site and stench so strong it broke through my terrible sense of smell. It was unmistakable; the garbage dump next to Pops' house.

My mom swore up and down she'd never go back there. She decreed even with a gun to her head, facing a lifetime of destitute suffering, and without the prospects of making a single dollar for the rest of her life, she'd never be caught dead within a thousand miles of her father's house. Yet there we were, less than a mile from it.

In that moment a thought ticker taped across the base of my brain: *we must be royally screwed.*

We hadn't been back for three years. We hadn't stepped foot in city, county, state, or even region for nearly a decade. So deep was Mom's hatred for her father, it had driven us 20 states away. Now, we had boomeranged back due to her hatred for mine.

*

We left the day her mother, my Nana, died. We left before Nana's body was cold in the ground. We left straight from the service, before they even buried her. "It's what she would have wanted," Mom said. She was right too. All Nana ever wanted was a ticket out of East Willow.

To call Nana a saint was a blasphemous insult. The patience she had, considering everything heaped on her, confounded reason and logic. It equaled her more to a demi-god than a lowly saint.

She'd made it over across the Atlantic from Czechoslovakia at three years old. She survived the bitter cold and crippling sea sickness to work in the filth and the muck with her five brothers. She could survive anything. She was a survivor; it's where my mom got it from.

Nana's family wasn't prepared for the torturous and brutal conditions of the mines and factories in which they'd slaved. Deplorable conditions, long hours, negligence, hunger, and disease picked them off one by one, until only Nana remained. Of all of her parents' children, she was the least wanted. That is to say, she wasn't wanted at all.

Still, she tried to make herself useful sewing garments for a few shekels, but even that was insufficient for her parents. Without a man to carry on their bloodline, a baby girl was useless to them. She was simply another mouth to feed. They searched for any way to jettison her dead weight.

Her frail body and narrow hips didn't ingratiate her to buyers. Desperate, they unloaded her on a miserable schlep for a pittance, and the girl was surrendered for less than winning second prize at a beauty pageant.

Their marriage was fraught with misery. She never willingly gave herself to him. He derived great pleasure in taking what he wanted from her. His nightly raping brought nothing more than miscarriage after miscarriage. After a dozen failed attempts, he cast her aside for a more malleable model.

Nana's parents refused her pleas for shelter. She lived out in the cold for a time before a kind-hearted man found her. A man she grew to love more than she thought possible. One that provided for her, cared for her, nurtured her, and believed in her. A man that died in battle serving his country and whose name she never took. A man that left her with nothing upon his sudden death in World War II.

Thrown into another tailspin, Nana fell into the arms of a new man; one gruff like her father: a dolt, callus and brazen, everything she hated about men; my Pop, a man who tried his best to love a woman that treated him with indifference.

She continued on that way until her death – or I should say the day she stopped breathing. She died the day her true love did.

As a good Catholic woman, she could never condone suicide. But she could smoke and drink and hope it would eventually catch up with her.

It took longer than she thought, decades too long, but she got her wish, gasping on the fluid-filled lungs that her emphysema brought; going to her grave with the bitter stench of the landfill which she decried throughout her miserably long life. The same particles my inefficient nose gathered as we drove up to Pop's house.

*

I don't understand how it can be so hard to create a loving environment for the people you claim to love. I know life is hard and people are hard, but if you love something, you should treat it with…love and respect, you know?

I know, I really, really know, that my pop loved my nana and my mom as much as my dad loved my mom and me. That's a whole heck of a lot. My dad loved me so much that my infirmities drove him mad; like literally mad.

I heard it in the way he talked about her after her death. "She was everything to me," he said the morning of her funeral. "I loved her more than life itself," he claimed when the coroner came for her body. "I gave her my soul," he said when he identified the body.

Those moments bore into my soul. They were so incongruent with the man he showed to Nana during her life. I never heard him talk to her with that kind of love. His voice was always harsh, grating, and mean. He screamed at her, berated her, and took out his miserable life on her. The same way my father took out his miserable life on Mom.

More and more, I believe that everybody has a miserable life, if not always then at least at times. Every single person on this planet is going to have a miserable life; misery follows people. Maybe it won't be as miserable as mine, but miserable none the less.

It's how you deal with that misery that determines if you're a good person or a bad person. Even bad people love. Even bad people care. Bad people miss people and bad people cry when their loved ones die.

But good people, they treat the ones they love well even in the darkest, hardest time. Even when all hope is lost, they default to love, they default to peace, they default to kindness.

That's all I've ever wanted in my life: a little kindness, a little compassion, and a little understanding from the ones I loved. I've gotten it in the best of times. I got it until I turned eight, until my diagnosis. But in the worst of times, even in the mediocre of times, when things didn't go their way even a little bit, my loved ones defaulted to anger and callous indifference.

I never saw Pop in bad times. I only saw him retired, living on a pension, getting fat. Pride swelled through him when I was around; his first and only grandson. It was easy for him to be good to me, and he always was. The bad times were reserved for Mom and Nana.

*

We pulled up to Pop's house; tears streamed down Mom's face. Without Nana, there would be nobody to deflect Pops' full-frontal assault. Her body shook from her head down to her fingers, which clenched the vibrating steering wheel.

"We don't have to do this," I told her. "Why are we even here?"

My mom's lips unclenched. She'd bitten clean through the skin. "Because we're out of options, kiddo."

Mom jammed the car into park in front of Pop's house. She was no happier than I at our recent turn of fortunes. Neither of us had any love for Pop, though admittedly my seething bitterness was borne second hand – stories told from my mother which turned Pop into persona non grata – a pariah that treated my nana and mother with such willful neglect it drove one to her premature death and the other into the arms of my abusive father.

The putrid stench of Pop's misdeeds stank more than the foul smell emanating from the landfill that abutted his house. There are many things I wished to smell again. At the bottom of that list would be the pungent smell which somehow stuck to my nasal passages. *Why couldn't roses smell so strong?*

"I can't do it, kiddo," Mom confessed, white-knuckling the door handle.

"You don't have to," I responded. "We can make it on our own."

"I know one thing, kiddo. No matter how much I try, we can't make it on our own." Mom's face sunk with each passing moment. It took several unspoken seconds for her to choke out two words. "You'll die."

I clasped my hands over hers. "I'll die either way."

"Not as soon. Not until you're an old man." She shook her head. "I'm not going to let you die young. I'm not going to let that happen, even if I have to die trying."

She meant it too. The day we learned about my prognosis, she offered her lungs – both of them – if I could live a normal life. She would have pulled them out herself, Temple of Doom style, except she wasn't a donor match.

My death would literally kill her. Maybe not overnight; it might be the slow death that befell Nana, but she would be as good as dead the moment my heart stopped beating. Mom didn't show much emotion, but I knew that much to be true. She still loved me, even if sometimes, she had a hard time showing it.

*

That truth led her to open the car door, though not without a deep sigh; one last, sweet taste of freedom, poisoned by the putrid smell of landfill.

Pop wasn't a large man by any measure. His age filled out his blue-collar face and midsection, but underneath the layers of flabby skin laid the skeletal structure and rippling muscle of a hard-working man. Years of lifting trash cans and hauling junk molded him into a little ball of strength that lasted into his old age. He must have been a fearsome sight to behold on the warpath, but I mostly knew him as a kitty cat, as least toward me. He unleashed the brunt of his assault on others.

His voice boomed and echoed across the distance at the sight of me. "MY BOY! How are ya?!"

He wrapped me in a bear hug. "You're crushing me," I groaned.

He dropped me. "Sorry. I'm just glad to see ya. It's been too long."

Pop always treated me kindly. He never raised his voice in anger and only resorted to insulting my mother in the harshest whispers when he thought I was out of earshot. If not for what I'd gleaned from my mother's life, I would have thought him a king, and I, his prince.

"It's been a long time," he said to Mom. They hugged like two strangers meeting for the first time. "You're so thin. Not like last time I saw ya."

"Don't start, Dad," Mom responded. "It's been a long trip."

"Didn't have to be. You shoulda called me first."

"You're lucky I called at all."

"No. You are. Otherwise you'd be dead in a gutter somewhere. Come on. Let's get you inside."

FOUR

Pop's house smelled of musk, born from years of neglect. Waves of stale air knocked the wind out of me. His house, though small, had always exuded the pleasant homey touches of my Nana. With her death, its once quaint touches fell into disrepair. Pop lived in another generation. He couldn't take care of himself any more than a baby could.

The door fought against us as we pushed inside. Dishes piled up in the sink. Stacks of newspapers lined the floor. Half gnarled toys and discarded junk lay strewn on the kitchen table.

"You can get those later," he said over his shoulder. "Earn your keep and whatnot."

Mom nearly turned back right then and there. Her fingers clenched my shoulder so tightly I winced. *Everything would be alright if I kept moving forward,* I told myself. *Never look back.*

We turned from the kitchen up a narrow hallway into a tiny bedroom that represented the worst years of my mother's childhood: a room no bigger than a prison cell, a cell she'd shared with boarders during lean times. There were many lean times.

"Here we are," Pop said. "Shangri-La."

Our suitcase landed on one of the beds with a plume of dust. "Sorry," Pop said. "It's been a while since I cleaned. You can handle that, right?"

Mom stood in silence for several seconds. Finally, her lips spread. "How about you unpack your things for a minute while Pop and I talk outside, Sammy."

"Dresser is all yours now, kiddo," Pop added

Mom pulled Pop out the door. I inched forward and leaned my head against the door.

"Are you kidding me, Dad? He can barely breathe as it is, and you want him to sleep in that death trap?!"

"It'll build character." "His whole life is character, Dad. Kid's got more character in his left pinky than most people have in their whole body—some, even after 80 odd years of life."

"You called me, remember?"

"Yeah, for help. And this isn't helping. I'm not your maid, neither is Sammy. This place is riddled with disease."

For the first time in forever Mom's words carried weight. Pride filled her voice – more than I had seen in the entire previous decade combined. I couldn't help but smile.

*

I slept in a tent for six days while mom disinfected, decluttered, and scrubbed every inch of Pop's house until it was Sammy proof. Pop just watched, baffled, like a child who'd just seen their first rainbow. The outside never bothered me as much as inside dander and other stuff. Even with the garbage dump, I was better outside of the dust filled house.

Pop never paid attention while Nana cleaned – too busy complaining about work, reading his newspapers or drinking his beer – too lost in thought to care how things got done; he only cared that they were done.

It was backbreaking work keeping a home for Pop. He was a stickler for a perfection no one could achieve, try as Nana might. He cursed and screamed at the slighted misstep.

Nana woke up at night drenched in cold sweat and in a panic thinking she'd forgotten some miniscule detail that would raise Pops ire. She often hopped out of bed to re-clean a pantry in the middle of the night.

It was a horrible, miserable way to live, but in death she got her revenge. I've never seen a man so distraught, so out of sorts, as Pop in the years since her death. Now, he lived in squalor.

"I loved that woman. Lord knows, I loved her. We were the love of each other's lives. She never wanted for a thing."

*

There's one thing I can't stand and that's a liar, whether to others or themselves. Pop was a master at self-delusion. Self-delusion is nothing, if not a lie we spin for ourselves. One thing I knew for sure, Nana wanted for something.

Nana had one dream in her long, miserable life; a dream that many people of her age and time echo, a dream to move to Florida. I don't know why that became the dream for so many of the "Greatest Generation", nor have I ever bothered to ask, but it drove Nana during her later years.

"We'll go next year," he told her over and over. What killed me was how much excitement Nana had for her plan. She always thought Pop spoke the truth.

He'd promised Nana year after year, decade after decade, over and over that they'd go. For all the misery she endured, it was probably that thought and that thought alone that kept her going.

She piled up brochures and pamphlets. She kept them stacked in a box next to her favorite smoking recliner. She'd pull them out at least once a day to check the bent and worn corners for overlooked gems of information.

Then one day, out of the blue, they were gone. Vanished. She went to Pop and asked him about it, but he stoned himself off like a wall. He'd even trashed the little Mickey Mouse figurine Nana kept on the dashboard of her car.

"I neva wanna hear you talk about Florida again, you hear me?" he said. "It ain't gonna happen!"

No explanation or reason, right out of thin air. Nana smoked double after that. She reeked of cigarettes so deeply that Pop couldn't stand to be in the same room as her without coughing up a lung, which was exactly the way she wanted it.

*

Our family often took treks down to the shore, a cheap replacement for Nana's crushed dreams. It satiated a need for Nana, a need to put her feet in the sand and hear the soothing lapping of the waves meeting the shore, but it also reminded her of the broken promises Pop had made.

I was a naïve child, completely oblivious to the tensions oozing from every pore between Mom, Dad, Nana, and Pop. I just loved being at the beach. Long boardwalks full of games, pretzels dipped in lye to accentuate their golden color, fries drowned with vinegar, and cotton candy bigger than your head.

I mean yeah, there were syringes and glass along the beach and the seaweed sludge made boogie boarding gross, but the BEACH! God, we loved the beach. Each and every one of us. I never heard Nana laugh harder or joke longer than at the beach, and Mom followed suit, which lightened the mood for both Dad and Pop.

Pop's luck determined the quality and vigor of our dinner. He loved the horses nearly as much as pounding slots, but really, he just loved the thrill of winning. He loved believing that something could pull him out of his crappy life and deliver unto him the untold bliss being rich afforded.

He brought that into the rest of his life, always looking for a quick fix, playing the lottery, scheming to find a way out of misery. "I'll give you twenty thousand dollars when I win the lottery," he told Mom, "and you'll move in with us and ditch that loser husbanda yours."

Mom placated him for a while, but Nana muttered back. "There's no amount of money that's worth being in his debt."

Mom and Nana spent their days at the shore sunbathing and watching the water lap along the beach, while Pop and Dad disappeared into the nearest casino; Pop to the sports book and Dad to the poker tables.

After a good session, we ate steak and they drank wine. They'd buy me a mug of soda, milkshakes, and anything else I wanted. After losing, which happened more often than not, we'd spend the rest of our time on the shore eating day-old hot dogs and sipping water.

*

The losses happened, shore or not. They happened so often that hot dogs and water became the norm. Dad only had enough cash flow to make gambling a vacation extravagance, but for Pop it was a way of life.

He spent every third Saturday at the track, hemming and hawing over which horse to pick. He'd visit the stables, interview the jockeys, and rub down the horses.

"I got a good feelin' about this one," he said right before putting money down on a loser.

He spent every Wednesday rubbing dozens of scratchers with his lucky quarter. "Loser. Loser. Loser." He'd shake his head and mutter under his breath.

Pop spent forty dollars a week on gambling, for about 60 years. In the nine years I'd known him, he'd only won three grand back. That's sixty grand in the hole over a lifetime, enough to build a nice, little house in Florida, but hearing the raw numbers of his defeat would kill every last bit of hope he had.

While he'd no problem destroying that hope in others, he needed it to burn bright for himself.

*

Pop was a master at ruining your day. He knew the precise moment to hit you with an innocuous bit of knowledge, after which your entire day would be ruined. He'd strike quick like it was nothing and scratch his head when you made a big deal out of it.

Whether it was during a good book, or after a good dump, he knew instinctively the moment of least tension, and let fly. I experienced it for the first time in those early days of our stay. I laid on the couch watching reruns of Judge Judy, when Pop plopped himself down next to me.

"Your Dad's not dead, ya know," Pop said.

Just flat out, like it was nothing. Like he was telling me he bought chocolate pudding or that my hair looked weird. Instead of that, it was the most important news in the entire universe.

I wondered why he waited so long to tell me, but in my gut, I knew it was the thrill of misery. It wasn't even a conscious need to see misery in others. It was so ingrained in his very nature that he reflexed to it, natural as breathing.

"He's not in a coma neither," he continued. "He got a couplea cuts and scrapes, but otherwise he looked fine."

I hoped for a broken leg or separated shoulder, but Dad was too lucky for such injuries. He inflicted them upon others, not sustained them.

"He spent a couple of days in the hospital for observation and they let him go." It was all true too. After his stay, the hospital shook him upside down a few times and found nothing but dust bunnies, so they let him walk free and clear; they can't take much from a man who has nothing. That should be my dad's motto.

Dad came to see Pop a few days after his release. He tilted at windmills though, and he left as quickly as he came. Dad knew it was hopeless. Mom would never be so desperate that she had to seek out Pop's counsel and shelter; not so early into her emancipation at least. It would take months for that level of desperation to sink in.

"I tried to reach out to your mother," Pop said, "but I was the last person she wanted to see. Just hoped that you'd come if you needed anything. And here you are."

All that running was for nothing. I couldn't believe it. *All that time looking over our shoulders for nothing.*

*

On a positive note, Dad's untimely recovery meant we could file for the Medicaid I so desperately needed. It was a risk to be sure, but my father wasn't known for his stick-to-itiveness.

We figured he'd given up and drowned his memories of us in vast quantities of booze.

We already searched the Amber Alert Website at the local library, the last bastion of connectivity for the hopelessly poor, and any outstanding warrants for my mother. We found nothing on either. Like I said, my dad was not known for his stick-to-it-iveness. He couldn't even file a police report right.

It's probably why he'd had 37 jobs the year before we left. That's more than a job every two weeks. He lost most of them before payday for a bevy of reasons: at least three he got the job and was too hungover to show up the first day, a half-dozen he cursed out his manager, another dozen he cursed out a customer, a handful he fought with an employee, a few he miscounted the register after his shift, and a couple just didn't like him. He blamed the government for it all, of course.

*

Twenty minutes after ripping open our Medicaid acceptance letter, my mom strong-armed our way into the nearest doctor's office.

Ten minutes after that, I sat in paper robes and socks, feet dangling off the side of the exam table, while a fiery-haired nurse named Susan Nohelty took my blood pressure. I got to know her well over the following months. She was saving up to meet her husband in Ithaca. He went there to raise Alpacas and ended up running for city council.

"You're a little low, kiddo," Susan said. "Have you been light-headed recently?"

"I've never seen him faint," Mom blurted. "I've never seen him stumbling or anything."

"You're underweight too," Susan continued. "Have you been eating regularly? Are you skipping meals?"

"I feed him three squares a day. I promise you that."

"I'm sure you do, ma'am," Susan said with a sigh. "Just be patient. The doctor will be with you soon."

The doctor never came in shortly. The nurses placated us with pleasantries, but they were clueless. They told us whatever they could to keep up some semblance of patience while the doctor took his sweet time ambling in. "Shortly" was a guess, at best. It could mean three minutes, three hours, three years, or three decades. I understand nurses have to say SOMETHING, but the lying pisses me off.

I paced around the room for a while; minutes, hours, years, decades I couldn't tell. By the time the doctor finally knocked on the door, I'd ran myself ragged. *Why did they even knock? What could I possibly be doing, except waiting for them? Masturbating? With my Mom in the room? Come on.*

"Good afternoon, Samuel. My name is Dr. Morris, but you can call me Phil." *Ugh.* I hated when they wanted us to be on a first name basis. *Newsflash; I don't want to be your friend.*

"You can call him Sammy," my mom interjected. "I'm--"

"Mom!" I shouted.

"Well, Sammy," he continued, unfazed. "Actually, do you like Sammy or Samuel better?"

"I don't care," I responded.

"I'm going to call you Samuel. Samuel is a strong name. You're a strong fellow, aren't you, Samuel? Of course, you are. Only a strong man could deal with all the…well, what we doctor types call crap…that's the technical term anyway…that you've been through at your age. Right, Samuel?"

"I guess you're right."

Dr. Phil flipped through the chart. "Of course, I'm right. That's why they pay me to hold this chart. Samuel, I'm going to cut to the chase. You have what we call in the business a huge bummer of a problem."

"That's an understatement."

"I'm not telling you something new, right, Samuel? I mean, you know that what you're going through sucks. And you probably feel kind of sucky, right?"

"I would say that's my normal state, yes."

"But do you feel any suckier than usual?"

I shook my head. "Not especially."

He threw down the chart. "Great! I'm going to order the usual battery of tests. I'm sure your familiar wit—"

"Bloodwork, urine test, stress test, breathing test— your general CYA tests."

"Yadda, yadda, yadda. Boring stuff, pretty mundane – unless it saves your life. Let's make a follow up in six weeks to go over the results and see how you're doing then. Unless you're dead of course. That was a joke."

"I get it."

"Of course, you do. Once the blood tests come back and we're sure you're not going to die on the spot, you can enroll in school. I'm sure a stud like you can't wait to be introduced to the general female population."

I gulped. *School. I hadn't even thought of school yet.*

*

Four days later my father received a call from the Medicaid office confirming that he wanted to enroll me in a different state. My dad was drunk off his ass, high on painkillers, and out of his mind. He said yes to everything they said. He would have said yes if they asked him to have sex with a donkey on national TV.

They hung up, he rolled over and passed out again. It would be three more weeks until he realized what happened. Three more weeks of peace.

FIVE

I hated school. I despised reading, writing, and 'rithmetic. Too much homework made me even sicker to my stomach than I already was on a daily basis. I loathed teachers and disliked the overwhelming majority of my classmates.

The thing I hated most was the simultaneous combination of pity, contempt, and ridicule seething from every corner, waiting to pounce and destroy me.

It wasn't blatant, of course. No, that would be too easy to spot; too easy to control; too easy to point out. This was more subversive, and thus more annoying. I was always five minutes from an, *"Are you doing alright, buddy?"* or a myriad of wayward, piteous glances.

Unpitying sorts saw an easy target and took full advantage of my weakness, taunting and harassing me ad nauseum. I didn't like the mean ones either, but at least I understood them; at least they treated me like something more than a baby, even if it wasn't by much. Funny how the pitying kind never defended me against the ridiculing ones. I wished they were more like Pop.

Pop never took me for an invalid. He never looked down on me or put me down. He never cleaned a bathroom for me, or held a door, or held back an insult from me for even one second. Even when I gasped, unable to complete a sentence, he never took it easy on me.

"You think you got it rough?" he always said. "Try gettin' old."

They were horrifically insensitive words, but I took comfort in them. Pop didn't give care what anybody thought of him. More importantly, he didn't understand why anybody would think he should care. He did what he wanted, when he wanted, how he wanted.

*

One night, Mom noticed Pop eating soup with a rusted spoon. Logically, Mom asked what he was doing. After all, the spoon was disease riddled and nasty.

"People don't respect things no more," Pop said. "This is a perfectly good spoon. Look at it. And somebody just threw it away."

"Wait," Mom asked. "Where did you get that spoon?"

"Where'd ya think I got it? The dump, genius. Some idiot just threw it away. I've gotten lotsa plates and stuff from over there. Used to have a whole set."

"Wait— the plates I ate on as a kid – were from the dump?"

"And the one you're eatin' on now—I found that a couple months ago. Let me tell you, the amount of waste in this county is crazy. We could literally power a city with the crap in that dump. And you want me to disregard perfectly good plates? Please."

My mother fasted for the next week. She washed her tongue out a dozen times, brushed five times a day, and gargled with gallons of mouthwash. Pop just laughed and sipped his rusted soup. I dug that about him. Then he would insult my mother, and my affections turned to disgust.

*

I remember that night distinctly. As Mom threw away the rusted utensils there was a knock on the door. I knew the knock well; the hard, loud thumping of a police officer.

"Ma'am," a booming voice shouted through the door, "we need to speak with you."

Dr. Phil must not have liked something he saw in the cut of mine or Mom's jib, because not 24 hours after we'd been sent off with a smile, a lady from child services and two police officers stood at our door.

"We have a few questions for you," she said with a smile. They shouldn't be able to smile. They are lying liars from Liarton, sent to take children from loving homes. In the off chance they find a needy child, it doesn't take long to lose them in the system, or ship them off to a molesting, rapist, pedophile sweatshop of a foster home.

They examined me, poked me, prodded me, and subjected me to very boring questions like: *"Does your mom ever hit you?" "Have you ever seen your mother angry?" "How do you feel living so close to a garbage dump?"* and *"Are you having trouble breathing?"*

Maybe that would've rattled a normal kid. They might've spilled that Mom had pounded half my stash of pills since we got the last batch, or that she was so angry once that she threatened to kill my dad – he beat her soundly for that one, but it still happened.

Not me. I didn't say any of that. I sat equally stunned and silenced. I acted as if I had no idea why they were there and kept pointing the finger back to my father like a good boy. If anybody was to blame, it was he, not my sweet, dear, pill popping mother. She was doing her best. That was the company line and I toed it with aplomb. The alternative was to be shipped off to my father, which was a fate worse than death. Actually, it might've just been death.

Eventually, they satiated their curiosity and took their leave, not before palming me their cards "in case of emergencies".

Mom was livid. She'd never been so embarrassed in her whole life.

*

The next day Mom ran into Phil's office like a woman on a mission. She didn't tell me what exactly happened, but I heard several muffled curse words espoused through the paper-thin walls of his office.

"How dare you – son of a—that's my kid—you have no right!"

If she'd had the choice, we never would have gone back to Dr. Phil. Of course, beggars can't be choosers. And we were the beggiest. Phil was the closest doctor our crap medical coverage took. The next nearest one was 20 miles away, and the waiting room took hours.

Mom couldn't afford to make that drive four times a week, so we were stuck. Friggin' medical coverage, man.

*

Mom took her frustration out on the house, cleaning it spotless and then starting again from the top. The dust and mold still overwhelmed my lungs and nostrils. Being outside helped, even though there were still nauseating smells, pollen, pet dander, and all manner of triggers out there as well. I escaped to the wide-open spaces of the outside multiple times a day.

It helped me think, being outside, but it was far from quiet. Behind Pop's house laid a train track. Trains ran through sporadically several times depending on the day. I'd watched them since I was a child, enraptured by whatever fascinated little boys about trains; their size, speed, and sound possibly.

To a little kid Pop lived in the coolest place in the world. Smack dab between a garbage dump and a train track that were perfect for exploring. It wasn't until I aged up that I realized the opposite was closer to the truth.

The tracks ran across a steep embankment behind Pop's back yard. Even though they were set far back from the property line, trains still rattled the house all hours of the day and night. It was hard for Mom to sleep the first few years after she moved away without the rattle rocking her to sleep. Since we'd moved back though, she found it impossible to sleep through it.

*

I loved trains. Not only were they fast and loud, but they carried all sorts of cool stuff all over the country. Maybe it was apples from Washington, or Ninja Turtles just shipped from China, or any manner of interesting fancies a child could imagine.

It was fun to imagine being the conductor, tooting that big horn, and barreling through every city and state in America. I fancied hopping a train, running off to some far-off world, and dying in peace.

It was just enough to be stuck with a condition I couldn't cure, that I didn't deserve, and developed through no fault of my own. But to be out on my own, without any discernible support structure, wore on me every day, every hour. All I wanted was a glimpse of those happy days when I was seven.

All I wanted was a loving mother and father who weren't too wrapped up in their own self-loathing to give a crap or two, aside from when the cops gave them a scare.

Yes, the train was a wonderful release. A wonderful thought. I could scurry up that hill, build up speed, and lasso myself onto the last car before it sped off. Then, in the bed of that car, I could die in peace as the world passed me by. It's a morbid thought now, but then it was a great comfort to me; not that I would ever do it, but that it was there if I needed it.

*

One night after dinner, while mom cleaned, I stepped outside to admire the night sky and taste the relatively fresh smell of the outdoors. The dust bunnies nipped particularly hard at my nose and tickled my throat, and the sweet, night air opened my lungs instantly.

I found Pop. He was outside wearing a rut in the yard. He jingled his change and paced back and forth. He'd done it for years. It drove my mother crazy.

"You're killing the grass," I said.

"It's my grass though. Probably the only good part about home ownership. This is mine."

"Your funeral. If you want awful looking grass, go for it then."

"I will. Wanna see something cool?"

"Who wouldn't want to see something cool?"

"Communists." Pop crouched into a three-point stance, ground his heel into the dead grass, and burst forth up train track hill.

Even at his age, he scrambled faster than I could on my best day. "Come up here."

I tilted my neck up. "If I try that, I'll die. Do you want a dead grandson?"

"No. I don't want a pussy grandson neither though."

"Well, you can either have a live pussy or a dead winner. Choose."

Pop sighed. "How about this? I'll come halfway down and hold onto a tree. All you gotta do is jump and latch onto my hand and I'll swing you up."

"What if you drop me?"

"Please, kid. You're two pounds of sickly bones."

I thought for a moment. "Alright. Don't drop me."

Pop inched his way down the hill and grabbed the hilt of a thick tree. He held his hand out. "Come on!"

I summoned all my strength and lunged for him. Pop grabbed my hand and tossed me onto the summit. I steadied my wobbly feet and looked down upon all of creation. "I did it. I did it! I did it!!!!!"

Pop brushed himself off and joined me. "Yup. It was all you. You definitely did it all by yourself."

"I know, right!!!"

"Watch your step." Pop pulled a penny out of his pocket while I balanced myself. "Ever seen one of these, kiddo?"

"Is that a trick question? I'm sick, not braindead."

"Take a look at this penny, smartass. Tell me what you see?"

I turned the penny over in my hand. I rolled it down my thumb. I felt for grooves along its sides. It was, by all accounts, a normal, everyday penny. "Seems pretty normal to me."

Pop smiled. "I worked six hours in a coal mine as a kid to get one of those. Now they're not even worth making."

"Well, not worthless. They're worth a penny. A hundred of them are worth a dollar."

"Don't be a smartass. I'm telling a story. And for my story – they're worthless. Got it?"

"Worthless. Got it."

Pop placed the penny on the train tracks and reached in for another. He pulled out a smooth, curved, elongated penny and held it up. "This penny though. It's different."

"Yeah," I chuckled. "It's actually worthless."

"You think so? I think this one's worth more'n the other one, because it's different, unique. There will never be another one like it. I've got a million pennies that look the same, but I've only got one of these."

"A million pennies. Now *that's* real money."

"Shut up, smartass. This one's been crushed by the train. A hundred pennies are crushed a hundred different ways. Every one is different, unique. This one's got character, because it came through that pressure; it came through being crushed and survived, molded by it. I'd take this penny over ten thousand of those fresh ones."

"I wouldn't. That's $100. You're—"

"—*WHAT ARE YOU DOING?!*" Mom screamed, rushing out of the cellar door toward us. "Get down from there! You're gonna get yourself killed!"

"Alright. Alright. Hold your horses. You'll have a heart attack." Pop plopped on his butt and scooted down the hill.

He brushed himself off and shouted to me. "Come on. It's easy!"

Mom shook her head. "NO! Don't even think about it!"

I smiled, plopped on my butt, and slid down after him. Even though an atomic wedgie nearly split me in half, it was the most fun I'd had in months.

*

I thought about what Pop said a lot, both when I was 12 and even onward to this day. It seemed sort of ridiculous that such a piece of wisdom came from a man who'd so clearly folded under pressure more times that I could count; a man that screamed, and struggled, and wore his heart on his sleeve with near contempt for anybody around him.

But the older I get the more pressure builds in my own life. The more I feel the pain in my chest, and the medications that dose upward and upward, the mounting pressure to be an adult. The thought that one day, I will be responsible for myself, for my own job, my own car, my own house, maybe even my own children, if I live that long. I probably won't live that long.

My dad, he crumbled under the pressure even more than Pop. At least Pop kept it together enough that his wife and child didn't run away from him. Not that it's a high bar, but it's a bar that even my Dad couldn't live up to; all because he couldn't deal with the pressure.

When Dad held a steady job, even though we were dirt poor, he was polite and even calm. When he had a healthy child and a doting wife, things were hunky dory. But when the pressure mounted, it became too much, and his raging ball of fury showed.

It's the same raging ball of fury I have inside me. Those things don't go away. It's something I worry about showing every single day. I feel horrible when it does.

I've seen that fury in myself once or twice before, when the pressure is on. When papers are due, or finals loom. I snap. I bite. I snarl. I always try to apologize after, but that apology is never enough.

There is no denying that pressure molded me. It crafted me in my even younger youth. I don't know of anybody else crushed quite as thin. I'm sure there are: child warriors in Somalia, AIDS babies in Rwanda, motherless orphans in Thailand. They exist, I just don't know them personally.

I hope that pressure gave me the ability to deal with my emotions better than my father and grandfather. Even if only slightly. For your sake, I hope that. And for mine.

SIX

On sleepless nights, I stared out into the abyss of the garbage dump. The moon rose right over it, sparkling like a jewel over the heaping mounds of stench.

Pop talked often about the majesty of the trash – that it lived, breathed, and took on a life of its own – that it was beautiful. I always thought him a kook, but since our return, I saw what he meant. There was a calm majesty in the silhouetted hills rolling into the distance – at least in the darkness you couldn't see the mounds of baby diapers and toxic sludge— in the moonlight the watery waste glistened and shimmered.

That night, the moon's rays lit the heaps of underwear and feces like the most beautiful moors of Scotland. I don't know if it was a super moon, or a harvest moon, or a blue moon, or just a regular, old moon, but the man living on it was more magnificent than I'd ever seen him before.

*

Mom snored when she drank, and she always drank in those days—at least until the last of our savings ran dry. It killed the majesty of the moment, so I do-si-doed around my curled-up mother and slipped quietly into the back yard. The grass glistened with dew and squished between my toes. I took in the man-made peaks and valleys illuminated by the moonlight and felt a calm wash over me.

I watched transfixed for hour long moments in the damp dew of the full moon, until a shimmering flicker caught the corner of my eye. I traversed the dewy lawn and picked up the smooth piece of moonlight.

Except it wasn't moonlight at all. It was a penny, pressed flat and ejected from the train's wheel to tumble down the hill, until its eventual sanctuary in my hand.

I ran my finger across its face. Mr. Lincoln's face contorted and elongated, distorted and unrecognizable; the edges of his face curled up and warped. The pressure had expanded the penny to twice its size – but Pop was right. I'd never seen its equal. I'd seen a lot of pennies in my short life, but nothing quite like that one. Beauty and elegance formed from the pressure of a million tons crashing down upon it.

I held it up to the moonlight and the dull hue danced upon my face. The moments turned into seconds and full on into minutes until a shadow fell out of my penny and danced across the moon and into the dump – ever so delicate and graceful.

It took me a depressing moment to realize the shadow wasn't that of Honest Abe at all, nor a raccoon, or a rat, or a scavenger dog, or even a vulture – though there were very few carrion birds their size in temperate climates like this one.

No. The shadow pirouetted between two garbage mounds and onto a rusted tin; I was sure it wasn't any of those things.

It was a person. But more than a person, it was that of a woman – no, not quite a woman, but certainly not a girl either. I'd seen many girls before. She was different. A limp in her gait, yet grace in her movement clearly showed somebody that had undergone immense, transformative pressure. I didn't know who she was, or what she was after, but I knew she was special; she was unique, like my penny.

I watched her sashay to and fro, tipping over bags, bottles, and all manner of funk, in a measured search for something unknown to me yet vital to her. She danced and pranced for an eternity, then in an instant I blinked, and she was gone.

I searched for her through the chain-link that separated her from I, but it was hopeless. As quickly as she came, she went back into the abyss. I stayed up all night thinking about her. I hoped against hope that I would see her again. I wished for it more than I'd wished for anything in my entire life.

*

My thoughts trickled into the following sleep deprived day. I paced and jiggled like Pop's true progeny. I'd been cooped up at Pop's house since our arrival several weeks before, with only brief respites to visit Dr. Chuckles von Funnypants. It would be days until my tests came back proving what I already knew; that I was no danger to anybody but myself and should be allowed into school forthwith.

I spent most of my time sitting inside, wasting oxygen, watching TV, reading comics, and watching paint dry. It drove me up a wall. That day in particular, I needed to fly the coop.

I hated wasting oxygen. Fate allotted me a few brief years on this floating marble. I despised frittering them away. That coupled with my raging hormones and amped up testosterone – let's just say I yearned for release. I couldn't go far, Pop saw to that, but we could walk to Mom's new job.

*

Mom spent the better part of every day going on job interviews and being summarily turned down. After ten thousand noes, she finally got her yes, thanks in no small part to Pop's charms and long-standing patronage.

She worked at a bodega down the street and under a rickety bridge from Pop's. An old family friend sold it off to a woman named Rosa, who handed it over to her daughter Rosalie when her aged infirmities prevented her from moving boxes.

Pop jingled his change in that store before Rosalie was a figment of a thought in her parents' brains. So, when Mom needed a job, but lacked any inherent skills, his years of patronage forced their hand.

"Alright, Pop," she said. Everybody called him Pop. "But if she sucks, it's on your ass."

With that warning, Mom became Rosalie's newest employee. It was a short walk, but I was grateful for the change of scenery. We passed neighbors watering their grass and taming their gardens. A few waves from Pop brought the oldest biddies scuttling over.

"Is this your son?" one asked.

"No. He's my grandson!" he exclaimed proudly.

"Oh, you're not old enough to have a grandson!"

The old biddies tittered away and wrapped whole tufts of hair around their fingers. They flirted incessantly with Pop. Each time, he would politely smile and walk away. Each time he left the old ladies disappointed.

"Why don't you talk to them more?" I asked. "They seem to like you a lot."

"Come on, kid," he responded. "Nana's the only one for me."

That was the one truth in all the lies Pop told himself. Nana was the only one for him. He only had eyes for her, even though hers roamed the world without ever leaving her home. He loved her. He just had no ability or inclination to show it appropriately.

After much more adulation from another gaggle of giggling grannies, we passed under the rickety bridge that separated Pop's house from the bodega. The walk took minutes in my youth, but that day it took over an hour.

Was it a factor of my youthful legs or Pop's aged ones that slowed our gait? Does time move faster as we age? Do years pass at Pop's age the same as they do for me?

*

Mom bagged groceries by the register as we entered. They'd busted her down from cashier for coming up short on the till three shifts in a row. Mom wasn't the most thorough of people, but she worked hard for her pittance.

"It's tough work," Mom said, clocking out. "Fun though."

She lied, of course. Everybody in my family lied all the time. The work was tedious, boring, and humiliating. She couldn't say that in front of Pop. Not after he stuck his neck out to garner her employment, terrible as it was, or around spying ears that could tattle to her boss for a taste of the momentary satisfaction of a compliment. She needed the money too much.

"How is it, kiddo?" Pop asked. He feigned only the slightest interest. It's hard to care about the doldrums of local grocery stores.

Mom smacked her hands together. "It's…good. And…your day?"

The only thing more boring than Mom's job, was Pops' lack of one. Rehashing another Bonanza rerun wasn't my idea of "seizing the day", so I took my leave of them. I needed school supplies anyway.

*

I hopped over a stock boy and nearly ran into a young girl huddled in the aisle way. She pulled her hair back in a taut ponytail and eyed the stock with intensity.

"Go away!" she seethed between her teeth.

"Sorry," I replied, but when I turned, she was gone – except she wasn't gone. I squinted my eyes and she reappeared in front of me. She blended perfectly inside the empty cabinets. Her eyed locked on a stock boy refilling soup cans the next aisle over. She glided elegantly without touching the ground, careful to avoid the dancing eyes of the head-phoned stock boy, blaring Rihanna loudly at an unhealthy decibel.

The song flipped, and the stock boy turned to scan the inventory. With his back turned to a box full of soup cans, the girl gracefully leapt across the aisle and snagged two cans of soup from the box.

The stock boy turned back without noticing his missing inventory. He whistled as he loaded another box of cans, and when he turned his back a second time, the girl ran across the aisle and stole two more cans.

Every turn of the stock boy led to another leap across the aisle, and two more cans disappeared from his inventory, until her jacket was full of cans.

This wasn't her first rodeo. She'd mastered her technique over years of study; her grace only belied by a slight limp in her gait that I recognized immediately; the limp of my Penny.

I only knew her from her silhouette, but I was sure it was her; her hair no longer wild and free as the previous night, her clothing hung loose, her dark eyes focused and determined.

She'd deftly removed nearly two full cases of soup before the stock boy took notice of her wobbled knees and lumpy belly. The cans clanked under her shirt and gave her away. A light clicked in the stock boy's head. He mentally counted his inventory; he found it wanting by two full cases.

Her frozen look of panic nearly shat a brick right there. She mustered a "hi" as she maneuvered the cans to her back to avoid detection.

"Where are your parents?" he asked. "What are you doing here?"

Penny clumped away from him, cans clanging under her baggy shirt. "What? Nothing. I just like the way you stack soup!"

The store patrons turned their gaze on her, the master thief that never wanted detection. "What do you have under there, kid?"

She backtracked toward the exit with a series of mutters and stammers. A customer entered, and the doorbell rang. She threw him aside with one motion and leapt toward the door. A can of soup dropped from her shirt and rolled across the floor.

"THIEF!" he screamed and ran toward her.

I panicked. They couldn't catch Penny. I wouldn't allow it. I had to protect her. I slid in front of the stock boy and stuck out my leg. It wasn't the most graceful or thoughtful move, but he tripped over my outstretched foot and slid into a nearby display of creamed corn, knocking it across the floor.

Mom's bony hand slid over my shoulder and dug it. I was in trouble. I didn't care. Penny was safe.

SEVEN

Thirty-seven minutes, fourteen seconds. Rosalie REAMED my mother for thirty-seven minutes, fourteen seconds.

That's longer than an episode of Mickey Mouse! It's longer than it takes to cook rice! It's longer than an oil change at Jiffy Lube – not on a Saturday though. It's longer than it took to eat dinner. It's longer than it takes to cook AND eat dinner, some days.

God bless her, Mom took it like a champ. Years of Dad's physical and Pops' mental abuse taught her well. She stood there, stoic, as vile bitterness washed over her. A crowd snapped pictures and recorded video, laughed and gasped, covered their children's ears, and shuffled them out of the store.

Through it all, Pop lifted no finger or so much as raised an eyebrow to help. He didn't twitch or shift his weight. He didn't defend his daughter. He merely shook his head when Rosalie's spittle drenched Mom's face. Only Rosalie's condemnation of Pop's judgment elicited a reaction.

"These are the type of people you vouch for? How could you?" she asked.

Pop dipped his head, red-faced. "She's my daughter."

He spoke only those words. Meanwhile, I sat outside with my knees curled into my chest. Rosalie's shrill tones carried out the open door and gave me a perfect vantage point of the verbal thrashings.

The moment Rosalie's insults stopped I would be in a world of trouble. I didn't care. I hadn't done anything wrong. In fact, I'd done everything right. I'd helped somebody steal soup. Nobody stole soup for glamorous reasons. Nobody reached baller or gangster or won any street cred stealing soup.

People only stole soup for noble reasons. There wasn't a soup stealing cabal in middle school. At least I didn't think there was; I hadn't actually stepped foot in my new school yet, so I couldn't definitively say one way or another. But I was pretty confident there wasn't a soup stealing cabal there. Even if there was, I could confidently say it was the worst cabal ever.

*

I spent the next half hour lost in thought; drifting between Mom's thrashing and trying to figure out the name of the soup cabal I'd convinced myself both definitively existed and definitely ran my new school. They bent the principal's ear, sold contraband to lunch ladies, and paid the janitor for after-hours access. They were the biggest bad asses in the entire world: *The Minestronians, The Chicken Dumpling Gang, The Fiesta Soup Crew, The Clam Chowder Bandits.*

I'd written down a pretty good list when a tight bun popped out from a bush across the street. Penny's head followed. Our eyes locked. I couldn't believe it. *She looked at me! Callooh Callay!*

I unfurled myself, ready to brave the intermittent traffic and follow Penny into the sunset. I took a step, but Mom's bony hand clasped tight around me.

"Quite a little stunt you pulled," she said.

"Y—but I—" "

"I suggest you keep your mouth shut."

I looked at Pop, hoping for sympathy, but found none. The usual warmth of his eyes was replaced with cold emotionlessness. I felt the fear Mom must have felt as a child. I was scared of what Pop might do to me. I felt the dread my mother dealt with her entire childhood.

My eyes darted from the immediate threat toward the bush that caused it, but the bun had vanished. I tracked the horizon and caught her silhouette scampering up a hill into the woods. She looked back for a moment, smiled, and disappeared.

*

My dad made a career of cutting Mom down when she was at her highest. Whenever Mom had a good day, Dad would be at his worst. It wasn't always intentional, I'm sure, but it was. I could tell he'd come home in a slightly foul mood, see Mom smile and turn himself into a tizzy.

The thing was— he fed off Mom's bad mood. In fact, when he saw Mom's smile turn to a frown, his mood lightened; he was a happiness vampire.

One night, Mom was actually in a piss-poor mood, some hangover or other sort of thing got her down. Dad came home in an even worse, kick the cat and the rat kind of mood. He got fired from one of his 500 jobs for cursing out a client or having them curse him out. I forget which.

Dad took two hours to bring my Mom out of her funk in one of the most magnanimous gestures of his life. I literally never saw him be so kind and pleasant.

Then in an instant, when Mom turned it around and plopped the slightest of smiles on her face, Dad decimated her, verbally, physically, and mentally tore her a new asshole until she was lower than a cricket's knees and twice as shaky.

Afterward, Dad smiled ear to ear for the rest of the night. That's the kind of guy he was.

*

Something changed in Mom after Rosalie laid into her. She'd been tampered down and trampled on long enough. Being screamed at, almost being fired, begging, pleading, and groveling nearly on her knees, for a job she hated destroyed her. She had no power; that she'd grown not even one iota since we left home. It crushed her fragile, little spirit.

I saw the twinge in her eye. Mom was never an addict. She stopped whenever she wanted. She never took more than she needed. I mostly had enough pills to get through any given day, week, or month; at least after my doctor refilled my prescriptions. Mom skimmed off the top, for the most part. After that day, a couple pills became a handful.

*

The blood vessels throbbed in Mom's neck well into the night. Her collections of starts, stops, "ers", "ums", and screams made not a lick of sense, but the redness of her face and vehemence of her intonations could've been correctly interpreted by a deaf, blind, mute. I felt like a kicked dog by the end.

Once she thoroughly berated me, the color returned to her face and the waves of guilt followed; she was no better than Dad in that moment.

With that realization came the wave of apologies. I was only a little boy, and what if it HAD been an accident, and she was just kicking the proverbial dog because she'd been unnecessarily yelled at, because she'd never been able to yell at somebody with Dad around.

"Oh my God," she said. "I'm a terrible mother."

Most children immediately corrected their Mom for something like that, but I knew how to play the game. I knew to let her stew for a moment, even two, before coming to her defense. I knew the longer I waited, the deeper her apology.

Finally, I eked out "no, you're not" and went to bed without another word. She wasn't a bad mother. She wasn't great, but she wasn't bad. She flailed and kicked and tried her best, it just wasn't good enough. I didn't have time to watch her wallow in the stew she brewed for herself, though. I needed sleep. The next morning began the ordeal of my school enrollment.

*

Dr. Phil's tests returned that I wasn't a ticking time bomb of disease, as we all knew, and he gave the green light for me to begin school.

When we first met, the good doctor made it seem like a simple process; that once the tests came back, I'd be rubber stamped for enrollment. Yet, even when the tests came back negative for Ebola, SARS, the Plague, and any other thing they checked for, my school schedule never came.

It turned out that once six-thousand and twenty-three years ago, a sickly kid with a condition WHOLLY DIFFERENT from mine– I can't overstate this, it was NOTHING like what I have – died after some student wiped a booger on his check – seriously, this kid had some sort of hereditary birth defect in his lymph nodes or something – and since then the school became rather cautious on the matter of enrolling students with preexisting conditions.

Before they could sign off on my "health", they subjected me to examinations by two independent doctors, a school nurse, a radiologist, oncologist, immunologist, gastroenterologist, chemist to certify my oxygen tanks safe for other students, pharmacist to ensure my drugs were necessary and proper, an occupational therapist, physical therapist, special needs teacher, a special needs consultant to verify their school was up to code for my needs, two vice principals, and the principal.

They forced me to sit for test after test to determine my aptitudes, attitudes, and even altitudes. They tested me for depression, schizophrenia, Asperger's, Tourette's, Downs Syndrome, and nearly every possible conceivable learning disability. They threw so many pieces of paper under Mom's nose that her hand cramped up from all the signatures.

At least they paid for it. Otherwise, I might never have gotten enrolled. It was hours, days, weeks of testing and diagnoses. Add onto that, the hours of paperwork forced upon my mother – seventeen hours in all – and we spent the better part of a work month certifying what we both already knew; I was neither a threat to myself nor were others a threat to me.

That certification cost East Willow taxpayers $37,621; government tax dollars at work. My Dad would have flipped his ship.

*

There must be something about aging that turns even the simplest of minds into founts of indescribable knowledge. Pop was never an eloquent man – at least not in my childhood – but once we returned to East Willow, I found a much more subdued, introspective person.

He sat outside, watching the sun make its way across the heavens, for hours. I couldn't believe how easy it was for him to sit still for a whole day, from the brisk first light of day, through the mid-morning sun, and into the crisp, pale moonlight of evening. I watched him fritter away every day like that, contemplating the ills and foibles of the world.

"Don't be like me, Sammy," he told me. "Do something you love; really love. I mean I liked the trash, don't get me wrong. It bought me this palace. But I never loved it."

"What did you love, Pops?" I asked.

"I like this," he replied.

"I don't think you can make a living watching the world pass you by."

He smiled. "You'd be surprised how many people do."

I kept that with me. I still do.

*

My favorite past time in those days, besides flattening $2.37 in change and listening to Popfucius, involved meticulously tracking Penny's comings and goings.

I originally thought that the one night at the dump was an anomaly, but her silhouette reappeared every night sifting through the garbage, avoiding the dogs, and leaping fences. It was always the same story, and she never left with anything. Ever.

She was elusive and unpredictable at first, but eventually patterns emerged. Penny showed up well after midnight and left before 1am, when nobody manned the yard.

She never stayed more than ten minutes. She dug systematically from right to left, always returning to where she left off the night before. Sometimes a thingamajig or a hooseimawhats caught her eye. She examined it against the moon light, shrugged, and discarded it; not what she was looking for, of course.

She came every night like clockwork and never found that for which she sought. I wished against hope I could help her, but also prayed she continue to come up empty, so she wouldn't disappear.

⁕

The night before school started, a realization hit me. Penny seemed my age – which made her nearly my grade – and if she lived somewhere between the bodega and the dump – it meant she was most likely enrolled in my school – and I would finally meet her – maybe we'd even be friends.

I ached suddenly for school to begin, so that I could find her. Every moment waiting felt like agony.

EIGHT

Finally, finally, FINALLY!!!! My first day of school came. I didn't care about classes, or shaking asses, or the terrible students I'd meet, or the ridiculous teachers I'd have, or the white glove treatment the principal garnered me, or how it would all be the WORST!

All I cared about was finding Penny. I was a man on an admittedly obsessive mission, but a mission none the less. I doubt there would be more than an outlier of a percent which called my actions less than obsessive – and those that did probably fell into the same camp.

Mom dropped me off in front of school with the trepidation she always felt in my absence. "Be careful. Don't play with strange boys. And cover your mouth if you see somebody sneeze."

I nodded. "I'll be fine, Mother."

It was at that moment that Mom caught glimpse of the principal and breathed a sigh of relief. "I know you will be."

My mother made sure of that – my mother and the principal, who combined to ensure I had no chance of fitting in. She mustered what remained of her parental instinct and sense of duty to be sure the responsibility for my safety landed squarely on the principal's shoulders.

"We've gone out of our way to make sure Samuel is well taken care of," the principal said at our last meeting. "I've personally overseen his schedule to make sure he has the least amount of walking possible and talked to his teachers so he can leave five minutes early from every class – and always excuse him without question, should he need to go to the nurse."

"And what about the bus?" my mother asked. "Is the bus safe? Do the children often get sick?"

"No more than any other buses, but I've been assured by his driver that every precaution would be taken to ensure his sensitivities are kept well in check. I'll make sure he's monitored at all times."

Translation: Sammy will have no fun, no friends, and no freedom; just like home. Mom loved that.

*

The principal trudged up to the car like Moses through a Red Sea of children. "Morning guys! Glad you could make it. We were worried when you didn't get on the bus we sent special right to your front door."

"Oh shoot," Mom responded. "It's kind of tradition to drop Sammy off the first day at a new school. I hope you're not mad."

She was. It seethed through her eyeballs and onto her acidic tongue, but she choked it down as best she could like a good bureaucrat toady. "No worries. You guys are here now, and tomorrow is another day, right?"

"That's enlightened," Mom said.

"I'm an enlightened indi—"

"—Can I please go to class now," I interrupted.

"Of course," the principal said. "How rude of me. Let me show you to your first class."

"Be careful!" Mom screamed just loud enough to elicit a chuckle from everybody in the vicinity; not a good start;

nearly as bad as a principal's escort. Eyes bore through my backpack and singed my shirt.

I followed the principal through the orange double doors. "Do you take such a personal interest in all new students?"

"Of course," she responded. "That's my job."

She reeked of lying smugness. I'd met three people's shares of educators in my short life. They rarely ever left their office unless a charity case presented itself – and even then, only because their job security depended on kids like me "acclimating properly" aka NOT dying.

*

We walked down the tight hallways crammed with children trying to make the first bell. Groups of like-minded sociopaths squeezed into corners to pass notes and discuss the nightly trivialities of their lives. Classmates pointed and stared, wondering who could possibly garner such attention from their reclusive and ill respected leader. Teacher's daisy chained a whisper to inform each other of my arrival. They smiled and waved as I passed; a local, infamous celebrity right in their midst.

"This is our music class," the principal said. "You clearly can't play the woodwinds or brass, but maybe we can find you a nice violin or drum."

"Maybe," I halfheartedly responded as we moved forward.

"Here is our gym," she pointed out moments later. "I've already talked to the teacher. You'll be excused to the library whenever you feel stressed."

Of all the crappy breaks and awful consequences of being sickly, getting out of gym whenever I pleased didn't suck – not at all. "You know, most exercise is too strenuous for me. Maybe we can just make it a second study hall instead."

"Hmmm… I'll think about it," she said. "And this is the lunch room. You're also welcome to bring your lunch outside, assuming the allergens don't interfere with your breathing or anything."

Mercifully, she finally stopped in front of the dull, blue, metal door just as the bell rang. "And here it is, just in time for homeroom." She opened the door. "Mrs. Featherbottom, I'd like to introduce a new student."

*

I squished in next to the principal as the other students funneled into the room. Once they were all seated, Mrs. Featherbottom called the class to order.

"Good morning, class," she said. "We have a special guest today."

The principal strutted forward with the pomp of royalty. "I would like to introduce your new classmate, Samuel. He's a very special student and I'd very much like you all to treat him as such. Samuel, wave to the class."

The room chuckled under their breath. I couldn't blame them. It was funny; humiliating to me, but funny to them. I had no choice but to turn into the skid. I smiled and waved like a good, little soldier. It was my worst nightmare, minus all the other ones.

"Say something, Samuel," the Principal demanded.

My throat closed. I choked on my own air. My chest heaved deeply, until my head deflated to weightlessness. I fell to my knees, which ratcheted the chuckles up to guffaws.

"Samuel!" the principal screamed. "Are you okay? What's wrong? Can you breathe? Do you need to go to the nurse? Should we call a medic?"

She cradled my shoulders until I sat up. "I'm fine."

"Are you sure?" She steadied me once more. "Maybe we should get a second opinion."

"Just a panic attack. Thought it might get me out of this. Guess not." I flung her off. "I prefer not to be touched though."

"Of course," she conceded. "Germs."

"Sure," I replied. "Let's go with that."

The principal cleared her throat. "If you're fine, then, why don't you tell the class about yourself and your – condition."

My chest tightened again. "Do I have to?"

"No, but I'm sure they all want to know. Don't you, class?"

They responded with a chorus of groans and the least enthusiastic "Yes, Mrs. Principal."

I had two options, faint again and show more weakness or grin and bear it; two terrible options. I chose the latter. "My name is Samuel. I think that's been clear from the screams and such. You can call me Sammy, put please don't. I hate that."

"Okay, Sammy," they blurted in unison. I walked right into that one. What followed it were blank stares and silence. Then, an ogre of a kid with an Australian accent called out. His shadow cast across the entire room, looming like a giant bear. His shoulders hunched forward to fit into the snug chair which made even the tiniest mass uncomfortable. It was one of the most ridiculous and surreal moments of my entire life.

"What's with that thing around your nose?" he asked.

"This is an oxygen tube. It connects to a tank in my backpack. I need it to breathe. No biggie."

Everybody's eyes went wide. The chorus of jeers turned to gasps. "Really?" they said.

"Yeah… ummm, you wanna see it?"

They nodded intently. I zipped open my backpack and pulled out the tank.

"Whoa" they said in unison before falling into silence. An Asian girl in the front row shot her trembling hand into the air.

"Why do you need that?" she asked. "Do you suffer from some sort of congenital respiratory condition?"

"Kind of," I responded. "It's because I'm a fish. I was born in the sea and just recently came back to land to be with my biological mother. My body can't process your oxygen."

The room fell into blank stares, except one Australian tinged chuckle and another masked by a bulbous, acned head. I tilted to glimpse at the single humorous person in the humorless masses, and there she was; chuckling away under her breath – Penny.

Of course, she would be there to see my most humiliating moment. At least she was laughing. She was LAUGHING! Really laughing. It was more like guffawing really. Butterflies fluttered in my stomach.

"Thank you, Sammy," the teacher said. "Sit in any open seat."

Featherbottom and the Principal parted each other with paltry pleasantries as I sat for the longest class of my life.

*

I fought my body's excited fidgeting until the bell rang. My feet tapped, my fingers jiggled, my shoulders shook, I fiddled with my pencil, and above all, failed to listen to even a single word of my teacher's lesson.

I tried, sure, but thoughts of my impending introduction to Penny kept me preoccupied. I knew how wily she was – how quick – and how easily she blended into a crowd.

I watched the clock. I needed at minimum a five-minute head start, just to get into position. The principal promised a five-minute lead on my classmates and for once I was glad for it. However, four minutes from the end of class the teacher still hadn't dismissed me. I walked to her desk and explained my condition, relayed to her the principal's expectations, but she remained unyielding.

Finally, after eons turned to millennia, the bell mercifully rang, and I leapt from my seat. I flung open the door at the front of the room and crashed headfirst into a sea of pubescent angst and sweat.

I inched forward as Penny speed walked out of the class's back door, head on a swivel. I kept Penny in front of me and gained on her slowly. I knew how stalkerish it was; I just didn't care. I needed to speak with her more than anything in the entire world.

I didn't care if she freaked out. I didn't care if she told somebody I stalked her. I didn't care that I could be expelled. I didn't even care if Mom found out. I needed to hear her voice.

I swam against the current, cut between two girls holding hands, slid under a group of misfits, and spun around a school of jocks. The anarchy logo on Penny's backpack deftly bobbed through the crowd so fast, I barely kept track.

Then, just as I snaked my way into arm's reach – BAM! – I connected with a meaty wall that flung me backwards. I slid six feet across the now sparsely populated hallway. Before I regained my balance, a giant lumbered toward me and Penny was gone.

I recognized him – the Australian behemoth from class – all the more imposing without his ill-fitting desk girdle. He dwarfed students and teachers alike by nearly half a foot.

"Well, well, well – if it isn't the fish," he said. "I liked your story, fish."

"Th-than-thanks— "

Just my luck, I thought, barely one class down and already the alpha bully knew me by name. I readied myself for a thrashing when the strangest thing happened – he offered me his hand.

"Sorry about all this, then. Let me help you up there, mate." He said. "Where you from?"

I accepted his hand. "Around."

"Popular place, aye? Know a couple people from 'around'."

I chuckled. "Yeah, it's a big place."

"So they say."

"Who's they?"

"No idea. The guys that make stuff up, probably. Sittin' around in their cabal somewhere around fig'ring out how big places are and how much time som'thin' takes. All very hush-hush o'course."

I brushed myself off. "Oh right. The guys from the place. I didn't think anybody else knew about them."

The behemoth stuck out his paw again. "Frank. People call me Franky. I hate it. Don't call me that, a'right?"

My hand disappeared inside his mitt. "Sam. They call me Sammy. Please don't call me Sammy."

"Alright, Sam. We have an accord. I'll be Frank. You be Sam, aight? Good to meet you. Where's your next class?"

I shook my head. "No idea. I figure I'll just wander until they send me to the principal's office."

"It's as good a plan as any."

The bell rang to class. "Whelp, I'll see you around. Be careful out there. Don't let them find out we're onto 'em."

I smiled; smirked even. Frank was easily the coolest person I'd ever met up to that point.

NINE

That first day, I decided to eat my lunch outside alone. Well, I didn't decide, the cliques, stone faces and stoned face alike, and averted eyes did that for me. I passed every manner of preformed cliché that movies warned about and others too inconsequential to mention. At every turn, they forced me away. Even the nerdiest nerds, geekiest geeks, and dorkiest dorks wanted nothing to do with me. Though in fairness, I had no interest in dorks either.

They forced me out of the comfort of the indoors, into the valley of freaks and rejects, where I was summarily rejected yet again, until no other option presented itself than the slow sting of loneliness.

Weirdos speckled the courtyard's grassy knoll, enjoying the sun's rays. I perched under the lowest branch of a small oak tree. I munched on the day-old bagels and jam Mom hustled a store clerk out of on our way to school.

They tasted vaguely of feet. Their secret ingredient, dirty socks, gave it that foot cheese kick. I ripped off a good hunk and tossed it to a flock of milling birds, yet none of them dared take a bite. Just another group with which I couldn't ingratiate myself.

They scattered from the radioactive bread as I grew accustomed to my solemn loneliness. A thin shadow grew out of their absence to replace them.

"Can I help you?" I asked. "You're blocking my sun."

"Yes, you may," it responded in a soft, feminine voice. No, it wasn't quite that. The voice was surely feminine, but a heft weighted it down making it almost gravelly.

The shadow said nothing else for several minutes. It simply stood in my way, blocking the sun's warming rays. I zigged toward the sun and it zagged to block me. I lifted up and it jumped to keep me in darkness. Mole hills turned to mountains and streams to rivers while our game of sun chicken moseyed on. Continents formed, and solar systems succumbed to the vacuum of black holes. Finally, once several universes blinked into being and returned to nothingness, the shadow stirred.

"Thank you," it said.

I finished chewing the last jaw breaking bite of my lunch and looked up. "For what, exactly, besides accepting your domination of the sun?"

"For—" A moment later the shadow turned into the light and I caught its profile. I would recognize it anywhere; Penny.

"Hey, you're P—"

I caught myself. I didn't know her real name; surely it couldn't be Penny. "You're that girl from the store."

She went to respond, but something else caught her attention; a sound on the wind and flash in her periphery. Without another word, she bolted, her pleasant shadow replaced by the Principal's rigid, unwavering one.

"You were supposed to eat inside, Samuel," she said. "We discussed that in quite minute detail, if I recall."

"We did," I responded. "But it's such a nice day, I couldn't bear the thought of being inside one minute more."

"I suppose I can't argue with you there. On another topic, your bullying incident is being handled post haste. We will not allow that sort of intolerance in this school."

"That's nice—" I said. "Wait, what incident was this again?"

"With that brute, Franklin, of course. Don't worry about it for another minute. Rest assured we are on the case."

Two guards escorted Frank from the yard behind the principal. He looked at me; wounded, hurt, a "how could you do this to me" look written across his face.

*

I scampered to the principal's office after her. Of course, I couldn't really scamper since my lung capacity rated right up there with obese chain smokers.

So, by the time I hobbled and wheezed my way through the school's labyrinth and passed the secretary's unmanned desk, the principal was already laying it on pretty thick.

"I can't believe you would ever treat an invalid like that! What would you think if that was your brother, or uncle, or cousin! You know he's not like other people. He can't defend himself. You should be ashamed of picking on somebody so weak."

—well, it went on like that, but you get the idea. Basically, everything I never wanted to hear another person say about me, screamed by one of the biggest authority figures in my life.

I flung open the door, my blood boiling with rage and my lungs weak from exertion. "Stop!" I screamed with the last vestiges of my breath.

"Excuse me!" she screamed. "This is a closed door— Samuel, what are you doing here?"

Frank turned to me. "G'day mate." Tears welled in his eyes. He fought back a case of the sniffles – that's not right, the man was crying, sobbing really, his nose bright red and dripping, sniveling like a baby.

I sucked a big inhale from my tank. "He didn't do anything wrong!" Another. "I accidentally bumped into him—" A third. "He helped me up and was nice to me. He's the only one who's been really nice to me this whole time!" Fourth. "He's the only one that didn't treat me like an invalid!"

"Is that true, Frank?" the principal asked.

Frank nodded. "Uh huh."

"Then why didn't you do anything about it—say anything about it before."

"You were—so mean."

"You didn't listen to me or anybody else. Just like you never listened to me – ever—you just decided I needed an escort—that I— needed special treatment. Did you ever— think that maybe I'm always treated like an outcast because you people in authority MAKE ME an outcast?"

"I didn't—"

I pursed my lips. I regained my breath. "Don't interrupt. If you'd come to me and asked what happened, I would have told you. But no. You treated me like a baby, like somebody that needed protecting, and you got it wrong. So, listen to the words coming out of my mouth. I don't need you to treat me differently. I don't need or want your special favors. And I certainly don't need your pity. All I want is to be treated normal."

I had nothing more to say. I slammed the door and walked out.

*

I never speak the principal's name. She had one I assure you but offering it up would be a sign of respect. Time and time again throughout my tenure I judged her wanting of such platitudes. I found her condescending, vindictive, and self-serving – three personality traits I don't value in the slightest. If not for her absolute necessity in explaining my time at East Willow Middle, I would have cut her out completely. She nary deserved a second thought, and I've rarely graced her with one.

Her crushing indignity toward me began in earnest the afternoon of our office encounter. During eighth period, she sent a cadre of office minions to read her declaration of my bus assignment in front of the whole class. Facts, figures, names, and dates might slip in and out of the addled adolescent mind, but the short bus's number stuck there like glue.

"Samuel Hickory. You have been assigned bus #231," they decreed. "The principal sent us here with special instructions. So you don't forget."

Bus #231- the short bus, a number seared into my consciousness. Three lifetimes hence I'd be some shoe farmer in a far-off galaxy, still woken up in a cold sweat haunted by the number 231.

Most of its riders were spared the humiliation of the bus's connotations and denotation either by lack of mental capacity or their ability to sneak out of class early to load themselves. After our incident, however, the principal summarily revoked my "get out of class early" pass.

*

It's important to note that I don't have the slightest hatred or prejudice towards anybody that rides the short bus; none at all. I rode with them in every school, at every grade, every day on my life. I only drew exception with the bus's explicit and implicit declarations.

Those kids were the bomb Donkey Kong actually: funny, nice, and happier than their messed-up odds gave reason. I barely lied myself out of bed every morning while paraplegics, like Joey Adams, laughed louder, longer, and more often than any "normal". You couldn't rip the smile off his face. I was so jealous of that.

They never judged or treated me like an inferior. In return I never thought myself superior to them.

The "Normals", however, were cruel, adults and children alike. They laughed, pointed, pitied, snickered, and treated us like pariahs. They talked down to us, embarrassed us, and gave us a hard time for not being like them – as if I had a choice in the matter. My screwed-up lungs and Joey's dead legs were no more a choice than some "normal" ability to throw a basketball or run a marathon. Their god given gifts just happened to win them adulation, while ours caused humiliation.

It didn't matter to me how I got home, but it mattered to them. It mattered to every single one of them. It still matters to every normal in the world.

*

Dad always wanted me to be a soccer star. He loved the game, even though it wasn't American. He never called it football.

He tried me at football first, as a little tyke, but I was too small and lithe, even then, to be anything but a kicker. I kicked well. Well enough for people to notice. Well enough for people to joke "maybe he'll go pro someday". Well enough for him to set his sights on his ticket out of Hell and onto easy street.

That's a lot of pressure on a five-year-old; be good enough at something to pull your entire family out of abject poverty, but it was something for Dad to rely on through my childhood. Everybody needed something to rely on. Pop had the lottery. Dad had me.

I think that killed him more than anything, when the diagnosis came. He no longer had an "exceptional". He didn't even have a "normal". He had a "special".

The day I was officially diagnosed, he was the first person that looked at me with that sheer, utter look of disappointment; that I was wasting regular people's oxygen. A look I've received every day since.

*

When the final bell rang, I swam up current toward the exit, focused myself on the task at hand; navigating my way onto bus 231 undetected. If only the principal hadn't spooked Penny, she could have given me lessons on stealth and evasiveness. If I could just get to my bus undetected, maybe I could still trick the five people at school I hadn't met that first day.

The bus line after school was chaos defined: kids fought each other for a spot in the back near the window, exhausted drivers broke children from their gossip circles, parents shielded poor schleps from the craziness, principals and teachers failed to keep order, crossing guards flagged down encroaching cars, dogs and cats lived together, it was mass hysteria.

The frenzy allowed me to blend in and slip unnoticed toward the special bus at the front of the line; bus #231. I weaved through the Milling Millys and Chatty Cathys and past the Stoner Sams and Jockey Jeffs.

*

I slowed to a crawl when #231 came into view. A haggard slag hopped off the bus and peered through the child-filled abyss directly at me.

"You Sammy?" she asked.

"No," I replied without thinking.

She glanced down at a white-knuckled clipboard. "Hmmm, I got a list here of all the kids ride my bus. I got 'em all accounted for 'cept one; kid goes by the namea Sammy, uses an oxygen tube or somethin' cuz his lungs don't work. Now, you got oxygen tubes comin' outta your nose, standin' in front of my bus, and it's you sayin' it's just a coincidence?"

I had no great affection for lying, but even less for becoming a pariah. "That's what I'm saying. Hope you find him."

I spun on my heels and disappeared into the thinned crowd. The assembled masses already dispersed onto their respective buses whether voluntarily or by force of authority. The sparse assemblage that remained left little cover for my escape.

I hopped onto the nearest bus as the driver turned the ignition. Two eighth grade girls giggled and snickered at me.

"Aren't you the retard?" one girl asked.

"Bus is up front, freak!" the other tittered.

I'd become a local celebrity within the span of a day. Bieber didn't even have such a meteoric rise.

"Sorry, kid," the driver cackled. "Insurance don't cover oxygen tank explosions. Gotta go. I'll tell #231 to hold for ya."

She reached for her radio, but I was already gone. I lifted myself onto the next bus in line just as I heard a crackle on the radio. "Please be advised we have a child in need of assistance. Lost. Wearing oxygen mask. Meant for bus #231. Please be on the lookout."

The driver smiled down on me. "Can I help you, son?" she asked through baked bean teeth.

I shook my head, hopped off the bus. I bee-lined for the end of the line and disappeared into a sea of straggling walkers. Several authority figures craned their necks to find me, but they soon disappeared into the horizon with the last crossing guard. It wasn't until the gruff bramble of the buses faded into the distance that it dawned on me; I had no idea how to get home.

*

Dying a slow death on the streets of East Willow beat out asking the principal for help. I'd begged on the street before. I was smart and resourceful. I could survive until I found a map.

"You following me, mate?" a familiar Australian-tinged voice boomed.

I smiled. "Don't think I'm supposed to be seen with you, Frank."

"Yeh," he replied. "Could get us in a lotta trouble, mate."

"Really? You think we could be in more trouble?"

"Dere's always more trouble ta get into, mate. Take this here. You don't know where you are, and I don't know where I am. I'd say that's more trouble, ain't it?"

The principal didn't enjoy having the screws turned on her, nor losing any perceived semblance of authority. To demonstrate her power, she'd revoked ole Frank's bus rights and forced him to walk home.

"Said it'd be good exercise, yeah? I disagree. Ima gonna diea heatstroke or somethin'."

"Why don't you just call your Mom?" I asked.

"I'd rather be lost in East Willow, ya know? – Hey, you hungry?" He patted his stomach. "I'm always hungry. Come on, I'll fix you up."

He threw his monstrous mitts around me and led me off. I had no choice in the matter. Luckily, I was famished.

TEN

It took two hours to walk into the middle of town. I used half an oxygen tank and needed seven rest stops, but eventually we made it. Frank and I barely shut up for even one second throughout the whole trip. When I had enough energy, I took the conversation lead. When I ran low on steam, Frank took over and I sucked wind.

Usually my brisk walks went from grand ideas to nightmarish quickly as my body couldn't hold up with my heart's desire. I wound up listening to the thumping of my heart in my ears and wishing for home. But I never did on that walk. I only wanted more.

We ended up at a kitschy little diner at the heart of East Willow's downtown called Barry's Diner. Frank didn't know the way home, but he could guide himself to that diner from anywhere on earth.

"I love everything about Barry's, ya know," he said on the way. "From the gen'rous portions, to the waitresses on roller skates, to the fact that at least once a day, a waitress slipped and sent those generous portions flying through the air, dousing customers and employees alike."

Nobody was immune to the pitfalls and pratfalls of the greasy spoon's floor; nobody except for Rosie. If there was ever a natural when it came to roller skating in a 50s theme diner, she was it. It was her divinely given gift. If you had Rosie as your waitress, you could comfortably order the big-as-your-head-monster sundae. Otherwise, best to stick with water.

It was my second time through the joint, so I didn't know the etiquette then. I certainly didn't understand the fist-pump Frank gave when Rosie slid from behind the counter and glided toward us.

"What'll it be?" she asked.

Frank's smile widened at me. "Get the big bowl, mate."

"Yeah?" I asked. "It's so much food."

"Trust me," he replied.

I looked up at her. "The big bowl, then."

She scooted off and we lost ourselves in conversation; everything from movies and books to our overworked and under available mothers.

"Mom's gonna be so worried," I said. "She's probably out lookin' for me right now."

"At least yer mum's got a legit reason to worry, yeah? My mum's prolly called the cops by now thinkin' I got abducted. Seriously, who is gonna abduct me? I'm biggen'n 90% of the pedos who'd try ta nab me, yeah?"

*

I listened to Frank gab on and on. His words mixed with the couple behind us talking about old movies and bowling scores. I recognized the man from the pharmacy down the street. He refilled my prescriptions now and then. His name was Scott Kent. He didn't say much, but his presence calmed me on my worst days.

The woman I didn't know then, but she handled setting up a life insurance policy for my mother years later. Her name was Victoria Kent and she made even the more boring health questions feel like a game.

I was happy to lose myself listening to the conversations around me for the rest of the afternoon. Then I saw it.

Rosie rolled out a tray with the biggest dessert I'd ever seen; ten scoops of every flavor ice cream they had, gobs of chocolate syrup, towers of whipped cream, and nearly every topping you could imagine from nuts to caramel to rainbow jimmies.

"You expect us to eat all that?" I asked.

Frank shook his head. "Nope. I expect me to eat all that… you can have a couple bites though, if I don't bite yer fingers off."

I thought he was kidding; he wasn't. The voracious vortex of Frank's stomach knew no bounds. He shoveled that ten thousand calories behemoth into his mouth faster than a turbo jet breaking the sound barrier. I shaved off a bit of sundae where I could, ducking deftly between his sticky fingers, only to be met by resistance and growls at every turn.

It took twenty minutes for him to finish guzzling the last drops from the bottom of the bowl. His face smeared with ice cream, his shirt decimated with chocolate sauce, and a smile as big as the highest skyscraper in New York. He didn't care how embarrassing he looked. I racked my brain with doubt and regret over every miscue and social faux pas. Meanwhile, Frank didn't care that he'd just taken a chocolate shower.

He slapped his belly. "I do love my food. Probably be a good thing if some guy nabbed me. Mom says I eat her outta house and home."

"I think you ate the house and home too, personally."

*

Another thirty minutes of gabbing and I paid Rosie her weight in gold for the sundae. It was a hefty price, but worth every penny.

She gave directions back to the dump. From there we could follow the perimeter back to our houses on opposite sides of the landfill. She asked if we wanted to call our parents to come pick us up. But we were having too much fun to do anything of the sort. Besides, we had directions. What could go wrong?

Answer: Much.

*

I don't know how it happened. Well that's not entirely true; a smudgy, chocolate hand had something to do with it. I wrote down the directions and gave them to Frank for safe keeping. Safe wasn't something Frank did well. By the time we turned left on Main and right on sixth, I'd forgotten what Rosie told us.

I asked Frank for the directions. He handed me a chocolaty mess, covered in goop and illegible under the quickly darkening sky.

Frank met my "what is this?" look with a shrug. "We can figure it out though," he said. "Town's not that big and the dump's got quitea stank to it, yeah?"

"Fine." I acquiesced. We wouldn't go back to the diner. We relied on our nose, or more accurately Frank's nose, to guide us toward the dump's stench.

Bad idea.

*

Frank's nose sniffed delicious sweet just fine, but disgusting stenches weren't his forte. By the time that realization hit, we were hours into our hike and turned around all until I didn't know which way was up.

We were, if anything, further from our goal –impressive since the town only rested on a few square miles. We had no money, no way to call home, and we'd entered the "sketchy" part of town.

"Sketchy" was a relative term. It would've been the nicest part of East Saint Louis. East Willow was a small, wholesome town whose biggest crimes were on par with paper theft. West Willow, where we unwittingly ventured, was the proverbial "other side of the tracks" to be sure, both literally as it rested across the rusted railroad track that separated the town, and metaphorically as it was known as a dump in more ways than one, but had no more penchant for crime than its sister city.

"No turnin' back now, ay mate?"

I liked West Willow's lack of Holly Hobby homes. There were no airs in West Willow, and the neighborhood Gestapo never came around to tell you how to color your window shades. Pop never stepped foot in West Willow, always strongly inferring, if not outright stating they were inferior to him.

I found that the height of irony, as most of East Willow rightly called Pops' house the epitome of sketchiness. Still, his house fell into the right zip code, thus he could justify his outsized feelings of superiority.

*

In later years a class project led me to the history of East Willow. I found that the homes that Pop and his ilk owned, that Frank and I populated, should have been labeled as West Willow, but a zoning snafu miscategorized their property lines for the east side of town.

When I told Pop that he was only right on a technicality, he scoffed "Yeah, but that's the best kinda correct, ain't it?" *No. It's not.*

By then I'd stopped arguing with him about banal matters. He long ago aged through his ability to change and I grew to accept it.

*

Another ten minutes of wandering through the "jungles" of West Willow and we were too pooped to pop with no idea where to go. We were exhausted, both mentally and physically. I'd kicked two thirds of my second oxygen tank and sucked deeply on what remained. Taking frequent breaks helped, but we needed to find a way back home and quick.

We made so many twists and turns that we couldn't find our way back to the diner if we tried. Frank's nose led us astray to a pizzeria, two different bakeries, and a rather pungent cheese shop, but no dump.

"Maybe we should stop'n get a map, yeah?"

"Good idea. There's gotta be one around here somewhere."

I was right. There was one right around the corner. It was there we ran smack dab into the most wonderful and puzzling coincidence of my entire life. We turned a corner and sitting there holding a sign was Penny, jingling a jar and holding a sign.

SPACESHIP BROKEN, NEEDS REPAIRS. ANYTHING HELPS.

There she was; right there in the open, panhandling. Panhandling? It didn't make sense. *Penny was homeless? How did they let a homeless girl into school? How does she get food? Where does she go to sleep?*

Of course, most of life's machinations made no sense to me. Simultaneously, it made complete sense; the disheveled look, the hours spent at the dump, the faint stench of mornings without showers, the look and posture of a woman much older than her age belied.

I peeked from behind a corner, careful to pull back before she saw me watching her. "I don't get it, mate," Frank repeated. "Whatcha doin'? We need to get into the store and get a map, mate. I'm hungry, yeah?"

"We can't. Look around the corner. Notice anything?"

Frank peered around the corner. "Yeah. It's—is that the weird bird from class? What's she doin' here?"

"Does it matter? Let's just go."

"I'm not goin' anywhere. There's maps and food in there, alright? What's the problem anyway, then?"

"You don't wanna know. Just trust me, we should go."

"Yeah. You want me to avoid food'n maps, gimme a reach."

"Fine." I explained everything – well mostly everything – to him. I left out the part about overtly stalking her at school.

I thought it best my new friend didn't find me a complete perv.

"So, you gotta crush on that girl over there cuz you found her dumpster divin' in the disgusting landfill next to ya house? That's flippin' bonkers, yeah?"

It was bonkers, but that made my feelings no less valid. Saying them out loud, however, proved how creepy they were. "I like her, alright? It's weird, but I do."

Frank smiled. "Alright then, I have an idea. When you see me, walk over to her." And then he disappeared around the corner.

*

I tapped my fingers and twiddled my toes for a few minutes, sucking down my panic with extra hits of oxygen, until Frank waddled down the street. He stopped at the corner a hundred or so yards from Penny. He threw his meaty paws up and gestured me to come over. I shook my head, but his waving escalated until I feared his hand detaching from his wrist.

I didn't know what to make of his plan – Heck, I didn't even know what his plan was – but I had nothing better. Sometimes you just gotta trust in friends, no matter how tight the gut knots.

I took a breath and willed my feet forward. They fought desperately against me. They felt 500 pounds each, but I wouldn't be stopped.

Frank pointed across toward Penny's corner. "Over there, yeah," Frank mouthed. "Get 'er at'n angle."

I shook my head, and Frank nodded his until I caved and crossed the street. Penny's eyes locked on the ground in quiet desperation. She jingled her change cup toward me. Frank waddled across the street to box her in.

*

She was no less beautiful covered in dirt than ready for school. Only her expression changed. Gone was the smile and confidence that exuded from her, replaced instead with shame. Her deep, dark eyes listed toward the ground, her hand jiggling an extended Big Gulp cup.

"Change?" Penny whispered under her hoarse breath.

I stood there for a long, awkward while. Long enough and awkward enough that she looked up and caught my eye; panic set in immediately.

She jumped onto the balls of her feet. "What are you doing here?"

Frank stepped across and blocked her egress with his lumpy, lummox body. "Relax, mate. We're not here ta hurt ya."

She scooted into a lamp post. "Famous last words. Wait, you two are here together? What, to abduct me or some crazy ish? I'm not into that ish. I don't care what you pay me. I'm not that desperate."

I held up my hands. "Whoa, whoa, whoa. First, yes you are. Second, nobody's here to abduct you. This is a complete coincidence."

"Sure," she said. "You just coincidentally walked three miles from school into the bad part of town to coincidentally find me begging for change. That's a believable story."

"You ain't gotta believe it, mate," Frank said, "to make it true."

"Well, it doesn't matter anyway. You ruined everything."

"Wait," I said. "What did we ruin?"

"I walk here from school every day to sit here so nobody – nobody! – knows what I have to do to get by. And you ruined it. Now you're gonna tell everybody."

"I'm not going to say anything. Who do you think I am?" I turned to Frank. "You gonna say anything, buddy?"

Frank shook his head. "I ain't gonna say nothin' mate. Ain't got nobody ta say things to even if I did, 'cept you, but I ain't no rat."

"Heard that before," she scoffed.

"You can trust us."

"Trust you?" she scoffed. "All I know for sure is you keep unexpectedly and unwelcomely popping up in my life."

"We can change that. I'm Sam. This is Frank. And you are?"

I held out my hand, but she didn't reciprocate. Her eyes darted to and fro. "Yeah, right," she said. "Listen, keep your mouth shut or I'll make you regret it."

She bolted without another word, bee-lining for the verve and underbrush between the buildings. A million interconnected and disparate thoughts clanged around my head until one rose to the surface. "Where are you going?"

"What's it to you?" she shouted over her shoulder.

"Are you going to the dump?"

She stopped. "How do you know that?"

"It's not important. We have no idea how to get home. If you're going that way, can you please help us?"

We must have been a pathetic, hapless sight for her to take us under her wing. Normally, I'm no fan of a piteous audience. Still, in some instances it worked in my favor.

"Fine," she sighed. "But don't say one word, got it?"

"Got—"

"Hey! Not one word. I mean it! I'm not slowing down for you either!"

She jetted off up a hill and nearly out of sight. It took every ounce of energy left in our tanks just to keep up with her.

ELEVEN

We walked and walked and walked forever. Neither Frank nor I were in any sort of shape to keep up the breakneck speed of Penny's little feet.

"PLEASE GOD! YOU'RE KILLING US!" I screamed.

"I thought I said don't say a word. I was very clear on that. Yet you've done nothing but complain for ten minutes."

"We're about to die!" I shouted.

"Well, maybe that wouldn't be the worst thing for me. Without you around, my secret would be safe."

I couldn't go anymore. I slid into the comfort of a tree and readied myself to die. Frank curled up next to me and held up my oxygen tank. Penny could have run. She should have run, maybe, but she stopped and looked back at us.

"Fine," she sighed. "But be quick about it. I can't have your deaths on my hands."

*

Penny sat on a log until I readied myself to stand. Darkness fell while she waited. Saplings grew into mighty oaks while she waited. Finally, I stood, resting on Frank's shoulder. "Okay. We can go."

"Finally," she said. "Let's go."

She led us deep into the woods. It would've been a great place to kill two nosey people. With our wheezing, gasping, and overall inability to move, we couldn't even put up a fight.

After the sixth hill, and our fourth break, my condition grated on her. Her shoulders slumped forward. Her teeth gnashed together. Her steps thumped with increased intensity.

"It's crazy, right?" Penny said. "I mean to think -- nobody around for miles, nobody to hear you scream, me strong as an ox, you boys weak as kittens. A quick snap of the neck and I'm home free. My secret would be safe forever. You really did not think this out."

"Well," Frank said. "Except for that part about you having a home, yeah?"

"And that's the opposite of not having our deaths on your hands," I added.

She was kidding; at least I thought she was kidding. When she grabbed the nearest tree branch, I had my doubts. She swished and swatted it within inches of our faces. "Don't mess with me, fat boy. You either, invalid. I can end you quick, because I'm better than you. Remember that."

She flipped the stick around handed it to me. "It will help you get through the worst of it. And there's some rough stuff coming up."

"So, you're not gonna kill me, right?" I asked.

She smiled. "What makes you think that?"

"What about me, then?" Frank asked. "Where's my friggin' branch?"

She darted him a look. "Sam's got a legit condition. You're just fat."

"I've got a glandular condition," Frank scoffed.

Penny trudged up a nearby embankment "That's what they all say, fatty. Now come on. Watch your step."

"She's a lovely lady, that one," Frank said. "Just lovely."

*

The way was fraught with peril; more hills than I walked in my life. Higher ridges, deeper valleys, I think a cougar even followed us for a spell. But eventually we passed through the wood and stood on the ridge overlooking the dump. It must've taken four hours to gather the strength. I conserved my oxygen just enough for the last leg. It wasn't easy. My lungs burned.

"We made it," I said, patting Frank on the back.

"Yes, yes," she said. "It's Homeward Bound with none of the charm."

Penny planted her feet on the ridge and surfed effortlessly down to the bottom. I tried the same but ended up rolling end over end over end.

Frank demonstrated less grace even than I, kicking up dust like a cannonball on his descent. Luckily, we all ended upright and unharmed save for minor scrapes and bruises.

Frank brushed himself off. "Ima take my leave then. I'd say it was lovely, except it wasn't."

*

I began trudging around the dump toward my house. "Goodnight," I said over my shoulder.

"Wait," Penny said. "You live on the other side of the dump?"

"Yeah. Across the big mound."

"It's easier to cut through. Save you ten minutes of walking time, give or take. Might save your life since that oxygen tank's pretty much kicked. Your choice though. Can you make it?"

I scanned the perpetual mounds in front of me, then felt my near empty tank. "Why are you being nice all of a sudden?"

"Because I'm nice, asshole. Do you want me to just leave you here?"

I shook my head. "No. Definitely don't want that."

"Well come on then if you're coming," she said.

Penny pointed out a hole in the chain link fence and I struggled through. She squeezed through after me and took the lead. She hopped from mound to mound as deftly as her silhouette. She turned back from the top of a particularly steep mound.

"Come on," she shouted. "What could go wrong?"

Famous last words.

*

If the dump smelt bad on the outside, then just like a Tauntaun it became exponentially worse on the inside. I'd been there before, but I'd forgotten just how bad it was. For all of the terrible things about Pop's house, at least it was slightly upwind.

"Come on," Penny shouted back at me. "I don't have all night."

Penny knew everything about the dump, which kept me calm, and saved my life, or at least my pants. The mounds were squishier than in my youth, when my tinier frame displaced less of the unstable masses.

"Don't step on that pizza box," she shouted atop a rickety toaster. "It's not supported by anything underneath. You need to find strong foot holds, like this one." She knocked hard on the upturned toaster supporting her. "See!"

"So, I can step on toasters but not pizza boxes?"

"Not necessarily. This toaster's safe. There's a chest of drawers underneath they brought in six months ago."

"How long have you been coming here?" I asked.

"Don't ask stupid questions. Stay close behind me. Only step where I step."

Penny stepped from the toaster onto a pile of worn out sunglass cases, onto a wobbly TV, and then onto a broken bunny cage. I followed in tow, sucking the rancid wind of the dump and coughing harder with each passing step.

"Alright, so make sure you don't step to the right of the sunglasses, because there's a pile of trash there from the hair salon and that will sink you."

Finally, I leapt from the bunny cage into Penny's outstretched arms. I'd never been closer to her. She smelt of pine needles and sewage. She radiated warmth and safety. I could have stayed there forever, had she not pushed me off after an unconscious moan.

"Whoa dude, what the heck was that?"

I straightened up. "Nothing. I just twisted my ankle on the jump."

"Don't do it again." *She bought it,* or at least played it off like she did. We continued trudging through the muck and the grime, I always careful to follow Penny's instructions to the letter. Eventually, we reached the fence line that separated Pop's house from the dump.

"That's me," I said.

Penny nodded. "I knew it! I've seen you over there, watching the dump. Well, technically, I didn't know it was you. I just knew some creepy kid watched the dump, but now I know it was you."

"Oh. It's weird, right?"

"Heck yeah it's weird. What kind of person watches a dump every night at midnight?"

"The same kind of person who comes to the dump every night at midnight."

"Touché."

"Can I ask you a question? Why do you come here?"

"I'm not answering that."

I sucked the marrow from the bottom of my tank. "Look, I could tell everybody about you. I could have for weeks. I could've told sanitation workers your schedule. I could tell my mom. I could tell the police. I could tell the school. I could tell the students. I could tell the teachers. I could tell the health department. I could tell the department of child protective services. I could blab it to anybody – but I haven't, and I won't. If that doesn't deserve at least a little trust, then I don't know what does."

She stared at me intently for longer than I was comfortable. "I'm looking for something. I know it's here somewhere."

"What? How? When? Where?"

She didn't want to answer; like really didn't want to answer, but something inside compelled her to anyway. She later told me it was because she needed to trust in somebody; she'd been alone for so long and she just needed to believe that everything, everybody, wasn't so horrible.

It fumbled out of her mouth almost before she could rationalize it. "It's like a bumper. A bumper that glows – like a firefly—but only in the midnight moonlight."

"Is it dangerous?"

"What? No. It's not dangerous. If it were dangerous, would I be looking for it without a mask on— you won't say anything, right?"

"Not a word."

"Goodnight, Sammy the Amazing."

"Goodnight—you. What's your name anyway? Your real one?"

"I don't think so, Sammy. Be safe." She leapt over a ridge and hopped the fence into the great beyond. I trudged off to face my punishment. Mom was lost in a drunken stupor most nights, but even she would notice me coming in past midnight.

*

I crawled through a hole in the fence between the dump and our house. Nobody wanted to get in or out, so the chain link fence was mostly for rats, voles, and raccoons. When the rust had caused it to buckle and snap, nothing compelled the city to spend hard earned resources on a fix. Instead, they just let it dwindle.

Pop sat outside catching the cool air when I strode up the patio. It wasn't even worth sneaking in. There might as well have been a giant spotlight on me when I crossed into the yard.

"Mom's been worried, kiddo," he said.

"She must be pissed."

"Worried. Pissed. Drunk. She's all that. Take a seat." I obliged him. I had no interest in facing the music, anyway. "You smell terrible. What was your plan here?"

I shrugged. "No plan."

He nodded. "That's a good plan. Had some of the most fun of my life without a plan. You have fun?"

"I did."

"Remember that when everything falls apart, okay?"

*

Pop led me by the arm inside to face my punishment. He smelt the garbage wafting off me – eau de dump – and a smile grew across his face, only for a moment—only in remembrance of a simpler time.

Mom laid face down on the kitchen table, half caught in the memory of a dream since forgot. She looked up at me. She stared into my eyes, and toward an old cuckoo clock against the wall – back and forth – back and forth. Her mouth moved, and her brow furrowed, but no noise came out. The only noise came from her head hitting the table.

Pop slapped me on the back. "You dodged one there, kiddo."

TWELVE

There was a time, though it wasn't long, wherein I was a
normal kid. I walked outside without risking infection and
everything. There were years in fact, though few, where I
could dance, play, and dive in the muck without a care in the
world.

In those first years before we abandoned East Willow,
Pop carried me dumpster diving through every disgusting
junkyard in three counties. Even then Mom hated it, but Pop
did it anyway. He dug that somebody loved it like him. It
wasn't until after my issues when he finally acquiesced to
Mom's demands for him to stop.

I adored those afternoons with Pop in the junkyard,
without a care in the world, without a thought in my head
besides what cool, unknown gem we'd find.

Pop didn't get giddy much. He was old school; a scowl
was his smile, a deeper one his frown. But in the junkyard, all
that changed.

He genuinely giggled as he dug through the piles of muck
and pulled out burnt GI Joes, shaved trolls, and even
decapitated Barbie dolls. We'd bring back our hauls and Nana
would squeal in aghast. *"Go outside and clean that off!"*

We found a broken scooter that Pops fixed up and resold
to a kid down the street for a sweet profit, after Mom
wouldn't let me bring it home. Pop gave me two My Little
Pony dolls after he repainted them black and gray. I left them
on my night stand when Mom and I ran.

Mostly, it was nice to bond with him in the days when my
innocence overrode his history with Mom.

"I like you most of all, kiddo," he told me.

He tried hard in those early years, he probably knew I'd sour on him eventually; that Mom's influence would drive a wedge between us. He was right.

Maybe he knew he was a bad person, or at least as much as somebody could be self-aware of something like that or at least that he would be seen as a bad person. I don't know if anybody can truly justify to themselves they are bad. He was though.

He didn't want me to see him as evil though. He wanted me to look back fondly on those memories and remember he wasn't a monster, not totally at least.

And I did. Even through the endless tales of Pop smacking around Nana and degrading Mom, even after witnessing the Hell he placed them through, even after all that, I still didn't think him all bad; he was never bad to me after all.

Plus, he just liked having somebody to dumpster dive with; lord knows he never had that before. Even at the DPW, his co-workers found him weird for collecting other people's discards. Pop still thought those pieces of junk had value.

Once I got sick, those days stopped. There were no more private moments, nothing to bond us, and we grew apart. He brought home trinkets and treasures with jubilation and excitement, but Mom threw them out before they ever reached me.

"He's too sickly and weak to deal with that filth," she said.

Pop kept trying, with gifts, stories, and visits, but Mom drove that wedge deeper and deeper. Pop couldn't fight against it. He didn't have the wherewithal.

*

It took six baths to wash out the stink from the garbage dump. I scrubbed for hours and still didn't get clean.

Mom pretended to care when I marched out to breakfast, but her drugged stupor made her numb in those days to even the most fervent emotions. She slurred and scoffed, but her machinations fell on deaf ears. "I fklj gobba spuggle," didn't really mean much to me, no matter how many times she repeated it.

Her frustration grew with each repeat of her words, but that caused her to slur more, which in turn created more frustration, and more slurring. On and on it went until she finally flung up her hands in frustration and hobbled off. It wasn't even 7am.

She came back with her coat on, a thick lacquer of vodka on her breath, jiggling her car keys. "Doctor," she shouted. "Now."

I should have been mortified, scared, and contrite, but the sight of my mother stammering like a four-year-old nearly brought me to laugh. Even Pop, usually so controlled in his anger, couldn't contain a wee little giggle through dead eyes.

"Come on, daughter of mine," Pop said between Mom's bursts. "He's just a kid. You keep him cooped up all day with an old fart like me. Kids need to explore; get their hands dirty."

I jumped up and steadied her wobbling knees, deftly detaching the keys from her loose grip. "Come on, Mom. Let's sit down."

I guided her to the kitchen chair and inched her into a seat. "Just want you safe," she said. "If anything happened to you—"

"That's bull," Pop blurted out. "Kids today are too spoiled. Need to get a little dirt on their skin."

Pop was right, of course. I tasted freedom and liked it. I learned more about myself that afternoon than the previous year combined. I told off a principal, ditched a school bus, hiked through the woods, mastered a garbage dump, and came out breathing at the end of the day. I'd learned one thing above all others, though, in my short years – always side with the woman; always.

"I'll be fine, Mom. I wouldn't leave you."

Mom shook her head and smiled, before passing out.

*

Mom woke up with a massive hangover and worse attitude. I'd lost myself in a heap of rapidly cooling mashed potatoes.

"He stayed out past midnight, Dad! He's gotta face the consequences!"

"He made a stupid move. Kid can't make a stupid move? He hasn't had a chance to make a bad move for half a decade. Cut him some slack."

"DAAAAAADDDDDD!!!!!"

No matter how old the person, or what station they were at in life, they reverted to children during arguments with their parents. It's happened to me, it happened to Mom, and it happened to the President of the United States. Nobody avoided it. All one could do was extend devolution's time. Mom lasted ten seconds.

Decades of fights meant that Pop and Mom knew each other's triggers and pushed them seamlessly and effortlessly. Pop wasn't known for rational and cogent arguments in the first place and blew his fuse after even the slightest uptick in his temper, which put him at a distinct disadvantage. Yet his erratic rage still scared Mom, which leveled the playing field.

Pop screamed, and Mom retaliated. Pop wounded, Mom cut deeper. The "blah blahs" and "yadda yaddas" continued endlessly.

*

I tired of them after the third consecutive hour. It was an epic showdown. I wanted no part of it. I excused myself to my room and basked in the moonlight's glow across the vacant dump. Hounds howled in the distance. Penny's appearance was still hours away. God knew how many more chances I had to catch a glimpse before she found her prize.

My eyes listed down toward the gate between Pop's house and the dump. A faint blue shimmered in the moonlight. It reminded me of the faint hue Penny talked about earlier. Without a second thought, I squeezed out the window and away from the argued whispers fading into nothingness.

I crept through the hole in the dump's worn fence; the same one I used to exit the dump the previous night. I tiptoed through the trash, careful of the rotten, festering piles of stink. The shimmering light protruded from a particularly nasty behemoth of bile and sludge.

I yanked and tugged until it spewed forth with globs of disgusting trash water. I slid off the excess ooze with a nearby newspaper and held it up to the shimmering moonlight.

It was cool to the touch, metal and shiny, almost like a car's bumper, but half the size. It couldn't have been a new resident of the dump. The sludge it sat under predated our arrival to Pop's, yet it looked brand new with nary a scratch or bit of rust.

I caressed its surface and felt a series of notched grooves. I tilted it into the moonlight. Several unknown, mystic symbols adorned its spine; nearly hieroglyphics but with images foreign to me: great sweeping behemoths, alien celestial formations unknown to our galaxy, and interlocked spirals too complex for man's hands.

*

I slipped back through the chain link fence without much fuss. It wasn't thicker than I, nor as bulky, so it fit through easily.

I didn't have to sneak the metal into the house either. Mom and Pop were still mid-meltdown and couldn't care less about my comings and goings. There were many things good about living in a house with such dysfunction. Lack of oversight was one of them. I would have gladly given it up, though, for a home cooked meal, and being snuggled up watching TV with a loving, caring family. The kind you see on TV. The kind that wasn't mine.

I slipped easily into my room and stowed the piece inside my backpack next to my oxygen tank. I bathed until I stank as little as possible, then I laid in bed, listening to the arguing. It was amazing how similar it was to my Mom and Dad; even Pops' cadence was the same as Dad's. I closed my eyes and could barely tell the difference.

When the fighting finally stopped, hours later, I was able to sleep. I dreamt of a family vacation, full of my loved ones, getting along.

The simpler things in life. The basest things. The things most families take for granted.

THIRTEEN

The next morning vacillated between torture and agony. "What's up wit' you, mate?" Frank asked multiple times, and with good reason. I twitched and jittered like a mescaline addict. I didn't break, though. I wasn't about to ruin the surprise. Frank was anything but a subtle fellow. If I let him in on my find he'd blow my reveal with his big mouth.

I went through the whole morning without seeing her. Finally, at lunch Penny made an appearance. She skipped homeroom and math. I nearly wrote her off as a figment of my imagination, except then Frank'd be in on the delusion with me – that didn't make a whole lot of sense.

Frank pointed at her "So there she is."

"I'll be back."

"Whatever. You gonna eat that, mate?" Frank asked, pointing to my pudding cup. The cafeteria staff's pity of me manifested itself as extra helpings of dessert. I hated all forms of pity, even delicious ones. I slid it over to him. He cannonballed it in one gulp.

"I have something for you!" I shouted at Penny.

She spun on her heels. "What could I possibly want from you?"

"I'll show you."

"I don't know what you think I am," she said, "but I don't have time to—"

"Will you trust me already? Have I not proven to you that I'm a cool cat?"

"Oh yeah. You're the coolest – fine but make it quick."

*

I led her into a corner of the dining hall and unzipped my backpack. I flashed her the bumper's corner and slid it down to reveal the hieroglyphics. "How cool am I? Admit it. Pretty cool. I found it last—"

Penny's eyes widened. She lunged for it. "Give it to me."

"Easy now. I went through a lot of trouble to get this piece. Tell me what it is first."

"Not a chance," she responded

"Then you're not—"

She wrested the backpack from my hands. My fatal flaw? I have the strength of a baby; a prenatal baby at that. I couldn't stop a bunny rabbit from choking me to death, let alone a human being; especially one with a fiery purpose behind her eyes. I'd have found it emasculating if I cared about that sort of thing.

"At least tell me your name!" I screamed at her retreating back.

"No!" she screamed.

"Please!"

A moment of silence followed a deep sigh. "Yva. With a Y. Now don't bother me again!"

"Thank you!" I didn't care that she was hard, gruff, or mean. I had her name; her real, honest name. Yva. With a Y—I liked Penny better, but Yva was good too.

*

The rest of the day lazily listed onward until fading from memory. The bits and bobbins blended in my memory. I'm sure homework existed, project due dates loomed, tardy slips accumulated. It all felt very important at the time. In retrospect, while the dread remained, the inconsequential details faded away.

The short bus no longer waited for me. After riding it a grand total of zero times, the principal cut her losses. However, she refused to lift my ban on the "normal bus", which left me with only two options; hoof it or force Mom to leave work and scoop me.

My previous misadventures at the dump put the kibosh on the former and left me dangling my feet on the curb waiting for her while the buses blew smoke in my face. The laughs of the walkers faded into the distance. The teachers piled into their cars and vacated the parking lot.

I didn't regret my actions — only the crap-storm that befell the poor bus driver. I never saw her again; not driving the short bus, not in line waiting for the children to load, not even at the only grocery store in town; not once.

Had I realized the extent of her trouble, I might have thought better of my escape. I already acquired the "freak" nickname, so what did I gain from avoiding the bus, really? Of course, then I never would have met Frank.

The principal strolled past me on her way inside. "Zip up. I worry about you catching your death from the cold."

The cold didn't get to me the first hour, or even the next half. Around hour two I'd stuffed my fingers inside the jacket lining. The lunch ladies offered a ride, but I knew Mom would go apoplectic if she came and I was nowhere to be found. Eventually, my fingers numbed, and I had no choice but to take actions into my own hands.

*

I should have known better than to trust Mom. She was unreliable even sober, and sobriety happened rarely in those days. Three hours came and went before I summoned my energy and leaped into action. I studied maps of the area until they burned into my retina. I never wanted to get lost in East Willow again.

I took the main road left until it cut along the train track, then followed it south until it ramped up a hill. I zigzagged through streets, avenues, and ways until the familiar pungency of the dump guided me. It took hours upon hours to muster up the energy to get back to our block.

*

A familiar glow illuminated Pop's house when I turned the street corner toward his house. I recognized it immediately; the red and blue swirling lights were undeniable and unforgettable. They'd danced in front of Dad's house at all hours of the night, warning Mom to behave and failing to protect her. My feelings toward authority were complicated and complex, but they stemmed from those lights and their failure to protect and serve.

My heart leapt into my throat. I ran through the likely scenarios in my mind as my feet followed suit along the gravel. There, on the grass, writhing in pain laid Pop; his face puffy, his nose crooked, his lip fat and bloody, a paramedic kneeled on either side of him.

I rushed toward him, but an officer held me back. I kicked, screamed, and flailed my arms, squirming every which way until I wriggled out of his firm grip.

Another set of arms grabbed me, softer and more tenderly than the officer's gruff mitts. It was my mother, face damp, her left eye black and swollen, her right bloodshot, and nose raw from the tissues. She wrapped me tight in her bosom, only my eyes cleared her narrow shoulder.

Then I saw him; sitting on the curb, surrounded by officers, my father. I immediately knew exactly what happened. Exactly.

*

EMTs lifted Pop into the ambulance. Two officers pushed Dad's head into their cruiser. After forty-five minutes the street's onlookers dispersed, leaving Mom and I lit by the moon. I brought her inside and pressed an ice pack over her eye.

She didn't twitch a muscle. Years of calluses and pill abuse acclimated her to the sensation. Her body neither welcomed nor dismissed the cold. It simply accepted it as a necessary evil, as she accepted Dad as one for so many years.

I held the compress to her eye. She stared off into space, synthesizing the series of events that paired her with a man so blatantly awful. I believed that that moment finally broke the cycle of my mother's abuse.

We sat in silence for a long while. We often sat in silence after she fought with Dad, me nursing her injuries, tears stoically streaming down her face.

*

The omnipresent fear of Dad's return haunted my waking hours since Pop relayed his miraculous recovery to me. However, not for the reason one might think. I knew that he would bear his teeth, bluster, and moan when he found us –

and he would've eventually found us no matter what we did. I conceded that eventuality.

My fear stemmed from my mother's inability to stay gone. She'd left before, though always haphazardly and ill-planned. She'd threatened to leave many more times on top of that.

On the precipice of every emancipation from Dad, or shortly after, came its eventual abandonment. Often due to my mother's sloppy design, careless tongue, or accidental reveal before it unfolded.

Whenever her plot revealed itself, Dad threatened death upon himself, professed his undying love, promised self-improvement, swore fealty to her beauty, and she bought it.

Time after time she succumbed, shattered her walls, and he waltzed back into her life like clockwork. I feared the inevitable eventuality apparent in any reunion with him. It was a tale as old as time and it happened every time. Every time until the last time; the time we finally made it out.

*

I replaced the cold water with fresh ice twice before Mom snapped from her zombie like state, confirmed what I already knew, and filled in the blank spots.

Dad showed up drunk, full of piss, vinegar, and a dozen pain killers. He hollered and stomped through the front lawn. He screamed vulgar profanities until Mom, defying Pop's adamant objections, confronted him outside. Dad dropped to his knees and begged forgiveness. He howled to the moon about the error of his ways; that the months without her tortured him unbearably.

He swore on his mama, and his mama's mama, and his children both born and unborn that he'd changed; that he'd seen the error of his ways and would never, ever lay a finger on her again, never ever raise his voice to her again, never again call out to her in anger. He found Jesus in the hospital. He'd found church. He'd seen the error of his ways. He's been saved.

"If Jesus forgave my onerous and hedonistic ways," he asked, "why can't you?"

An easy question to answer, of course. Jesus never sat at the business end of Dad's open palm. Jesus never developed ulcers from worry, laid in traction for days after a devastating right blow, or needed fake teeth after Dad knocked out three of his originals. Jesus had it easy forgiving Dad.

"Then he smiled at me," Mom said. "I hadn't seen a smile like that for years, maybe decades. It was like the man I fell in love with came back—"

I couldn't believe it happened again. We were on our way back to that death trap with the most dangerous man in our world. I'd never be free of him; we'd never be free. The knot in my stomach shrunk my body into a little ball of fear and frustration.

"—then Pop punched him in the face."

That's right. I'd forgotten the end result of their little dalliance; with Pop on a stretcher and Dad in a police cruiser.

The bullshit train might have done its magic on Mom, but Pop saw right through it. He punched Mom and Nana's first-class ticket for decades. Maybe it takes a monster to stop a monster; Godzilla tried to convince us of that for years, yet we never listened.

*

There's a tipping point in any argument where forgiven became not only an option, but a certainty. Mom lived there, always denying its existence until it happened despite her. Pop knew the moment equally well, having effectively deployed it for decades on all manner of willing and unwilling shmucks.

He saw that moment in Mom's eyes; the moment of forgiveness. It compelled him to act, with one swift punch to Dad's face, Mom snapped out of her blissful haze. *I remained eternally grateful to him for that.*

The fight didn't last long. Pop landed a couple of swift punches, but his age and infirmity couldn't keep up with Dad's festering rage. Watching his brutal animalism unleashed convinced Mom of his unworthiness of her.

Mom shook her head. "I was with him so long; so many wasted years."

*

Dad spent the two months after we left screaming for Mom to fix him dinner, dress his wounds, and do his bidding. Her lack of answering pissed him off, but the haze of drugs made him forget quickly. He wasn't much for movement, knocked out as he was by the painkillers, and he was never much for intelligence. Combine that with shock, and Dad never knew we were gone.

After the pain subsided, he came to terms with our desertion intellectually, but not emotionally. He knew we were gone, but still instinctively shouted to Mom when he came through the door and looked for me in my room every night.

It was a slow decline from denial to acceptance, filled with bitter, vile hatred, bar fights, shouting matches with everybody Mom knew from childhood friends to ex-lovers (he even beat up two of them thinking they'd won her back).

Finally, he came to terms with it; drugs and booze helped. They helped a lot. He had just got over the hump when a call came from Medicaid asking about my enrollment.

Two more weeks passed until it dawned on him it wasn't a dream. Another two days to piece it all together. And one more to get on the road.

When he got to East Willow, it only took him a couple minutes to ruin everything. He'd became exceedingly efficient at ruining people's lives as he aged.

*

I didn't want to see Dad after that. I wanted to leave him in jail to rot. I wanted the police to ship him off to some solitary work camp in Siberia. No, I didn't want to see him, but I needed to see him. I needed to look him in the face one last time.

I couldn't help myself. I had to see him behind bars. I walked down to the town square and into the police station. I told Frank my plans the previous night and he insisted on joining.

*

Plenty of opportunities presented themselves to send my father to jail before, but never materialized. Mom always found a reason: "where would we be without him working", "the police never believe me", and "it's not that bad," were her favorites.

Even when she received bruises so vicious they could only be caused by a man stomping on her chest cavity – she still never pressed charges.

Sometimes she thought about it. It's hard not to when somebody strangled you inches from blackout, but whenever tried, the police officers made her feel so bad about it that she recanted.

"You probably said something to deserve it," an officer once told her. More than one actually. Almost all of them. Almost all of them men. Even the women thought like men. "Deserve it" was a ballsy thing to say to somebody.

Mom developed a complex because of their callous and flippant attitude toward her beatings. She didn't deserve them, but if you're told something enough, especially by people with authority, you start to believe it. Mom believed it. It was her own little version of Stockholm Syndrome.

Dad struck Mom in the privacy of our home, devoid of prying eyes. This beating was different. Everybody saw it. Everybody was a witness. Nobody was scared of him. Not in East Willow. They barely knew him from Adam. They just knew he beat up a beloved member of the block.

*

We sat a long time as the desk clerk bounced from task to task until he finally had time to help us. I wasn't in a rush to see my dad, so the delay didn't bother me. He could have taken a week and I would have waited patiently.

I got to know Paul Jarman, the clerk, well during the next couple of months. He was the first person to throw in on pizza and always willing to hear me tell stories about my day, even if they were excruciatingly mundane.

That first day in the station, I was scared. I didn't know what to expect. Paul clasped my hand tightly inside his and promised it would be okay. His voice was so confident that I believed him…at least for a moment.

The closer we got to my dad's cell, the more my heart fluttered. By the time Paul went to open the cell, my heart pounded inside my brain.

"No, don't," I whispered. "Leave him locked in there."

For the first time in my life, I looked on him without fear of reprisal. If the cell door opened, he'd unlock the monster.

"Suit yourself," he said. "Hurry up. We're talking him to county in a half hour."

*

It shocked me to see Dad behind bars but disturbed me less than I expected. After all, I wished for this moment. I'd dreamt of it. I fantasized about it. The orange made him look like an oompa loompa, further dissipating my fear.

"Sammy!" he screamed jubilantly. "How've you been, my boy? I thought you were dead."

"Not dead. Doing fine." *Keep your answers short and sweet; emotionless.* Years of his manic-depressive swings taught me that.

"You gotta get me out of here. Where's your mom?"

"She's home; doesn't know I'm here."

"Well get her down here, man. Somebody's gotta get me outta here. I can't go to county. You know what they do to guys like me in county?"

A smile crept across my face. They did not take kindly to wife beaters in county. "Why'd you do it, Dad? You want me to help you, tell me why you did it."

"You know me, my temper, Sammy. I didn't mean to— but you gotta understand my position."

"Tell it to me."

"Your mom left. She ran me over. With our car. Which left me out of a job. I thought you both were dead. DEAD. That's a pretty awful thing to do to somebody. And then, your grandfather – he lied and said he didn't know where you were—

"Then one day I get a call, you got medical insurance. I didn't wanna be mad. I just wanted to see you. I just wanted my family back and your mom would've come back with you. Your Pops completely lost it – and then I lost it – I know that's not an excuse, Sammy. I truly know it's not, believe me, but it's a reason. It's my reason. And I'm sorry. Now, please, get me outta here!"

I'd never seen fear in his eyes before. I saw nothing, only rage and anger with brief moments of interspersed joy. His wide, scared eyes were gratifying in a way I didn't think they'd be. He'd be the lowest man on the totem pole in prison. I pitied him then. I hated all forms of pity, especially those toward a monstrous sociopath.

"I can't help you. Bye, Dad. Enjoy prison."

Dad's fear flipped back to rage; familiar rage. He lunged for me through the bars. "You little shit!"

He reached though the bars. I jumped back. His arms swung wildly but remained out of reach. I grabbed Frank's shirt and walked away. Having Frank there, even in silence, eased my beating heart. Leaving Dad to wallow and rot was the greatest rush of my life. I still think about it with glee all these years later.

FOURTEEN

After Dad nearly killed Pop, things were understandably weird around the homestead. Mom catered to Pop's every whim, no matter how small. She was at the hospital every day and twice on Sunday. His momentary bravery regained emotional leverage he lost years prior and like any good sociopath with an inch of power, he grabbed for the whole mile.

I, meanwhile, vacillated between a massive emotional range all the way from shock to awe and back again. I pitted Pop and Dad against each other in my head, like some epic manga brawl. After grooving on it though, it sucked plain and simple.

Pop certainly saved Mom from future heartbreak, agony, and pain both physical and mental. He came to her rescue at a moment of weakness and should be lauded for such bravery.

However, he historically treated my mother like a pariah for way longer than Dad did and molded her horrible self-image during her formative years. He made her sleep in a dog kennel for a whole week twice on a whim—that's right, it happened twice. He hit her so hard once she forgot an entire summer; he dressed her in a trash bag and sent her to school when she spilled gravy on a new dress. He just generally treated her like wanton scum.

Pop deserved to get his ass kicked, maybe a couple dozen times, but not like that; in his youth, sure, when it mattered, when it could enact change, but not now, not as an old man. Now, enfeebled, I pitied him; and I hated that. I hated that he garnered my pity.

Meanwhile, Dad undoubtedly deserved prison. He deserved a lifetime of salad-tossing and dick-licking for everything he'd subjected Mom to. He should be used like a pair of Chinese finger cuffs and passed around like a doobie at a P-Funk concert

But Mom ran him over, and we did jet away without the slightest regard for his wellbeing. He thought we were dead or worse; not the most Christian thing to do. We poked the bear. How could we be surprised when he poked back?

Moral gray areas sucked. Life needed to be clear cut black and white, like comic books. Superman=good. Joker=bad. There were no middle grounds.

*

They transferred Dad back and forth from the prison to the police station to the courthouse and back again two-three times a week. I became friendly with the clerk and he tipped me off whenever Dad came back for one reason or another.

I sat in the shadows as they dragged him through the station. The first time his eye was swelled three times its size as he limped past me; the second somebody had ripped a chunk out of his hair; the third his front teeth were missing. By the fourth, his soul had vanished.

Every time he came through his head sunk lower and lower, until he dragged it behind him like a dead leg. He called me every time he came back from lock-up, left messages, cried, whimpered, and cursed his lot in life.

"I didn't deserve this, Sammy. You know I didn't. I was always good to you. Never laid a finger. God will set this straight."

"I'll be back to you, Sammy. It all comes back to you in the end, and this'll come back to your Pops 'n yer Ma tenfold."

"I'm setting to get straight with you, Sammy. You, your ma, and the lord. Gimme a call back, ya hear. Please."

"I'm a bad man. I'm sorry."

*

After a month they released Pop from the hospital. He was old and frail by the time he came home. The vim and vigor left his eyes, replaced with quiet desolation. They left him for observation too long, they poked and prodded him until his veins gave dust. Sure, he was alive, but at what cost?

Upon his release, the hospital handed us a bill of the itemized charges of Pop's medical stay. Whether Pop deserved a beating or not, nobody's deserved that kind of horror.

We choked with every passing page. In Pop's stay he'd racked up $326,842 dollars of charges.

> •IV BAG (That's basically salt water.) = $450 x 115 = $51750
> •PT (usually about $100 per session): $90 x 834 = $75060
> •JELLO: $11.75 x 160 = $1880

Over $10 for a tin of disgusting JELLO! It went on like that for 1,000 pages. They even charged us for PRINTING THE BILL! $89 to print a bill! It was right there in the fine print.

I wasn't a scientist or an economist, but it was excessively ridiculous. Even with the deductions, they expected nearly $46,000 in payment. Pop's pension benefits were alright, but he certainly didn't account for tens of thousands in hospital payments. Who had that kind of money? *Not us.*

Especially not after Rosalie canned Mom. They never liked each other, but once Pop came home from the hospital, Mom lost days caring for him and others drinking the pain away. Rosalie loved Pop and all, but she ran a business, and without a trustworthy and prompt employee, there was no business to run. So, Mom was summarily fired.

*

Without the bodega, we lived off Pop's Social Security checks and pension; a whopping $2200 bucks a month. Luckily, Pop had paid off his house some years ago. It was the last bit of pride he had left, that house.

"I worked my fingas to the bone for this place. It's all mine, baby," he said often.

Unluckily, that still left only $2200 bucks pre-tax to feed, clothe, and nurture 3 people – Pops had barely gotten through the month when it was just him.

*

We might have been able to do it except the hospital kept bilking us every day for every dollar. They wanted their money and they were sure going to get it – even if they had to take blood from a stone.

We'd tried pleading our case to a very nice cashier, who bounced us to a less nice clerk, who became a downright rude internal collections agent, which morphed into a downright vicious outside collections officer.

"We don't have the money to pay," Mom argued.

"I don't care," the officer replied over and over.

He called all hours of the day and night – waking Pop from sleep, me from my studies, and Mom from her daughterly duties. He had no compassion.

"We will take your house," he told us. "You'll be homeless and destitute."

Dad had nothing, so they left him alone. The hospital wasn't about to put resources into a money-losing stone. Pop, on the other hand, that stone had a house, and a house could be bled and hard.

"If you don't pay, we'll tank your credit and leave you with nothing. You'll be left bankrupt. We'll freeze your pension and your family's Medicaid health plans until payment was made in full. We'll destroy your credit."

"It don't matter much," Pop said. "I don't got many years left. I don't need no credit."

But he worried still. He never welshed on a debt in his life. Pop was nothing if not a prideful man. Welshing on a debt was the worst hit his ego could take.

Now, I know the collection agency couldn't do that; they can't just take your life away. Maybe they can garnish wages, but that's it.

We didn't know any better though. Back then we didn't know collection agencies would say anything to get us to pay. Not that it would have mattered even if they could take everything. It didn't change the fact we had no money. *None.* Not even a little bit. If we even gave a little bit to him, we'd have nothing left for little niceties like food and water.

*

Mom managed to pick up jobs in the short term, but Pop needed constant care. It wasn't long before she racked up Dad levels of job desertion. She patched together paychecks with three days at one job, with nine at another, with another where she still owed on the uniform. It wasn't even worth it, but she couldn't afford not to do it.

She had no time for me, or Pop, or even a shower between the many hats she wore and the weight of her burdens.

All she had were the pills to give her relief. We filled my prescription bi-monthly before she lost her job, then we moved to weekly, and quickly needed to fill up twice a week. I told the good doctor my pain level shot higher than usual. It made sense. Everybody thought I was dying; that it was just a matter of time. They wanted to make me comfortable. So, he upped my dosage without a fight. I'd rationed myself just enough to get through the week and left the rest for her.

She needed the pills to sleep. She needed them to get out of bed. She needed them to make it through the day without lodging a bullet in her brain. She needed them to live.

I'm not proud of letting her abuse my stash. I should have said something. But I was just a kid. I wanted Mom to get better. I wanted her to be happy. I just wasn't equipped for the ethical or moral gray area she waded.

*

Yva didn't come to school for a long time. She didn't go the dump either. I thought she had forsaken me. I lived for the excitement on her face when I showed her the piece I found, but that excitement soon waned and left me with no joy in my life.

Finally, at the end of a hard month of wallowing sleepless nights, Yva reappeared in the cafeteria. She jetted right up to me like she'd only been gone an hour.

"I have something to show you," she said. "Come with me."

"I want to be alone," I replied. "Where have you been?"

"Don't care. Not my concern. Come with me."

I turned from her. "Why? So you can just abandon me again?"

"Oh, come on. Don't be a baby."

But I wouldn't budge. I didn't budge. I didn't even make eye contact with her for a solid five minutes.

"Your granddad – was very brave."

"That's what bravery gets you."

"He takes a punch like a champ, if that's any consolation."

"It's not. What were you doing back at the dump anyway? Miss the smell?"

"You missed a piece of the bumper when you yanked it out. I had to go back and get it. It was really buried in the muck. Got it out eventually; took forever. Now, I want to show you something. Come with me."

I shook my head. "I can't."

"Can't or won't?"

"Pick."

"Fine. Will you meet me after school?"

"Maybe." I pushed her away. "You can wait and see if I come."

Let's be fair, there was exactly zero chance I wasn't going. No matter how bad I felt and how low, I still loved Yva deeply. If she wanted me to jump into the sun during Pop's funeral, I would have been there, but a kid couldn't seem too eager, you know?

*

I paced outside the school steps while the students filed out. Yva didn't even appear for a long while. I'd nearly given up on her when a gaggle of gossip queens parted toward their respective buses revealing herself in the aftermath. She beckoned me, and I followed without another word.

We walked in silence for a long time. We walked until we trudged, then trudged more. Our last hike ended with a near bludgeoning. This time she was much more accommodating. We stopped often for me to catch my breath or change my oxygen tank.

"Come on," was all she said. "We're losing the light."

She dragged me from whatever perch I'd landed and pushed me up the next hill and into the next valley, until weariness overtook me, and we'd start the process over.

"You're going to kill me, right? This is it for little, ole Samuel, huh?"

She laughed. "Trust me, if I wanted you dead, you wouldn't be here. Now come on." She tugged, until finally we reached a point I couldn't go on. I fell down, exhausted.

"There's only one more ridge," she said. "I promise."

"You said that six ridges ago."

"Yeah, but I was lying then. Big time. Now I'm not. So come on." She pulled me harder until I couldn't resist. Her infectious enthusiasm spread over me like rabies.

"Alright," I shouted. "But if this isn't more than fabulous, super, great, and incredible combined, you're going to have some explaining to do."

"It's going to be fabupercredigreat. And if you don't think so, well I could always kill you."

"Not funny," I said.

*

Finally, we reached top of that last ridge and looked down at a valley; a valley, of nothing except junk; worthless, terrible junk.

"This is not fabupercredigreat. It's barely okay. You have some explaining to do."

She entwined my fingers in hers. That was, frankly, fabupercredigreat. "Just shut up and wait."

The sun set over the junk pile and the junk pile stayed a pile of junk. We stood for a long time, fingers entwined.

Then the moon rose and something magical happened. The junk pile glowed; a faint blue at first and then brighter and brighter, until it lit the whole valley like iridescent jelly fish.

There, between the worthless junk, scattered clothing, and noxious odors, the moon revealed something incredible. A spaceship. A. Real. Life. Spaceship. Just like in the movies.

"Told you," she said, smiling. "Tell me that's not fabupercredigreat."

I couldn't. Because it was. "Okay, Yva. You win."

FIFTEEN

I've only been left awestruck three times in my entire life. Three measly times.

Once, Dad woke up with a big ole smile on his face and unilaterally decreed we take an impromptu trip to the Grand Canyon. We packed up the car and drove across three states. We must've broken down and/or overheated six times easy. I kicked and screamed. Mom's tongue bled from biting down so hard on it. Dad realized halfway through New Mexico what a terrible idea he'd had, but by then, we'd passed the point of no return.

After the 300th "I will turn this car around" from Dad and 600th mournful sigh from Mom, we finally reached the Grand Canyon. I harbored little expectation; it was a hole in the ground after all. I shut my mouth right quick after witnessing its majesty though. Not a month went by I didn't think about that view and the sense of awe it inspired in me.

The second happened over the Great Plains on our final sojourn to Pops' house. We crested a cliff and beheld a great fire. Hundreds of fire trucks battled the blaze, but it continued to rage on and on and on. The flames danced across the brush and brambles without notice of the nuisance it fought. I watched it for hours until the road reopened.

The third time happened looking over that ridge at the glowing spaceship. The unset screws, pins, bits, and bobbins illuminated the thatch like the bottom of an iridescent ocean.

*

The ship itself, save for the glow, would have been considered a clunker in all but the poorest intergalactic circles. It wasn't even fit for the Yugo name. A Yugo wasn't hand-cobbled together by a pre-teen.

A spaceship was still a spaceship, though. Even Dad's derelict rust bucket seemed impressive to a tribesman who never saw such technology. As such, I was a rightly impressed tribesman.

*

Yva eased down the hill with grace. I barreled after her like a child on Christmas morning. By the time I reached the valley below my humbled silence vanished into jubilant exclamations.

"I can't—It's like – Is this—No way!!!!" I screamed and wailed gibberish in excitement. I spoke in tongues and nonsense. I forgot my breath hurt and my lungs ached. I forgot my tired legs and lost myself in the glow.

I crawled underneath. I climbed up top. I rubbed my hand along its surface and felt the grooved characters embedded along every inch.

"It's my language," Yva offered.

I turned to her. "You can speak this?"

"No. My parents though— could—I guess—"

"I can't believe you built— the detail. How did you think of this?"

"This is what brought us here. The three of us. Mom, Dad, and I."

I chuckled. "Yeah, right. And I'm Han Solo."

"I didn't bring you here to make fun of me!" she screamed. "I brought you here to help. I've been to 15 states and three continents to find every little nut, screw, and bolt that fell off when we crashed here 11 years ago—I'm so close— the pieces I haven't found yet. They're all here, in East Willow. I know it."

"You need my help you track them down?"

"No." She unrolled a sheet of paper kept hidden in her back pocket. "This is a blueprint of the ship. I've done the best with the math and science, but half of it is written in my parents' dead language. I've tried everything, but I can't decode it. I'm no good at words or language. Without knowing what it says— let's just say I could die before I left the ground. I—"

"I'm no good at language either. Have you seen my grades?"

"Better than mine. There's nobody else I can trust. Please."

I cupped her hand in mine. "Do you know anything about your language?"

She shook her head. "My father—he spoke it to me as a baby – told me children's stories – But I never read it. Can you help me?"

I pursed my lips. "I'll try."

She wrapped her arms around my neck. I heard her cry; not a sobbing, weeping cry but soft and gentle; wistful, thankful even.

"Thank you."

*

I spent well more than several bleary-eyed hours staring at Yva's blueprint that night. I jumped off the deep end. I spent days and weeks admiring Yva from a distance, stalking her, and that was cuckoo crazy banana pants in and of itself. Believing her an alien from another planet, however, was a deeper, more troublesome story altogether. *Or was it?*

I mean sure, there were millions upon millions of uncharted galaxies in the universe, but up until this point, aliens only corn-holed bumpkins.

It stood to reason that intelligent life existed. Infinite planets circled infinite stars nestled inside infinite galaxies. If even a fraction or a fraction or one percent contained life, and only a fraction of those contained intelligent life, and only a fraction of those contained intelligent life advanced enough for intergalactic travel, our universe would be filled with millions of interstellar species. *Was it so crazy to think one might be a bad driver?*

Our galaxy, while old, is one of the younger in the universe. Others are easily a billion years or older than the Milky Way. *What would humanity do with a billion more years of evolution?*

If a family of three were to make that trip, and their Yugo blew a gasket, couldn't Earth conceivably pull them into its atmosphere, and couldn't they then crash land, dispersing their parts across multiple states and continents in the process?

In the end, it didn't matter whether she was an alien or crazy. The blueprint was a really cool logic puzzle; a really cool logic puzzle I couldn't tell anybody about lest they thought me crazy.

Except that—it was impossible. At least Cracker Jack boxes gave you a decoder ring. I had nothing. It was like trying to decode Russian into Sanskrit back into Arabic and then into English without a Rosetta stone, the actual one from history not the stupid infomercial.

*

Yva showed me the number system she'd worked out. If she measured 13.2 feet from bow to stern, and their diagram shows three squiggly lines, a moose head, and two shafts of light, that mishmash of ridiculousness HAD to measure 13.2 feet.

Math was universal and absolute. Words were not. Even the same word in English could mean seventeen different things, be spelled four different ways, and modify fifteen different words making even more complex compound words.

I spent study halls for the next week browsing the internet for different cyphers and encryption breaking algorithms, but every scenario involved a decryption key. Without one, nothing made any sense.

*

I stayed up late or through the night every single night working on the cipher, which made Dad's arraignment all the more fun. It became a game I like to call "Don't fall asleep". The rules are simple: don't fall asleep. If you do, somebody elbowed you hard in the rib.

The DA left Dad in rot as long as possible, but eventually "due process" won out and they had to stand him in front of a judge to read out the charges; stupid Bill of Rights.

We agreed to go and watch Dad's face when he couldn't make bail. If I took bet on whether he'd do the right thing and plead guilty, the odds would be $0 : \infty$. That's right, a bet of

$0 returned infinity dollars back. That's not a good bet for the bookie, which was me. I still liked my odds though.

They dragged him into the courtroom in his orange jammies and without counsel. The prosecution drolly greeted an aged judge. Dad looked defeated. He'd stopped calling me weeks ago. He never even made eye contact. He never even looked up.

"You've decided to act as your own counsel?" the judge asked.

Dad nodded. He'd fallen into a classic blunder. Even a cursory glance through TV history proved appearing as your own counsel to be the worst legal move imaginable.

For one, Dad came from out of state and had no idea the procedures and laws of this particular jurisdiction. For another, he was wholly unlikeable. For a third, he was an idiot that reveled in his distaste for the intelligentsia.

The judge read aloud the charges. I didn't understand what any of them meant, really. I don't think anybody did.

They were all fancy ways to say over and over that Dad beat up an old man. He skirted attempted murder by the skin of his teeth, but the litany of charges, thirteen in all, kept the judge spouting legalese deep into the night. For a man with a third-grade mastery of the English language and a first day ESOL student's literary level, a single chapter could occupy him until kingdom came.

"I know this must be difficult for your family," the judge asked. "Are they prepared to drop the charges?"

We sat stone faced. Pop gave the slightest head shake. "Very well," he continued. "How do you plead?"

Dad looked at us; through us even, or possibly into our souls. Nothing but contempt dwelled within them. "Not guilty, your honor."

My bet held and that was it. The judge set bail for some exorbitant amount and they whisked Dad back into the holding cell for transfer into county. *He'd be lost in the system before long,* I thought. *Maybe they'll rape him to death before trial. That would be sweet.*

It was a terrible thought to have toward your own father. But then again, he was pretty terrible.

SIXTEEN

I'd missed 60% of school days since I started at East Willow Middle, so when the principal pulled me into her office I wasn't surprised in the least. What surprised me was that she waited so long to do it. She'd let me look over my shoulder for three periods and lunch in complete and utter terror of running into her.

"We're concerned," she said. "It seems your condition is worse than we'd first realized."

Of course, that was a lie. "I thought I was doing quite well."

"Your absences are astounding. Truly the most I've ever seen for a new student, or any student for that matter."

"They're all excused."

"No, they're all excuses. It gives me more reason for pause," she continued. "If you cannot properly focus on your schoolwork, you will fall even further behind."

"My assignments are completely up to date. All my teachers are informed when I'm out. Have I fallen behind?"

"No more than any other average student, but you're not trained in education, Samuel. My job is to take a holistic approach of your studies. I've enough certificates to fill a wall, and have seen my share of problem children from every walk of life—"

It was the sort of bluster I neither condoned nor appreciated, and she had it in spades. I understood my lot in life, and that I, in fact, was a child in her eyes, but I'd more than learned to deal with my deficiencies and problems – something a person like her could never understand.

"Have I done something to personally offend you?" I asked.

She smiled. "Your contempt for my school is not reason enough to be offended? No, Samuel. I am looking out for you. One day you will appreciate every string I've pulled for you." *I never have.*

"If you continue on this path, it could lead to your expulsion."

"I'll keep that under advisement."

She didn't know. She couldn't know what it took to be me. She just looked at stats and figures, and what it took to keep her job.

*

On the trudge down the hallway, I felt a light tap on my shoulder. "Where have you been?" Yva asked. "I've been looking everywhere for you."

I swallowed my feelings of hatred toward the principal and plastered on a smile. "Hello to you too, ET."

"Who is ET? Never mind. Don't care. I need your help. Do you have the blueprint?"

"Of course. I'd never leave home without it. I've been working on it in secret every day." I pulled it out of my back pocket. "I didn't get anywhere yet bu—"

She laid the blueprint out on the floor in front of a gaggle of onlookers. "—I don't care about that— that's it! I found it!"

"Found what?" I asked.

"Found a piece. Come on!" She grabbed the blueprint in one hand and my arm in the other and ran off, leaving the huddled congregation scratching their heads.

*

I coughed blood the entire hour of our hike. It happened more regularly in those days since I exerted myself more. As with the rest of my condition, I absorbed it into my everyday life and hid it away from the world. *I even hid it from my own memories.*

"Alright, so here's the plan," she said when we came to rest in front of my favorite arcade. "You follow me. When I cause a scene, you run like the wind into the stairwell and onto the roof. Are you with me?"

I shook my head between coughing fits. I sucked the dregs of an oxygen tank and popped open another. "What— are you—talking about?"

"Pay attention," she continued. "All you gotta do is run when I say so. Alright? Easy Peasy."

She sprinted toward the entrance without another word of explanation. I didn't know what the heck was going on, but I didn't care. I loved a good arcade. I spent a couple evenings a week stuffing quarters into those old birds.

I dug PlayStation and Steam too but sinking my quarters into the old school cabinets gave me a special thrill. It pained me when that arcade closed three years later due to lack of interest.

*

I trailed Yva inside the arcade. The adrenaline kept my lungs and wobbly knees in check. Behind the counter, a pimply, oil-drenched teenager debated with a kid and his mother about their paltry ticket collection.

"I don't know what to tell you," he said. "You don't have enough tickets to get a teddy bear. You can get a comb or a mustache."

"But I want one!" The kid stomped and cried. I bumped the kid's shoulder as he ran past me in tears. "MOMMY!!!!!"

"How could you be so mean to my son?!" the woman shouted. Yva turned to me with bug eyes and shooed me off.

*

I made my way over to Sunset Riders and stuck in a couple of quarters. I barely got through the load screen before a big shadow blotted out the artificial sun.

"Mind if I join, mate?" Nobody else but Frank used the word 'mate', nobody in East Willow, nobody that loved Sunset Riders as much as me, at least. I bonded with Frank over it into the wee hours of the evening. Together, we were an unstoppable team: I on the shotgun, he on the pistols. Outlaws didn't stand a chance. Unfortunately, I was in no mood for bonding. I had a mission; a secret mission.

"Saw your bird flying around somewhere. That why you haven't been around?"

"Nope." I intentionally jumped into a stray bullet and died. "Rats. I'm all outta quarters. Gotta go. Good seeing you again."

*

I hotfooted to an ill-maintained, dark corner that housed all the seventies-era cabinets. The arcade bought a whole lot from eBay for a song, trying to ride the retro wave of gaming that never came.

They sat unused, but mostly functional. A castle defense game appropriately titled WHERE IT'S KEPT – very pun filled indeed – sported a deep crack down its face, fritzed out half the time, and represented the crowning jewel of the lot. ASTEROID, PONG, and DONKEY KONG also lined the wall.

Management turned down the lights in that corner to hide their shame. I loved them, though; you could play like a king for hours in that corner using only a couple shekels.

I stuck a quarter into the GALAGA machine just when the woman at the register screamed bloody murder. "I demand to see the manager right now!!!!"

I knew a cue when I heard one. *Get to the roof.* That was my mission.

The manager's office guarded the roof's only access door. He was a heavy sleeper and a terrible worker. That's why he was an arcade manager deep into his forties. Only a burning building roused him from afternoon slumber; a burning building or at least the vocal stylings of a screaming woman.

The woman's shrill voice cut through the air. "Get the manager out here right now or I'll sue!!! I swear!!!!"

The maintenance door swung open and an aging gentleman life had shat on popped out and bee-lined for the disturbance. "Please calm down, ma'am. What's wrong?"

I raced up and grabbed the door before it swung closed. I snuck inside and pulled the door closed, but it never clicked. I yanked and squeezed, but a fleshy mitt held it open. Frank's mitt. He swung the door open.

"Let's have it then," he said. "The truth."

"Can you close the door first?" I asked. "I'm kind of on a mission."

"I'll think about it – after the truth."

He deserved the truth, but it wasn't mine to give. Yva had trusted me with vital and damning information. I couldn't violate that trust. On the other hand, being her sole secret keeper gave me ulcers. *Besides, if you couldn't trust your best mates, who could you trust.*

"Alright, fine. Just come in!"

He snapped the door shut behind him. "Out wit' it."

"I'm not crazy. Just remember that."

"I'll determine that, yeah?"

"Thank you for your service!" the woman blustered. "I'm very satisfied with how you handled this situation. Are you satisfied, son?"

Crap! The manager was coming. I heard his footsteps clopping back. "We have to go. He'll kill us if he sees us."

Frank knew I was right, but his obstinacy outshined his survival instinct. He immovably guarded the access roof even as the manager's footsteps grew louder and closer. I pulled, yanked, and shoved to no avail. His fat fingers glued the door shut.

"Please, Frank," I finally begged. "I promise I'll tell you everything alright? Just not now. I'm sorry."

He smiled. "Was that so hard, ay?"

Frank released his grip and the door flew open. I disappeared, and Frank followed lock step behind me. The door slid closed as the manager fell back into his coma.

*

We skipped up the steps and onto the roof. Safely away from momentary danger, I swung around to him. "Like I said, I'm not crazy. The thing is— Yva's an alien. Like a real, full-fledged alien. She needs my help to rebuild her ship and get out—"

"—No more. I don't wanna know. This is bonkers, mate. It's certifiable. You're going off the deep end. You really believe this girl's from space! That's more nuts than I thought you could get."

"Don't you think I know that?"

"No. I need to hear ya say it. Say yer laffy daffy banana pants."

"I am laffy daffy banana pants. Now can you help me?"

"And what do you think that makes me, helping a guy who just said somethin' daft like he was laffy daffy banana pants?"

"A friend."

He snickered. "Yer an arse."

Yva shouted up from the street. "You up there??"

"Stay put, alright?" I said to Frank and ran over to the ledge. "And be quiet."

Yva smiled up at me. "You got up there! Awesome! Did you find it?"

"Find what? What am I looking for?"

"Oh, right." She held her arms out chest wide. "It's an antenna. About two feet long. Glows in the dark."

I took a quick look around. Frank mouthed, "What does she want?"

At least I think that's what he said. It also could've been "Slather me with cream pie", but that didn't make sense. Still, on the list of things in my life that didn't make sense, that request wouldn't have been anywhere near the bottom.

"Did you find it?" Yva shouted.

"Not yet! Gimme a minute." I counted seventeen antennae on the roof of the arcade: TV antennae, cell phone antennae, possibly CIA antennae; none of them looked particularly "alien" to me.

*

I scoured the roof for thirty minutes with no success as the sun crept below the horizon. As night fell, a slight blue tinge emanated above the roof. The faint hue towered above the other antennae on the tippiest, toppiest ledge with the tiniest foothold of the entire building.

"Found it!" I shouted.

"Well hurry up then," Yva shouted from the ground.

"Boost me up, buddy." I said to Frank.

Frank sighed and held his hand together and boosted me above the access door. I carefully slid onto the narrow ledge that held the antennae.

*

Several symmetrical cylinders complicated the shaft, but otherwise it didn't seem particularly alien to me even close-up. It seemed, in fact, that any Radio Shack antennae in the greater Tri-State area could've done the job. Except at its base. The base was intertwined, intermingled, and ill fit among the other cables, attaching to them like the roots of a tree attached to the ground.

I yanked hard at the base and it budged slightly, pliably, like it was alive. There wasn't time to be delicate. So, I yanked. I yanked hard. Sparks flew as the antenna wiggled free.

"That's a bad idea," Frank said. But I didn't care. "This is looney tunes banana pants, man!"

I was acutely aware, even then, the degree of craziness it took to rip an antenna off a building. I *needed* that antennae though. It was my mission. Yva's mission. I couldn't fail. I pulled harder, loosening the antenna slightly with each yank until eventually it popped off into my hand, electrical wires nipping a dying burst.

That's when everything went fuzzy, before it went dark.

*

I woke up in my own bed a few hours later. I wasn't a fan of blacking out, but I'd become accustomed to the sensation. It never became a more pleasant experience, though; especially when you've just stolen the communications antenna of your favorite arcade.

Truthfully, I had no idea how unpleasant or awkward it was until Frank told me. The manager came to check on the interruption in his radio feed and found my unconscious body. He assumed the worst about Frank. All his bumbling and babbling did little to allay the manager's fears. He left to call the paramedics. That's when Frank pocketed the antenna, threw me over his shoulder, barreled out the building and fireman carried me the four miles home. Yeah, that's right. Four miles.

*

I had no love for cops, nor their intrusions into my life. They always seemed to side with the aggressor and discount the victims. So, when they showed up at my door later that night with a wiry CPS officer, I pleaded the fifth. They just wanted to "ask me questions" and "make sure I was alright". I've played that game. The manager of the arcade knew me. They were there to probe me about the recent theft.

"Do you have a warrant or anything?" I asked.

"Well no. We just want to talk. Do we need a warrant to talk?" the CPS officer said.

"Inside, you do," I said. "We can talk outside though."

Never let officers into your house. Not when you have something incriminating to hide. That was rule #1. For years Dad physically and mentally abused Mom, not to mention emotionally tormented her. However, the most he ever got was a quick talking to by a laughing cop and a pat on the back. He never let them in.

"Do you know anything about a robbery at Morton's Arcade this afternoon?" one officer asked. "A communications antenna was taken, and the manager described you specifically fleeing the scene."

I chuckled. "I was at the arcade earlier, but I have no need for a communications antenna. That seems crazy."

"It does seem crazy," the CPS officer stated. "But it's our job to follow up on things like this."

CPS officers were the worst. They rotated like a mentally taxing game of duck, duck, goose, passed around until the pain of their ineptitude swallowed them up. I didn't bother learning their names. I was on CPS officer #8 in the short time we'd lived with Pop.

"How are you doing since my colleagues' last visit, Samuel? Your principal seems to think things have degraded. Is everything going alright at home?"

I didn't bother answering their questions. How could I? The truth would have only led to me being removed from my mother, Pop, Yva, and Frank.

"Everything is fine. If there's nothing else, I have a lot of homework to do."

"Of course," the CPS officer said. "If you need anything, you have our number."

The one nice thing about being an invalid; people don't think you could do anything wrong. They believe you incapable of lying and applauded the sheer moxie it took for me to get up in the morning. Had I displayed the antenna proudly, there's at least an outside chance they would have thrown me a parade.

I went back to bed, counting my blessing the shock didn't blow up my oxygen tanks. If I didn't have an incurable disease, some might even say I was lucky.

SEVENTEEN

I caught up with Frank as he opened his lunch pail on the rickety bench where we set up camp every day. I opened my mouth but choked on my words. Exhibiting human emotion was never easy for me, especially when it wasn't blind rage. *How could I tell him how much I appreciated what he did? How he stood up for me? What it meant to have a friend like him?*

"Thanks," I said.

He nodded. "No problem."

That was it. We switched gears to video games, and football (real football, not the American kind), and how rugby was the best sport in the world I never watched.

We fell back into a natural groove built in the days before Yva's secrets. I'd spent too much time worrying about lying to him, I didn't even give him a chance to be a confidante.

Frank wolfed down his first lunch pail by the time I sat down and was nearly halfway through his second. He let out a sigh as Yva sidled up to us. "Feeling better, I see."

"No thanks to you," Frank responded. "I had to whip that guy with your antennae just to get out of there. And me mate almost died of electrocution."

"He was fine."

"How'd ya know that, then? Since all you did was run off the first signa trouble?"

"I didn't bolt! I saw you had it under control and made a strategic getaway! Do you have it though? The piece. I really need it."

"Oh yeah. I got it. But I wanna see this thing Sam's riskin' life and limb for before ya get it, yeah?"

Yva gritted her teeth. "Fine. After school. Don't be late."

*

Ten minutes after the last bell, Frank and I were on our way to Yva's ship. Frank remained unimpressed, pouting, the entire trip until we crested over that final ridge and the ship presented itself. It wasn't quite as magnificent without the ethereal blue glow, but it did the trick to wash away his cynicism.

"That's flippin' incredible," Frank said.

"Now do you see why I believe she's an alien?"

"No, but it is really cool none the less."

We scrambled together down the hill. Frank examined the ship from every angle, rubbing his finger across the grooved letters I'd still made no progress in deciphering.

"Can I have it then?" Yva asked. "The piece."

Frank pulled the antenna out of his backpack and handed it to Yva. "Still don't like this, yeah?"

"I don't care," she responded. "Ready to see something cool?"

Yva crawled up to the roof of the ship and plugged the antenna into place. She was equal parts precise, delicate, and nimble.

"Alright!" Yva finally said as she straightened the shaft. "It's done." She hopped down and unearthed a car battery from underneath a mound of leaves and blankets. She wired the positive to the battery and held the ground in her hand. "I think this'll work."

"What do you mean, you think?" Frank said.

"Well, it's not like I can read the instructions now, is it?" She looked at me. "If this doesn't work and I fry myself, don't take me to a hospital, okay? I won't become a lab experiment. Promise?"

I nodded. "Yeah. I promise."

"Good enough." She crawled under the ship and flipped open a latch. She mumbled something under her breath, closed her eyes and clamped on the ground cable. It crackled and fizzled to life.

The ship screeched and hummed. Strings of gibberish spilled out of its radio; beautiful, elegant, gorgeous gibberish. "Kfhedfh edfhlewfh;ehfgkleh Kalei Yva Altalien. Nem."

It continued like that for several loops. Then, it popped loudly, and crackled, and went silent.

"What was that?" I asked.

"That was my language," Yva said, tears in her eyes. "My home language."

*

I'm not a true believer — actually I'm not any kind of believer. I flatly disbelieve in religion all together. I don't believe in God, angels, the Devil, Heaven, Hell, or any of it.

I haven't since Nana's funeral, when some idiot shook my hand and said. "I'm very sorry for your loss," then mumbled "That's a shame." as he walked away.

I haven't since I found him afterwards to ask what was such a shame, hoping it was a Knicks loss or broken shoelace tied or because he spilled chocolate sauce all over his tie before the service.

I haven't since he turned to me and, with a straight face, told me "Because a priest didn't absolve her sins. So, she's not going to Heaven."

I stood hornswoggled and flummoxed for a good five minutes. There were lots and lots of people that aren't going to Heaven: murderers, rapists, ruthless dictators, abusers, but Nana not going was a travesty. After putting up with Pop for most of her life the LEAST God could do was open the gates wide for her.

My Nana was a saint akin to Mother Theresa. In fact, Mother Theresa couldn't handle my Pop. Nobody could. Nobody did. Except for Nana; and if she was going to Hell – no. If that was what religion preached, I wanted none of it.

I tossed my Sunday school books, stopped going to service and quit church altogether. I previously loved the idea of religion, or an eternal reward for earthly suffering. I found God in everything in my youth; from the sunset to a simple flower to the way electricity worked. After that day, I found him in nothing.

But on that day in the woods, when I heard that radio crack and the most beautiful sounds that had ever filled my ears lift my spirits, it was hard not to believe in the divine. It lifted my soul to dance.

And I cried. I cried all the way home. Frank too. We'd never heard anything like it in our lives. Some days I wish I could hear it again. Just one more time. For one more second.

No, that's not true. I wished for it every day. Sometimes every minute. As the years went by the sounds grow dimmer, like the bells from the Polar Express. But the feeling of joyous rapture never faded.

Those words. Those letters. Those vocal cords which produced them came from another plane. Every doubt I had about Yva being an alien vanished in that moment. I was convinced.

And I saw it in Frank's watery eyes. He believed as well. We didn't have to acknowledge it. We just knew. We were changed.

*

I barely walked through the door when Mom pulled me back out. I'd barely caught a glimpse of the lottery tickets littered across the kitchen table. Pop frantically scratched more vigorously enough to leave a groove on the table.

"Loser, loser—Come on! Another loser!"

His hope addiction crossed over to necessity in those days. The hospital's collection agency called twice before I dropped my bags. They were ruthless, relentless, and brutal. Our only hope of repayment became Pop hitting one of those worthless scratchers.

Mom took three odd jobs to make ends meet, which kept her out all hours of the day and night. Even with them, we still drowned in our accumulated debt. No matter how we dug ourselves out of a hole, another one presented itself. The bills washed over us again and again.

"Where are we going?" I asked.

"Out. I just need a witness, and you're the only one I trust, okay? Quit asking so many questions."

Ironically, that was the name of the payday loan company she parked in front of. "THE ONE YOU TRUST PAYDAY LOANS", *we give you cash 'til payday, with a name you trust.* Payday loans. They were predatory and awful, but we needed relief quick.

Just like a drug fix. Drugs for those in poverty. You knew it was wrong, but it brought momentary sweet relief. I begged Mom to pawn some jewelry or sell her blood. She could've even sold my blood. I told her to sell an ovary or two. Anything but take out a payday loan we couldn't repay.

"What do you think I've been doing the past month, kiddo? I ain't got no blood left and there's only so many experiments the body can endure. I already pawned everything of value."

I thought about it for the first time. I'd been so oblivious to our family's machination, so transfixed on Yva and her ship, that I didn't see it.

Still, it was clear as day when I looked back. Over time, Pop's house became sparser and sparser. I'd never put two and two together. We ate on paper plates instead of Nana's ceramic ones. A white stain hung in place of our clock. Pop's TV downgraded from plasma to a cheap black and white CRT model. He loved that.

"Ah," he said, "TV like it was meant to be."

I'd been too busy with Yva to notice our family circling the drain. So low we sunk, that payday loans became our brightest respite for home. Payday loans with job collateral Mom probably wouldn't have on payday.

They said all the right things: "We're here to help.", "Your satisfaction is our guarantee.", "We'll work with you if you can't pay.", and the like. Of course they'll work with you. The longer it takes to pay back your loan, the more interest grew and the further into their clutches we sunk.

Still, even with all of that. Even with every knot in our stomachs squeezing tight, Mom took the money…we had to eat, we had to drink, we had to live. We were the ideal client; we had no other option.

*

We brought home a KFC feast fit for no man with hope in his heart. Halfway through dinner, Pop screamed "SAMBUCA!!" and pointed to the basement. He asked for everything in short, annoying declarations and expected them fulfilled in five minutes.

I looked at Mom; she was too worn from three straight twelve-hour shifts to move a muscle. So, I dutifully trudged to the cellar. Mom hated it down there, full of childhood traumas I'd never experienced. I'd always liked the basement, though.

Eyeless dolls, broken plates, and other relics from the past caught a glint of the light as it passed by and haunted more than one of my nightmares. Still, it was peaceful and quiet. The insulation drowned out Pop's incessant demands, and by opening the cellar shutters even the dust and dander didn't bother me much.

It filled my imagination with wonder, actually, to picture the children who played with five-foot-high stuffed dogs and burned the heads of GI JOES.

In his younger days, Pop collected knick-knacks from trash cans along his route. In his later years, rummaging through the dump for lost treasures became an obsession, especially after Nana died. He displayed the best of the best and kept the rest in boxes labeled "COOL OTHER JUNK STUFF". Coffee-stained and tattered books and trinkets filled those boxes, not unique enough to display, but too sentimental to trash; every one a memory of somebody's life.

"Hurry up down there!" Pop shouted.

I scrounged the minibar and found a half-drunk Sambuca bottle. I never got the appeal of disgusting licorice flavored booze, but if it calmed Pop down, I wasn't complaining. I delivered the bottle to him just in time to hear the answering machine click.

"Sammy, it's your dad. Please pick up, son. I gotta talk to you. I only get one call a day and I'm usin' it on you, buddy. Come on, my man, pick up. Pick up! If you don't, I'll have no choice—alright. I warned you. See you soon. I love you. Bye."

His desperation bordered on the pathetic. Patheticism that boiled over the following day into downright stalker type stuff.

EIGHTEEN

I sat at lunch in silence, staring off into space. Frank prattled on about one thing or another: school, movies, video games, some test he took. He complained about some teacher or student. I was in my own head, so his words floated and flittered into the ether. I caught every other sentence or so.

"Can you believe Featherbottom's test, mate? Killer. Can't believe she expected us to know the opposite angle of a right triangle. How'my supposeda know that, ay?"

"It's ridiculous—" Yva slammed down her tray. Frank called her "Hurricane Yva, the Alien". Every time she made landfall, our lives were about to be tilted asunder.

"You even go here, mate?" Frank asked.

Yva chortled. "Course I go here. You think they'd let some random chick walk through school?"

Frank nodded. "Starting to. I barely ever see ya in class 'cept for test days."

"Maybe I'm just really good at hiding—ever think of that? Unlike your fat ass, I don't lumber around."

I remembered back to that day in the bodega. She hid in plain sight; not even the stock boy recognized her until she took two cases of soup.

"Little strange though, ain't it?" Frank asked. "I mean, if you're an alien, how'd you get into school, huh?"

Yva rolled her eyes. "I faked a passport and got a homeless guy to act like my dad. It's not that hard."

"Bullocks."

"Really? Because illegal aliens do it all the time."

"Well they ain't from outer space, is they?"

"Same problem, though, ain't it?"

"Why'd you even come ta school anyway, yeah? Don't you just wanna get off this blue marble, ay?"

"I like learning, jackass. I don't have to defend myself to you anyway!"

Frank elbowed me. "What chu think, mate? You bein' awful quiet."

I was quiet. My mind was still awash in thoughts of the heavens. Then I saw a glint of him in the shadows of the fence separating us from the outside world.

My father stood on the other side of it, cloaked in shadows. There he was; no police sirens or anything, like it was the most normal thing in the world.

*

I drifted like a ghost across the playground. I caught a whiff of "normals" smoking cigarettes. It deflected my anger from Dad for a moment toward their destruction of their perfectly useable lungs, what a waste. *I hated them.*

I fought my body and tried to turn away from the fence, but it wouldn't listen. With each passing moment I inched closer, despite myself. I screamed and shouted for my legs to walk somewhere else; anywhere else. Instead, it ended up inches from dear old Dad, only a fence between us.

"Just like old times," I said. "You made bail."

"I hired a lawyer," he responded.

"You mean they appointed a free one for you."

"Same difference. You've been avoiding my calls."

"Should I feel bad about that?"

He shook his head. "No."

"Good. Because I don't."

"In prison—they taught me some things."

"I'll bet. Like, don't drop the soap."

"Like how to control my anger. And how badly I treated your mother and you. And how it was wrong. I wanna see you, man."

"You needed prison to teach you that?"

"It's a little depressing to admit, but yeah. I know you don't believe me, but I'm a changed man."

"I've heard that song and dance before, a few hundred times. I don't buy it."

"I know. Neither does your moth—"

"You leave her out of this!"

"Then have dinner with me. It's all I ask."

I white-knuckled the fence. "Fine. But keep Mom out of this. You go near her again, and I'm walking out. I'll punch myself in the face, make Frank beat me half to death, and I'll blame it on you. I'll be so convincing you'll never make bail again. Got it?"

He nodded, and I promised to pick up next time he called. Then, he walked back into the shadows.

*

It took three calls with Dad to broker the peace. "No, I'm not going to a fancy restaurant." "Because then you'll hold it over my head." "You will absolutely not pick me up here. I'll meet you around the corner." "Fine. Barry's. That's acceptable. Mom doesn't find out. Once we're done, you'll never bother her again, agreed?" *Agreed.*

I hated going behind Mom's back, but it was for her own good. She did stuff for my own good all the time that I hated: she force-fed me veggies, poked and prodded me like a human pin cushion, and forced me to bathe way more than a reasonable amount.

My rendezvous with Dad was just something loved ones do for each other; a moral gray area we all lived in from time to time. This one just happened to be a very deep gray. Besides, she was half dazed from sleep deprivation and pill depravation.

*

I met Dad three blocks away from Pop's. I was ashamed of him; and myself. Dad drove a new hoopty. It popped and crackled through its rusted innards. Something had gnawed through the seat belts, and cigarette burns dotted the upholstery. If it got closer than three blocks from Pop's house, Mom would know everything. I couldn't have that.

"I won it in a prison card game," he said. "If I'd lost, I would've had to take one in the mouth. Thank God I didn't lose, right?"

"I don't want to hear that," I responded. "You know I'm your kid, right? I don't want to hear how many loads you took while you were in the joint."

"Three. Only three…I'm joking." But I heard truth behind his jokes. I placated him with muted murmurs and chuckles at his dumb jokes the rest of the ride to Barry's.

*

Our waitress's chocolate-stained dress carried the well-worn sign of a newbie. Dad eyed the young thing with the mournful lust of an aged man on the prowl.

"Leer much?" I asked.

"If she didn't wanna be stared at, she shouldn't have gams like that."

"That's disgusting. You realize I'm your son, still, right? And you're married to my mom, still? You know what, forget it. Can we get down to business? What do you really want?"

He sighed. "Well I was hopin' ta get a little more sugar in your belly before I told you this—I want you back. I love you. You're my boy."

"Since when?"

"Since forever." He leaned in. "I know I ain't treated you that good in the past, but I'm a changed man."

I leaned in to meet him. "Last time you said that you gave Mom a black eye a week later. Time before that you sent her to the ER with a cracked rib. Time before that—"

"I don't need a history lesson, Sammy. I know I been a complete turd muncher."

"You think? You just beat my grandfather half to death. That *just* happened. He still can't walk right or eat solid food. So, what's changed then?"

"Jail changed me, Sammy. I ain't never been inside. I don't never wanna be there again. There's some real assholes in that jail, man. I didn't wanna be like one of them. I ain't like one of 'em."

"Alright, you wanna be my father again. What medications am I on, Dad?"

"That's a good question, Sammy," he responded. "I don't know the answer."

"How often do you need to refill my oxygen tanks?"

"Once a month, maybe? Man, you're caught up in the details."

"Wrong. Do I take my pills with food or on an empty stomach?"

He slapped his hands together. "Alright, I got this. 50/50. With food."

"Wrong. Last question, how long did it take you to start looking for me when I was gone?"

He stuttered and stammered for a good three minutes after that. I'd had enough. "You got none of them right. 0 for 4. Goodnight, Dad."

He grabbed my wrist before I could leave. "I'm better for you'n your Mom. I wouldn't have taken you out of school, kept you on the run without doctors or held you up in motels fearing for your life. I wouldn't pop yer pills neither."

"No. I just would've feared for my life every day from the comfort of my own house. Now get off me before I cause a scene."

He released me. That's when I saw her – Mom. In that moment I witnessed her heart tear apart.

"Let's go." That's all she had to say. Her heart was broken in two. No amount of explaining could fix it. It was only something that healed in time, with a lot of pills and booze.

*

Early the next morning, I woke bleary eyed to a loud rap at the front door. Mom told me to stay in bed, but I tagged along anyway. A bushy haired woman stood at the front door wearing a scowl. I learned she was a process server too late.

She handed Mom a bright yellow envelope. "You've been served."

Process servers are dicks. Their jobs were twenty different ways of awful, nobody wanted subpoenas served on them, and more than once they'd been pepper sprayed or beaten up, but come on man – can't a brother get a cup of coffee before you wrecked their lives?

Mom ripped open the letter and read it aghast. It was from my dad. He was suing for full custody and filing for divorce.

Divorce. Dad threatened to kill himself if Mom ever brought the idea of divorce up; if she even uttered the word in his presence, he went nuts.

But there it was, on court documents in black and white. Mom's brain spun and flung around. She blubbered and stammered. The letter fell from her hand and floated to the floor.

"I can't—I just can't deal with this today—"

She was right. She didn't have time to deal with anything else because it was Doctor Day; the worst day of the year.

I didn't think Doctor Day could get any worse, but Dad found a way.

*

Every two weeks I spent an evening having blood drawn, peeing in a bottle, and pooping in a cup. Every other month I went through a chest CT, MRI, and ultrasound. Every six months I endured a stress test. Twice a year they fell on the same day. Doctor Day.

I spent about 10% of my life in doctors' offices. Since I spent another 33% of it at school and 33% sleeping, I spent 1/3 of my remaining free time with medical professionals, so I got rather chummy with the receptionists. By and large I hated them. They patronized me, asked stupid questions, and nearly never earned their keep. They kept me waiting with an unpleasant smile that screamed contempt for their job.

They had the social skills of a 5th grader and the physique to match. They chatted like catty school children, and they read magazines written for babies.

On this particular Doctor Day though, there was nobody in Phil's office except the good doctor. He picked up a never-ending string of phone calls. "Excuse me. Yes. I— Hold please. How do you work this thing?!!!"

Mom grabbed the phone from him. "The doctor will call you back. Yes. Please hold. I'm sorry he's busy on that date, possibly the following week. He'll call you back. Good day."

By the time she hung up, Phil clapped. "That was incredible. Even my old receptionist couldn't do that. You have a gift."

"Sure. Sure. We're late though. I've got another job later and I know these tests take forever. Can we hurry this along?"

Phil eyed her for an uncomfortably long time. "Maybe this can be your job."

"Don't mess with me, doctor. I hate you. I know you're not fond of me either."

"I wasn't fond of my last receptionist too and she was here four years." Dr. Phil smiled. "I'm dead serious. She just didn't show up today. Said she's moving to Tahoe with some ski instructor. If you want the job—."

Good things didn't happen for my mother; especially not on Doctor Day; especially not after being served. She didn't quite know how to react. Luckily, I did. "She accepts!"

Dr. Phil smiled. "Good. You start right now while I examine Sam. Don't curse."

The phone rang, but Mom didn't move. I grabbed it and stuck it in her hand. "Talk."

She sprung to attention. "Dr. Morris's office. How can I help you?"

"Come on, Samuel. Your mom's got work to do. We have a big day." He led me by the shoulder into the nearest exam room while I mouthed "Congratulations" and gave a thumbs up.

We ran through battery after battery of tests. I ran treadmills and blew into lung testers. They drew pints of blood and gallons of other fluids. After hours of non-stop testing, we were done. The smile hadn't fallen from Mom's face all day. Sitting behind a desk, gossiping, throwing her feet up – white collar work suited her.

*

Mom drove me to each of her three terrible jobs, grinning from ear to ear. The word "quit" barely escaped her lips before she left a cloud of dust behind her.

Then we drove to the supermarket for the fattest steaks we could find. It was the first of the month. Our newly loaded EBT card usually meant ramen and milk. Lots of milk. Why did they make us buy so much milk?

Mom hated it. She hated the sideways glances, the shame of needing government assistance, and the embarrassed pity others felt for her. But mostly she hated the checkout sigh. There was always a sigh – whenever we pulled out our EBT – whether from the check-out girl, the bagger, or the man in line behind us. As if it wasn't a pain in the ass for us to use it. As if that was our master plan, to make so little we needed food stamps.

But not on that day. Mom smiled through the checkout. She stocked up on delicious, fresh fruits and veggies, she bought thick-cut meat and deli-counter cold cuts – not those vacuum sealed ones. She blew hundreds of dollars easy.

And she didn't use that EBT card. When we got home, she cut it up and threw it away. She hated that card. It was a great day. The kind our family didn't see often.

The kind of day where we forgot about dad, and tests and even my condition.

*

Dad came around the school every day at lunch for the next week. I tried avoiding him. I tried telling on him. I tried throwing food at him, but it wasn't enough. He wasn't going anywhere. By Wednesday, I gave up and ate my lunch across the fence from him.

"Why are you divorcing Mom, Dad? Why now?"

"I told you I changed, Sammy. Mom deserves better. I deserve worse. We all deserve a new start."

It was the most intelligent thing he ever said. It was the most mature he'd been since I was seven. In that moment, I really, desperately wanted him back. I wanted that guy to be my dad. I really wanted that glimpse of him being magnanimous to last forever.

*

But it couldn't. It couldn't even last the week before the suck descended on us again. That was my father – one nice thing followed by ten terrible ones. He not only wanted a divorce— he wanted custody— full custody – and he wanted alimony. Her new job smell hadn't even worn off and Dad already wanted to rub manure into the fresh scent of success.

"Your mom got that job whiles we were married. Only fair I should get my cut."

He stopped just short of demanding her license and passport, so she couldn't flee the country. Mom might've fled too, if her case wasn't so airtight.

No arbitrator ever sided with the father, especially not when they demonstrated a violent temper repeatedly and with malice. He was on trial for assaulting an octogenarian. No judge in his right mind would rule in Dad's favor.

Except Dad had a lawyer. Somehow, he convinced his bleeding-heart assistant DA to take the case pro bono. The lawyer wasn't great. He wasn't even good. But he was better than Mom.

She couldn't afford a lawyer, so she was stuck with herself as a client. It's the worst mistake in the book, defending yourself. Dad learned it the hard way and quickly became Mom's teacher.

The lawyer asked lot of questions, none painted Mom in a flattering light.

- Did you run over the plaintiff? *Yes.*
- Did you intend to cause bodily harm when you hit my client with your car? *Yes.*
- Did you take my client's son without telling him? *Yes.*
- Did you make any attempt to contact my client to let him know where his son was? *No.*
- Did you live out of a car while you were on the run? *Yes.*
- Did you fill up your son's medication and oxygen tank regularly? *No.*
- Did your son regularly see a doctor? *No.*

The longer her testimony lasted, the less airtight Mom's case became. Dad's lawyer did a bang-up job of painting her as a flighty, ill-equipped mother. Then he went in for a death blow.

• Do you use your son's medication? *I don't recall.*

• Don't or won't. *Don't.*

• You realize you are under oath. *Yes.*

Mom did the best she could with her examination of Dad, but she represented herself and Dad's lawyer had rebuttals for every possible scenario. They already rattled her.

• Did you beat me repeatedly? *Irrelevant. My client never laid a hand on the child. Hearsay.*

• Have you ever intended to cause bodily harm to Sammy? *My client's prior state of mind is not relevant here. He's admitted prior wrong-doings and will pay for them.*

Mom squirmed in the breeze. Dad got off on torturing her. He must've busted ten nuts. I couldn't stand by and let him get off an 11th.

"Why do you want me, Dad?" I asked.

"You're my son, kiddo. I want to see you. I want to be in your life. Isn't that enough reason?"

I shook my head. "It's the worst reason."

"Fine. I want to be better. I have five years of being a horrible father to make up for. I can't do that part time. I can't do that across the country. I can't do that unless I'm with you every minute of every day."

"If you've really changed, really, really changed, I'll come with you. I'll stay with you. I'll move in with you three nights a week. I'm not leaving Mom though."

"What's the catch?"

"No catch. All you gotta do is win your trial. Meanwhile, show me you're in counseling, have a real place to live, and that you have a real job. You get a job and a real place to live and I'll come stay with you once. Just once, before the trial ends. You're not getting more than that. No alimony. No child support. Nothing. I'll run away every day if you take me out of East Willow. Deal?"

The lawyer whispered into Dad's ear. Dad grinned ear to ear. "Alright, Sammy. You got a deal."

"A real job, apartment, and counseling?" I smirked. "Guess I'll see you when Hell freezes over."

He flashed a toothy smile. "We'll see."

He and his lawyer left, and my mother collapsed into my arms. "What have you done?"

I stroked her hair. "It will be alright." But even I didn't believe that myself.

NINETEEN

After real heavy stuff like betraying your mother, it was always good to see Frank and Yva. Well, it's really good to see them both separately. Frank never much liked Yva, nor vice versa. So much so that it made it very difficult to hang out with them in the same room, bickering as they do.

Frank thought Yva made me risk too much, do too much. He thought that she played off my affections toward her to manipulate me to her will.

Yva thought Frank was a pussy. I mean he was definitely right about all that other stuff. She freely admitted she manipulated me for her own gain.

"That's how life goes, Frank," she said. "I manipulate him. He will manipulate some other girl. She manipulates some fat oaf. It's the circle of manipulation."

I loved her more than anything on the planet. Yva forced me through my previous shortcomings. She made me walk longer, stay out later, swing a hammer, hold heavy equipment, and entrusted me with all her secrets.

With her I did more than I thought possible. More than I thought would kill me and it didn't kill me. It made me stronger, more confident. I could fart in front of Frank and act like a dude, but that became less interesting than the thrill Yva provided.

Some days I needed them both. On those days we argued, bickered and settled on throwing pennies at passing trains. Yva tired quickly of the tedium in it and Frank quickly found the solace. I placed pennies 10 deep and watched them flutter through the air like magic with each train, catching the dying light of the sun like little stars.

On the day after my deal with a devil, Yva started chucking her allotment right into the cabins of the passing trains. "Three points if you get it through. Five if it lands in the cabin."

Frank loved a good game. Competition was the only thing that bonded him and Yva. A game was afoot, and he wasn't about to lose to some silly, little girl. "Five bucks for the winner."

Frank failed to get even one single penny into one single car, every single time. Yva never missed. The advantage of being an alien, clearly.

Frank fumed. Not only had he lost miserably to a girl, but it was Yva no less. He pulled out the last five dollars in his tattered wallet and forked it over, head on his knees.

Yva looked at it and smiled. She handed the money to me. "You know, I could use a milkshake. Yeah, a milkshake would go real nice. How about everybody else?"

A smooth smile crept across her face and perked up Frank's. It was those things that made me love her. She was homeless. She had nothing. And yet, she still saw that Frank was hurt, somebody that I cared about, and she mended a fence.

*

Not to mention I got a milkshake, which was dope. Milkshakes made me forget, for a moment, my terrible judgment; my terrible deal.

Dad couldn't though. He strutted around school more and more after that. He waited outside when the last bell dismissed and hung off the fence during lunch. "Ay Sammy, I got some big news comin'! You wait!"

On my more accommodating days, I met him there and listened to his crap "I got three interviews tomorrow, buddy. You'll be proud.", "I'm meetin' with a psychologist tonight too.", "We're gonna be together soon, buddy."

I threw him bones every now and then, but mostly I hated him. "You know what you did to Mom is worse than anything you've ever done before?"

"You do know that you're takin' her side? There are two sides here, Sammy. I lost my son. My son was homeless and without medications. Nearly left for dead. Can't you, even a little bit, see it my way?"

I couldn't.

*

Mom's mood tilted manic in those days. Dr. Phil's hours were much more lenient than her previous jobs, and she'd get home before the sun dropped below the horizon. Her life's misery broke a bit, and even her pill habit calmed. I even had enough to get me through all but the worst days.

The fog cleared from Mom's head and the last few months came into stark focus: my abject disregard for her rules, my betrayal, and my eminent departure from her womb. No amount of my professed undying love calmed her mind.

"You got a funny way of showin' it," she replied to my every comment.

But I did show it. I stepped in front of a bullet for her, instead of the other way around. That's real love. She loved me, but her love became even colder and even more distant. I wondered if her wound would ever heal.

She was everything to me once, and now she wanted nothing to do with me. Before, I could handle it; the pills kept her numb. But without them, her seething indifference cut deeper, much deeper.

*

In those days I took solace in Yva's stories. She told me about her home planet; it was created 7,000,000 years before Earth. In the cosmic scheme of things that's not that much, but when you look at all we've accomplished in a single thousand, it's remarkable to think what could be created given seven thousand times more.

Her species created amazing things; over and over again. But every time their civilization advanced through to a certain point, it was decimated by famine, disease, and war. Robots destroyed their civilization once, mutated viruses another, and a disastrous asteroid a third. Once they were wiped out by famine, and another by interstellar scavengers.

Each time they survived, rebuilt, and remade their civilization anew. They learned from their mistakes, and each time built their world better and more resistant to change. Their governments became more unilateral, less wavering, and warier of outside influence. Once that even became their undoing.

Luckily, even on the verge of extinction, their technology survived. They advanced quicker and quicker with each genocide, until they made it past the extinction level events that brought them ruin before.

They created greenhouses filled with food, weapons to protect their people, and even strains of vaccines to prevent them from diseases both known and unknown. They even protected against known unknowns.

They got so good at protecting against extinction level events, that it became their undoing.

*

The principal pulled me into her office again that afternoon. "Sammy, I'm sounding like a broken record. I've tried to help you, but you make it very difficult. Not to mention that your parents have been uncooperative at best. What are we going to do about this?"

"Have some sympathy, maybe," I responded, "to everything we're going through."

"I do have sympathy, Sammy. I wish you could understand where I'm coming from. I have—"

"Boxes you need to check. I know. You have things you have to report for, plus—"

"Plus, I care about you, Sammy. I want you to do well. And you are not doing well. You're behind every student in class."

"Am I suspended?"

"No, Sammy. I'm not suspending you. That would be too easy. I think you would like that. I want you to try harder. Will you do that for me?"

"No. Can I go back to class now?"

"Will you go back to class, Sammy? Will you?"

"I guess we'll see."

*

I asked Yva once why she wanted to go home. "Why don't you just stay here? I mean it can't be that bad here."

"It's pretty bad, Sam. It's really, really __*pretty*__ bad."

"I'm here."

She smiled. "Yeah you are, but it's not home. Ever since I can remember, I've felt a twinge of pain and loneliness, like I don't belong. Haven't you ever felt like you don't belong, Sam?"

"Every day of my life."

"And if there was a way to end it, to find somewhere you fit in, wouldn't you take it? Wouldn't you do everything you could to end the torment."

"I would."

"There's your answer."

*

I found Yva every chance I got: before school, during lunch, and after school. Then one day, she was gone, without a trace. I looked for her and asked about her. Nobody knew anything; nobody even remembered her.

"You're being a wanker," Frank said. "She vanished before. She vanished a buncha times prolly, all over the world. She's that kinda girl. You gotta get over her. She ain't no good."

But I knew better. She wouldn't abandon me.

At night I fruitlessly scoured online journals and I rummaged the local papers during 'classroom' reading time every morning before math studies. I checked the obits and the police blotter, hoping for a clue.

I found it three days into my search. A tiny article in the smallest print at the lowest corner of an abandoned page:

LOCAL TEEN LEFT BEATEN AND BRUISED AFTER ASSAULT

Late Tuesday night a local teen was found assaulted and unconscious by local law enforcement at the corner of Willow and Pine near the famous Barry's Diner. She was taken to a local hospital for further observation. No suspects have been detained. Best efforts to identify the teen have failed.

It was Yva. I knew it. *Taken to a local hospital.*

It had to be County General. It was the only one close enough. Two counties and two dozen miles separated it from East Willow Middle; too far to walk, too far even to bike, even with my newly improved stamina.

My friend, my Penny, laid in a hospital room alone. I had to find her quick. She'd once made me promise I'd never let her be a lab experiment.

If they drew blood even once, they'd know she was an alien. They'd take her to Roswell, or Area 51, or the more secretive Area 52; they'd torture her to death, revive her, and do it all again. I couldn't let that happen. I needed a car.

All I had was a hoopty.

*

Dad trolled the fence line that afternoon like every one before it. For once I was glad to see him. "I need your help."

"You sure, buddy?" Dad replied. "I ain't quite found a job yet."

"Don't care. I need a favor and I need you not to ask me any questions. Can you do that?"

"I think so. You ain't gonna kill nobody, are you?"

"No questions. Meet me out front."

I walked away. He screamed over my shoulder. "You sure I can do that?"

I didn't respond. I was too busy eyeing the stiletto wearing roadblock that was my principal.

"I've been meaning to talk to you about that gangly father of yours patrolling our walls. It's against policy to—"

I didn't break my gait. I'd barreled right past her mid-sentence. In school suspension would be an upgrade from what she put me through.

"We'll talk later then," she said.

*

By the time I reached the front door, Dad had his hoopty parked in the bus loop. "Where we off to, buddy?"

I popped open the passenger's seat door. "Away from here."

"Alright, kiddo, but you gotta tell me eventually. I'm drivin', remember."

I kicked away empty beer cans and half eaten potato chip bags to take a seat. Before I hopped in though, Frank slid into the back seat. He came out of nowhere like black smoke.

"Where are you—?" I asked.

"If ya needed me with a cage between the two of ya, you need me more now."

I couldn't argue with him. Frank came and went from school at his leisure, one of the advantages of a broken home; especially when neither parent wanted you. He missed out on the love but gained the independence; a terrible trade I wished I could renege as much as he did.

I slid the seat back and scrunched Frank's legs to his chest. His knees buckled under his chin. "Cozy," he grunted.

I heard the clickety clack of the principal's stilettos. "Oh, Sammy," she beckoned. "Hold a minute for me before you run off."

She pressed her hands onto my open window. "Now, I can't just let you run off with any old Tom, Dick, or Harry, can I? Especially one that's been causing such a stir."

Dad smiled a toothy, hillbilly smile. "Well, I ain't just anybody. I'm Sammy's daddy."

"I'm aware of that fact. You know it's customary to sign students out of class, correct?

"Well, heck. I sure didn't. Can you let it slip this one time?"

The sides of her lips curled. "I suppose so. After all, it's nice to see a parent take an interest in his child's education."

"Well, thank you, ma'am. It's easy, as I'm between terms of employment now. I want to get as much time in with my little buddy as possible."

"That's a very interesting happenstance. As luck would have it, I've recently laid off one of my janitors. With your desire to be close to your son, it might be a perfect fit – if you're willing and interested, of course – not the most glamorous work – not at all. Good work though. Honest work."

Things always went Dad's way – and against mine. "I just might be at that."

"How about you come in tomorrow morning? Talk to my secretary."

"I'll do just that."

He had the job before she even bent down into the car; another way for her to mess with me. The principal clomped away—like a tornado – if tornadoes clomped that is. Dad threw the car into gear and tore out of the parking lot before she changed her mind.

*

Every teenager worth his salt learned the subtle art of obfuscation. The smart ones learned it sooner than later. My master course began that day. Dad asked at least twenty questions per minute every minute until we reached County

General, and at every turn I redirected his concerns right back to him.

For every, *"Why the hospital?"* I returned, *"Reminds me of Mom's broken jaw, remember that?"* Each, *"Are you sure we should've clocked you out of school?"* there was a, *"Didn't seem to mind when I missed for your trial."*, and I countered *"We should tell your mother."* with, *"I'm sure she'd love to bring that to the arbitrator."*

*

It took less than 15 minutes to reach General, but it felt like an eternity. Walking would have taken Franko and Samwise a good two days. The price I paid, though, barely netted any gain.

"Wait here," I told my dad. "We'll be back."

Dad pushed the locks closed. "Actually, Sammy. I gotta ask a favor of you, too."

Of course he did. What would a favor be if he didn't have some ulterior motive? "I think you're too in the hole to ask for a favor, Dad."

"Maybe. But I'm askin' anyway." I braced for a plea for money, or something else I was equally unwilling or unable to give. "Can you just understand what I'm doing for you? That I'm tryin'. That's not too much to ask, is it?"

It wasn't. It really wasn't. But it was too much for me to give. I pushed open the door and ran off without another word.

*

Frank and I boot scooted into the hospital. There were no special snowflakes in the hospital game, only slightly different versions of the same one. I knew exactly where the ER was and how to navigate to the ICU. Depending on the architect, I could almost do it blind.

A nurse stuffed herself waist deep into a pizza at the admissions desk. She shot-gunned another slice and massaged her throat to choke down the piece whole.

Her temporary rapture distracted her just enough, that I snuck behind the desk and caught a peek at the patient roster. All the technological protection in the world couldn't protect from the antiquated processes of philistine technophobes.

Yva wasn't on the admissions list. But there was a Jane Doe admitted to the ICU, unconscious with severe head wounds. The time line matched with the newspaper article. It wasn't good news. The ICU isn't a place you spent a lot of time. You left pretty quickly one way or another; either to a normal room or the morgue.

*

The elevator to the ICU opened to blue flashing lights. Coding sirens blared. The ICU erupted in chaos. Nurses, doctors, and orderlies scuttled around at breakneck speed. Doctors shouted "CLEAR" over the screeching flat lining of monitors. Nurses injected God knows what into God knows where to save some poor man's life.

They barely noticed me squeeze into the nurse's station. I scrolled down their roster and found Jane Doe. She'd been move from the ICU the day before into room #1513.

She wasn't dead! My heart skipped two beats. I nearly coded in jubilation, though nobody would have been available to save me as they were all occupied saving some lucky schlep's life. That would have been irony.

*

I knew what to expect walking into Yva's room. I'd seen my mother in the traction more times than I liked to remember. I've seen casts, protective vests, crutches, and metal braces for both mouth and finger.

I was an old pro at my tender age. But the expectation never prepared me for the sight of somebody I cared for enfeebled and helpless. The shock cut just as deep every time. The emotions choked back just as difficult.

You had to be strong; strong for them. They needed your encouragement and positivity. Any breakage in that veneer irreversibly set back their recovery. We weren't responsible for the injury, but the mental scars lingered just as long.

Just a few months ago, Pop had laid in a similar bed, on a similar floor. The white, sterile room was anything but warm and inviting. To me, it screamed sick, pasty, feverish, and dying. I wish just once I could walk into one painted blue, or pink, or green, instead of sterile white. You only found them in the children's ward.

*

Yva's injuries were much, much worse than I expected, maybe the worst I'd ever seen. Both her legs hung in stirrups. Doctors encased her face in mummy-thick strips of gauze. They perpetually suspended her right arm toward the sky; her left drooped by her side.

I saw the violence of love for a decade, if there was such a thing, but this was violence of utter, vile hatred. The sight of Yva's condition initiated the possibility that perhaps Dad's deep-down love for Mom stayed his hand ever so slightly.

It didn't excuse his actions even one tiny iota. It merely opened a grateful possibility that Dad was only the second to worst kind of monster.

*

We sat with Yva for a long while. She didn't wake; she didn't stir. She laid motionless save the gentle rise of her sunken chest. Frank and I spoke not a single word. I simply laid my hand on Yva's and bowed my head to pray.

> *Our father, whom art in Heaven*
>
> *Why is thine will so screwed up?*
>
> *Mine friend is pure,*
>
> *Your will unjust,*
>
> *On Earth as it is everywhere.*
>
> *Give me this day a solid reason,*
>
> *To not hate you with my whole being.*
>
> *And I'll forgive you*
>
> *For trespassing against us.*
>
> *Lead her back to consciousness,*
>
> *And deliver her from pain.*

Amen.

TWENTY

I sat with Yva all night at the hospital. Nurses tried to kick me out, but I growled at them until they backed off. I recounted stories of Yva's home world. They always made her smile. She was never as joyous as when she thought about home.

By the 11th iteration of Yva's home world, people believed they'd figured out all the loop holes and problems of the past. They were confident their world would not be destroyed again.

They had contingency plans for every scenario from global warming to revolution, to not having enough tea with dinner. They automated tasks that needed automation and fixed those pesky bugs which led to no less than three robot revolts.

They left the population sparse – they'd learned to control their population after the 7th destruction of their planet – to contemplate fabulous innovations in technology like outbound space travel and faster than light drives.

They poured their money into funding innovations in technology and developing the means to escape the planet and explore the vastness of the solar system. And eventually, they succeeded.

The greatest minds of their planet reached out and explored the universe. Only the ignorami remained on the home world; a governing body full of slack jawed yokels and idiots. Wars reigned as dum-dums battled for power over worthless land and resources. The worse the wars, the more fled into the peaceful settlements in the outskirts of the galaxy.

They colonized nearly every inhabitable planet over the next million years, including Earth. They hated Earth; a backwater planet in a backwoods part of a poor galaxy. It held no strategic or structural advantage. It wasn't even that pretty.

*

I went to Yva every chance presented to me: before school, after school, at lunch. I never left her side unforced. Sometimes stray passersby peeked into the room, but otherwise we were alone. One gray faced, gaunt heroin addict passed by multiple times. He always peered in and looked around, but even he scattered off once he saw me.

Frank came with me from time to time but waited in the lobby. He bored quickly of my silence. I liked to believe Mom cared about me never coming home before nightfall, but Phil demanded more of her with each passing day. He piled project after project on her. Every time she didn't break from the stress of his workload, he asked more and more. She didn't know how to say no, from decades of practice in being a doormat.

She couldn't say no, though, even if she wanted. We needed the money too desperately.

*

We were in mountains of debt to the payday loan company. Our simple payday advance turned into two, three, ten, and twenty. Before long we were $10k into them and it went up astronomically every month.

Even with Mom's new job and increased salary, there was no money. Half her paycheck went toward repaying loans; the other half toward feeding us. We thought things would be better with a steady paycheck, but so many months dangling on the tip of a needle had caught up with us. Every dollar in went out faster than it came.

"Let me help ya," Pop said on repeat.

Mom didn't want him involved. "I'll figure it out," she said. "It's my quicksand."

"But ya haven't figured it out, have ya?" he responded.

*

Pop was a man of action. Words did not become him. Months with no resolution on the debt front compelled him to action. He took out an equity loan on his house and paid off our debt in one fell swoop. He used every penny of that stupid loan to get us even with our payday loan debtors.

"See," he said. "Now I can get some peace and quiet."

It didn't last for long. Once the equity loan hit, the collections for the payday loan replaced itself with collections from the hospital. They laid dormant for a spell but came back in full force once the prospect of money presented itself.

Pop had no choice. He took out a second equity loan to pay back the hospital. Eventually he owed more in mortgage payments than he'd paid for the house. "I only paid fifty grand for this place," he said. "It took me thirty years to pay that off. I ain't got thirty years left."

Nearly his entire pension check went toward paying his newly acquired debt. Money we needed to survive. Money we counted on to eat, clothe, and feed us.

Eventually, something had to give. We had to eat. We had to drive. We had to visit the doctor. After all that, there just wasn't enough to keep a roof over our heads. So, we stopped paying the mortgage. We had no other options.

Long story short, Mom and Pop had more important things to worry about than a broken alien. Dad didn't, but I didn't want to rely on him. He was notoriously unreliable.

*

I couldn't rely on my family for rides to the hospital. I quickly learned the city's bus schedule.

After that I didn't need anybody, especially not Dad. He interviewed and landed that janitorial job at school, so his days filled up anyway. He started in the wee hours of the morning and worked well into the evening. We met in passing when he emptied the trash cans of my prison, or as he cleaned the toilets during my supervised bathroom breaks. I reveled in pissing on the floors of the bathrooms on his route.

To his credit, Dad showed up to work every single day. It was the longest he held a job since my diagnosis by a factor of three. He even seemed polite, almost content mopping floors and taking out trash.

"It's an honest day's work at least. And it's work I understand. People gotta have empty trash. People gotta have clean floors. It's good, hard, honest work."

*

Yva's injuries were a constant reminder of Dad's brutality. The longer she remained comatose, the more my anger toward him grew, the more I rebelled, the more piss I spilled.

I worried about Yva being taken by the government, experimented on like some lab rat. She didn't want that. She'd rather die than meet that fate.

I showed up every day with the knowledge she could be gone; moved to some remote location in Utah or Uzbekistan, yet every day she remained. Perhaps she was too fragile to move and risk damaging – such a fragile and priceless subject needed the upmost caution.

Her recovery was slow, but my presence helped – at least it seemed to. By the end of my third visit she'd tightened her hand around mine. By the beginning of the fifth, she mumbled through her dreams. Three days later her arm twitched.

The next, her eyes fluttered. She couldn't speak through the plaster cast, but a glint of appreciation floated between us. Her eyes grew darker and heavier with every passing visit, but the soul behind them remained as vibrant and powerful as ever.

The cacophony of weirdos never stopped passing by her room. The gray faced heroin addict came by six times a day. His beady eyes caved into his head. They darted back and forth. He mumbled under his breath when saw me and scuttled off. I called him Creepy Grey Dude. I named some of the others as well: Waddles the Nurse, Crazy Hair Lady. None of them very original. Cut me some slack, though. I was only 12 at the time.

The nurses and staff grew to know me over the weeks. They mostly let me be. The nurses shuffled me out well after visiting hours ended and allowed me access well before they began.

It was only when forcibly that I left Yva's side, and the nurses knew that. They hadn't the strength to fight me. A hundred dragons couldn't fight me away.

Then one day, it happened. I opened the door to her room and her bed was empty. I nearly collapsed. *Where had they taken her? Had they taken her in the night?*

*

Yva wouldn't just leave without telling me. How could she? She was an invalid. The only solution was somebody took her by force. My mind raced with possibilities of Yva's capture and how to save her. *If they only took her last night, maybe they were still in town. I could find them and free Yva. She wouldn't be healthy enough for long transport. She needed medication. They'd have to drive slowly. They couldn't have more than an 18-hour head start.*

I was ready to launch a full-frontal assault on the federal government when the bathroom toilet flushed and out walked a fully functional Yva. I couldn't believe it. She was perfect; like she hadn't received so much as a scratch.

"What?" she said, like her miraculous recovery was anything but; like she hadn't just spent days in the hospital in a full body cast.

"I know you're confused," she said. "But you forget, I'm an alien. There's all sorts of complex mechanics that go on inside my body that you don't understand. I don't even understand them."

I had so many more questions, but Yva simply didn't have any answers. As the only member of her race she knew on Earth, it wasn't like she had a manual. She just knew that any injury repaired itself very quickly. She'd been beaten, bruised, and left for dead countless times before and always fully recovered.

"It's just a shame. By now they must know who I am. They're coming for me. Right now. Two guys in suits just swung by here. I ducked in the bathroom to hide…and pee, but mostly hide."

Just then two men in dark black suits peered inside. They wore dark sunglasses. An earpiece dangled behind their neck. Their chest bulged with the indentation of a firearm.

Yva quickly jumped behind the door. "Have you seen the girl that used to be in this room?" one of them asked.

I resisted my eyes' natural inclination to glance over at Yva and shook my head. "No. They said my mom was in here; must've gotten the wrong room."

He scowled at me and kept walking down the hall. When I finally looked over at Yva, her eyes were big as saucers. "We have to go."

*

Yva's recovery was miraculous, but even her alien physiology weakened and atrophied after days of inactivity. She drooped and sagged against the door as we plotted our escape. I slung my arm over her shoulder in an attempt to prop her upright, but my strength remained anything but legendary.

"It's no use having a plan," she said. "Let's just go."

"I wish Frank were here. He'd carry you no problem."

She smiled. "You'll have to be enough."

We held each other up and peeked out the door. The two black suits hadn't passed again, but they could reappear any moment. The elevators were too central; too easily guarded. We were sitting ducks in there.

The stairs were our only legitimate option. Yva wasn't strong enough to slide down 20 stories, let alone walk it. It wouldn't be a picnic for me either, but there wasn't a choice.

"We'll just take it slow," she said.

*

We scooted across the hallway into the stairwell. We barely made it down one flight when Yva's energy left in a rush. Her legs turned to jelly. She'd run out of fight. She slid against the wall. I fell with her.

"Just leave me," she said.

"Never." I dragged her down two more flights of stairs before my tanks ran dry. We ducked into the next floor, across the hallway, and into a storage closet. I snapped the lock closed behind us.

"Come on, Yva," I said. "Stay with me."

Yva's eyes rolled back in her head. "So…hard."

"I know it is. You used a lot of energy getting better. I know I'm asking a lot, but you made me promise I'd never let you be a lab experiment, right?"

Yva nodded, then pointed up to a box of scalpels. I knew what she wanted. She wanted the sweet relief of death. She knew she would be caught. There was nothing that could stop it. We were two enfeebled children against the weight of the federal government.

She opened her mouth to mumble just as the door jingled. I covered her mouth, sure that even the smallest peep would give us away.

"Jack!" I heard from beyond the door. "The storage closet's locked again. You got a key?"

"Get ready, Yva. We have to move. We have to get you out of here. You with me?"

She nodded. I grabbed Yva around the waist and lifted her to her feet. The door opened quickly. We burst through the nurse and janitor and back into the hallway. The startled scream of the nurse alerted everybody on the floor to our presence.

We were three floors down by the time anybody came to check on her. My adrenaline kicked in. I'd sucked through three quarters of my tank since we'd left Yva's room. By the time we reached the ground floor it was kicked, and I reached for my spare.

Winded and gassed, I pulled Yva the last remaining feet into the brightness of the outside. The suits would be on us before long and the hospital wouldn't take too kindly to one of their wards leaving without proper discharge paperwork. Forms and procedures bothered me not. Yva was out; she was safe.

*

After we left the hospital, Yva was spent. She barely moved more than a few paces without collapsing. I didn't do much better. We crawled into the verve and collapsed until nightfall.

It was a much different experience than our first meeting. She was so proud, so determined, so strong then. It wrecked me to see her so wounded and vulnerable. She was a larger than life figure; trekking through the woods for hours was nothing to her. Now, she barely crawled.

TWENTY-ONE

Yva and I woke to darkness, neither of us wanting to move. "They didn't find us?"

I shook my head in disbelief. "We have to move."

We lost ourselves in the woods. Yva droned on and on about her ship. I answered curtly. *"It's not been taken, has it?"* "Frank watched it closely." *"Has it rusted?"* "It's as new as when you left it." *"Take me to it."* "Not yet. It's not safe. I have a plan."

I dropped her in the woods opposite the train tracks from Pop's. She complained and tried to continue onward, but I wouldn't hear it. She struggled in vain against my help, trying to escape back into the woods, but her energy hadn't returned. She crumpled on the ground and passed out.

*

I hopped the track and jumped down the stairs to the basement. I grabbed a pop-up tent, two sandwiches, and three granola bars. The house was empty save Pop's snoring. No prying eyes questioned me as I made my way back to Yva.

I knew very little about camping, but I'd learned how to crudely set up a tent from Pop; not that manufacturers made it difficult. They cringed at difficulty. Had I needed to construct a shelter using only forest materials it might've been another story. As it stood, fifteen minutes after I started, the tent was erected, and the granola bars devoured by Yva.

She crawled into the tent and laid her head on a pile of leaves. She'd nearly drifted off to sleep when she mumbled under her breath.

"I found it, you know," she said. "I found it, I stole it, and I hid it. You have to get it back."

"What did you take?"

"Another piece, silly. Another piece of my ship. That's how I got into so much trouble. I took it from him."

"Where did you hide it?"

She smiled. "He was following my every move. He chased me for over a mile. I finally ducked him and found a safe spot— the arcade – tucked away – consoles you love so much- hieroglyphs – carved front – You'll find it appropriate."

*

That caused a problem. I couldn't be seen at the arcade without causing a stir. They banned me after the communications antenna incident. The cops would be called if I walked in there again. Even with no proof, businesses had the right to bar anybody from their establishment.

I needed help. I needed a distraction. Yva couldn't help; she could barely move 100 yards at a time. Frank sat shiva at the ship. Mom couldn't help; she spent every hour of her day trying to dig us out of our financial hole.

Pop gave me the cold shoulder after I warmed mine to Dad. He shunned me as only those from the Greatest Generation could. I had isolated and turned away every other person in town, which left me only one choice for help.

*

I found Dad scrubbing a particularly nasty vomit stain out of the boy's bathroom. He'd extended his record for the most work he'd done in years—decades even. "Did you know they want me to work for the next, like, 35 years of my life? 35 years! That's crazy. That's more years'n I been alive!"

A sobering thought for sure, but one I couldn't properly appreciate for years to come. I needed his help, and I wouldn't accept no for an answer.

"Sorry, Sammy. I got work to do where I'm appreciated."

"Really? That's the game you're playing? I need you for once and your loyalty is to this crappy school and that terrible principal?"

"Who's been nothing but nice to me since we met. More'n I can say for some people."

"Well, I never hit you, so there's that."

"I never hit you neither. Remember that."

"Not for lack of trying."

"Granted. I already admitted I was not a great person. I ain't like that anymore though, which you'd know if you spent any time with me."

"I'm asking to spend time with you now. Quality father-son time."

"Hmmmm…alright, Sammo. I'll help you. You owe me though."

"I'll deduct it from your tab."

*

That afternoon we kneeled in front of the arcade like I did with Yva a lifetime ago. I hoped I didn't reek of vomit and bleach quite to Dad's level.

"All I need you to do," I said, "is go in there and cause a scene so big it draws everybody's attention. Got it?"

"No," he replied

"Just be yourself. Now go."

I pushed him toward the entrance. He gave me a quizzical look, but after a moment he walked into the arcade full of gusto and bravado. It didn't take long for the commotion to ensue.

"MY SON LOST ALL HIS MONEY AT THIS ARCADE!" he screamed. "I DEMAND SATISFACTION!"

People gathered like moths to a flame. The registers emptied, and the manager flew out of his office like a world class sprinter. "What can we do for you, sir?"

"You can quit being a gutless prick for one!!!!"

I snuck through the front and toward the dingy, dark, little corner that housed the old, worn out games. Yva told me she'd stuffed the package inside one of the old cabinet walls.

"You'll find it appropriate," she told me.

Dad ranted and raved like a true pro. It was a good show. He knew the character well. "My son came in here with my bank card three days ago and your guys just let him withdrawal hundreds of dollars! My son is 10. What's he doing with a bank card?"

"I'm sure I can issue you a store credit—"

"And what am I going to do with a $900 store credit to an arcade!?!"

I finally scanned the cabinets until I found one dripping in irony: "Where it's Kept". I chuckled. She was right. It was appropriate.

I felt around the cabinet. My fingers caught a loose, bulging hinge that housed in it the electrical innards; not quite broken as much as jammed. I pried it with my fingers but couldn't get a solid finger hold.

I felt around for anything that could wedge itself into the hinge and came up with a crusty, old knife, caked with years of food. I rammed it inside the crevice and pried it open. The hinges cracked, creaked, and finally snapped open. The hinge flew away, and the innards fell out, so much eviscerated intestines.

"DO WE HAVE TO GET THE POLICE INVOLVED!!!!??!! Cuz I can do that?!!" Dad laid it on thick.

A little too thick. They'd call it chewing the scenery in any High School Drama class. But he was captivating. I'd give him that. He wholly kept the manager's attention.

I rooted through the intestines and guts of the old bird until my fingers wrapped around a little, rectangular box, the size of a credit card.

I yanked it hard and pulled out several wires and plugs along with the wedged box. I felt the hieroglyphics Yva told me would be carved into the front. I didn't even close the door. I only waved my tiny hands in the air to signal dad and jetted out of the door before the manager caught on.

*

"What is it, Sammo?" Dad asked.

"I can't tell you that. Not yet."

"That's not a lot of trust you have in me."

"It's not, Dad. But it's growing. Give it time."

"I got time, Sammy."

*

Dad didn't ask questions on the drive home. I appreciated that. "I found a head doctor," he said after a long silence. "I've been seeing her a couple times a week."

"Yeah?"

"I made an appointment for tonight. Will you come?"

"I have other things to do, Dad. Good for you though."

He sat in silence for another long moment. "Oh. I see." He cleared his throat. "Well I'll just drop you off, then, and let your Mom know what happened; vandalizing an arcade, stealing and all."

"You wouldn't. You promised to leave her out of it."

"I promised a lot of things, Sammy."

*

Twenty minutes later we sat across from a bespectacled psychiatrist with a toothy, unnatural grin. Degrees lined her walls from every prestigious university in America.

"You know I hate this kinda stuff, right, Sammy?" Dad asked.

I nodded. It brought me great pleasure to watch him squirm. Truthfully, the simple fact that he was sitting in a chair, across from a shrink, showed me that he might've changed. Old Dad never would've done something like that.

"I do."

"That's gotta count for something, right?"

"Something, Dad. I don't know what yet, but it counts for something."

"Now, Sammy," the psychiatrist said, "let's talk about you for a moment." She pounded me with questions about my family and my social life. She asked about friends and family, loves gained and lost.

"I'm really not comfortable answering that. Let's go back to Dad."

"I already know about your father. I want to hear about you."

"Well I don't want to talk about me."

"Tough."

At every turn, I obfuscated. She was better than my Mom at redirecting me for sure. She was better at digging through the half-truths than anybody I'd ever met, but I held strong. I circuitously steered to conversation back to Dad at every turn.

"How does your parents' estrangement make you feel?"

Except for that one question. I couldn't stop myself from answering that one. I tried to leave it alone. *"That's not really something I want to discuss right now?"* and *"we're not here for thats"*, were bandied around, but she needled over and over again.

"It's very important that we talk about it, Sammy. It affects everything in your father's life."

"Fine," I started. "They both seem happier now. They were terrible for each other. I certainly like not having my Mom beaten to a pulp every month; I think she likes it too. I like not fearing for my life. I really like not fearing for hers."

"Now, Sammy," Dad said. "That's not fair—"

"You wanted the truth. That's the truth."

He didn't want the truth. That was okay. It shut them up. Not another word was spoken until he dropped me off; even then he only said "goodnight". I hurt him. I really hurt him. I didn't think words could hurt him. I didn't think anything could hurt him.

I certainly couldn't hurt old dad.

*

Mom passed out on the kitchen table waiting for me. She might not have waited for me, honestly. She was so tired in those days that she could've passed out mid-dinner with no warning.

"Where have you been?" she asked.

I didn't have the energy to answer her. "Out."

She didn't have the energy to fight. Her eyes fell, wounded. "It wasn't always like this, was it? We used to be close once."

"We used to be. We used to be a lot of things though. I'm sorry, Mom. I have something I have to do."

"I made food. It's cold." She pushed the plate toward me. "You have to eat. I won't talk, I promise. I'll just sit here."

I pulled the plate close. "I don't want that. Tell me about your day."

And she did. It was a nice moment in a sea of abysmal moments.

TWENTY-TWO

Two plates of cold food and three hours of gossip with Mom made me massively late to meet Yva. She complained daily about the cold, hard ground. She complained about the cold cricks in her neck from sleeping on a pile of leaves. She did a lot of complaining, which was out of character for her, but I understood how somebody used to being independent got cranky when they were helpless.

I scoured the basement for an extra blanket and pillow. The only set I found was old and ratty. It smelled of mildew and had aged near paper-thin. She accepted it ungratefully, but I found her snuggled up in it every time I saw her.

She healed up a bit, but her body still lacked strength. Even seated, she teetered and tottered, wibbled and wobbled. Most days she barely sat up. That night was no exception.

"Do you want to hear a story?" I asked. "Or tell me one?"

"Not really," she replied from under her new blanket. "I just want to go to sleep."

She fell asleep fast. I curled up next to her and did the same. It was cold and the crick in my neck shot down my shoulder and into my fingers.

*

Dad held his helping hand over my head the next day, and by the evening I was again sitting in his therapist's office. We gabbed for half a session, swirling and whirling around insignificant facts and figures.

"When you look at your Dad," she asked, "what do you see?"

"I'll be honest," I responded. "I don't think I'll ever be able to look him in the eyes without thinking him a monster."

It was harsh, I knew it. I felt bad I didn't feel bad. I had read a lot on the concept of spousal and child abuse since Dad walked back into my life. "But at least now I can look him in the eyes."

"I didn't know any other way, Sammy," Dad admitted. "My dad hit me, and his dad hit him. We're a hittin' kinda family."

I never considered that before. Dad's upbringing certainly played into how he treated me. There seemed to be two camps of children, those who reject every aspect of their parents' lives and those who grow into them. I fell into the former (I hope), while Dad drifted toward the latter.

"Now, that ain't no excuse," he continued. "But I'm tryin' to change, buddy. I am."

I believed him. In that moment, I believed him. I believed he tried to change. *I also believed a leopard never changed their spots, no matter how much they scrubbed.*

*

Dad dropped me off down the street from Pop's house. It was late at night by the time he turned off the engine. All the lights were off save a faint blue one from the living room TV.

"I'm not a monster, Sammy. The world ain't black and white."

"I know, Dad. I'll give you this, you're trying."

I said my goodbyes and turned back to the house just in time to see Mom walking up the stoop. She wasn't alone. Dr. Phil cupped the small of her back and guided her up the stairs.

They smiled at each other in ways that employers shouldn't smile at employees. She giggled, and he laughed.

The driver side door of Dad's car slammed shut. A blur flew down the street faster that my eyes tracked. "How could you sleep with some other man?!"

"What are you talking about? He's my boss. Besides, you're the one that filed for divorce," she replied. "So, nothing I'm doing is wrong, but I'm not doing nothing anyway!"

"Don't mess with me. I saw how you looked at him with those eyes. I heard that laugh you make when you wanna get banged. He ain't the first wealthy prick to go dumpster divin'."

Dr. Phil stepped down the stoop. "Excuse me, sir. I think you should go."

Dad shoved him. "Don't tell me what to do. You think just cuz you screw my wife you can tell me anything? I'll kill you."

"Ex-wife. Soon to be ex," Mom chimed. "And we didn't do anything!"

Dad clenched his fist and swung wildly. Dr. Phil blocked his punch. "I don't want to hurt you."

Dad laughed and threw another awkward punch. "Like you could."

Dr. Phil ducked it and cold-cocked him across the jaw. "I don't want to hurt you, but I will."

He could certainly hurt Dad. The good doctor's punches staggered Dad, who reset and threw a haymaker that had frequently knocked Mom on her ass.

Phil blocked it and jabbed him in the face, busting his upper lip. "Go home," Phil pleaded.

Dad rushed Phil like an obstinate bull. Phil dodged his horns and slammed Dad into the side of Pop's house. He stumbled, concussed from the impact. Dad wasn't used to losing a fight. He wasn't used to picking a fight he couldn't win.

"Enough!" I shouted. "I thought you weren't a monster? People that aren't monsters don't fly off the handle!"

"But he—"

"Dad, go home."

He sniffed and sneered, full of piss and vinegar, but acquiesced to the stronger fighter and stumbled off into the night.

Dr. Phil picked up his jacket. "I'm sorry. I simply can't be associated with any of that. Good night, Miriam."

*

The good doctor gave Mom her walking papers the next day. We lived in a right to work state, and Dr. Phil exercised his right to fire anybody for any reason.

"I've seen this sort of thing before," he said. "I think it's best for you to find another doctor and another line of employment. Thank you for your service."

And that was it. He dropped both her and me like it was nothing. He called the Medicaid office and spun some crappy excuse that he couldn't be my doctor. That left us driving 30 minutes to find the next closest one.

Just like that, I never saw him again. He seemed so calm, so collected, and so cool for so long – he even seemed to like me – but something out of our control ruined it all. A monster of a different kind.

*

I wouldn't see Mom for another week and a half after that. She fell off the wagon and hard. I looked for her with every waking breath. She left me a note before she ran off with only the clothes on her back.

"I don't want you to see me like this. I love you. – Mom."

She took all my pills; every single one of them. Every day was agony, every movement pain, every breath fraught with difficulty.

Frank and I searched every hotel, motel, and flop house in three counties. I didn't show up to school. I didn't see Dad. I didn't sleep. I didn't eat. I only pained and searched. For a small town, East Willow swam in every form of shelter imaginable.

*

The search was hard work. I went through my oxygen tanks three times over every day combing the city. Frank and I came up with a systematic plan, starting at one end of town and walking east to the other. When we reached the end of a street, we turned around and went back again. Every day we went further and further. Every day it was harder and harder.

We called Pops every day when we were done searching and he came to pick us up. He thought we were crazy. "What's the point? She's a grown woman. She'll be back."

"Before she kills herself?"

"Probably. She ran away when she was younger a couple times. Always came back before long."

"Before Dad finds out?"

He was silent after that. Dad couldn't find out. He'd use it against Mom. He'd get full custody. And with his trial coming up, we needed to maintain every sense of righteousness we could, to show that Mom was a capable adult; at least more capable than Dad. I didn't have many capable adults in my life.

*

Eventually, we found her—in the worst pile of villainy and scum in three counties; filled with felons, junkies, and the soon-to-be homeless. The place someone like Creepy Gray Dude would shoot up in, fresh from a stint out of the hospital.

Mom emptied our meager bank account in a week and made a wicked dent in our credit card balance. She snuck back into the house when nobody was home and took one of Pop's credit cards.

That's how we found her. If she had more money, she might've gotten to Nebraska. As it was, she didn't even get out of town.

The room smelt of vomit, piss, sex, and booze, in that order and magnitude. I didn't know how much of that was from Mom's stay and which was a mixture of the fluids from past residents. Pill and alcohol bottles, half empty, spilled across the floor.

"Come on, Mom," I said. "It's time to go home."

"What's the point, Sammy?!" she screamed. "Nothing's ever gonna change for us!"

She looked horrible; sweaty and pale, the clothes pasted to her back. Frank and I peeled them off and dragged her into the shower.

"Why is it, Sammy? Why is it that I just can't catch a break, huh?"

"That's not our lot in life."

I washed her hair and she came back to consciousness. She apologized. She cried. "I'm so sorry, Sammy. I didn't mean to do it. It's just so hard, you know?"

I didn't want to hear it. I was just so sick of being the adult.

*

I washed and cleaned her up enough to be presentable; enough to get down to the courthouse. It was Dad's trial date finally; he'd finally pay for what he'd done to my Pop.

I popped three days' worth of pain pills and antibiotics. I wrapped her around my waist and Frank steadied my gait. Mom's head listed from one side to the other. The pills she'd popped still hadn't completely worn off as we took our seats in the back of the courthouse.

"Just maintain, Mom," I told her. "Nobody's gonna ask you anything alright?"

Mom nodded and quickly nodded off. Frank and I waited. And waited. And waited. Dad never showed up. Pop was there, ready to give testimony. Mom and I were there to watch him rot. Dad's lawyer was there. Dad, however, was nowhere to be found.

And if there's one thing I knew about the court system, not showing up is never a good sign. Dad was some scared, little coward that saw his life slipping away. He'd surely be found guilty.

So, he ran. He was an idiot. But that was a very smart decision on his part.

TWENTY-THREE

After a couple more weeks, Yva grew strong enough to sit up and take short walks through the forest. She foraged for her own food, fixed her tent, and mended her broken bones. I spent my time going through the old blueprints Yva gave me. I'd given up ever translating the words properly and focused on the diagrams.

It's not like decoding the word TRANSDUCTION MAGNIFIER would give me any insight into its use or purpose. I certainly didn't know what an INDUCED BERGINATOR did or how it was related to the NRIGIL FASMAGRAPH.

Even after months of studying, of reading electrical engineering books, the wiring diagrams were gibberish. I cross-reference the diagrams to those of trains, planes, and automobiles, to little success. I couldn't tell 15 amps from 20 joules. I didn't know how a joule translated to a Verne. It was like translating Arabic to Swahili. I still couldn't speak Swahili.

Yva did an admirable job cobbling the ship back together, but it became obvious the longer we studied it that she wired something wrong in the undercarriage. The communications relay fritz and fried out on the regular, and every time we thought the engine would turn over, instead we got the joy of a small fire. Shockingly, three average to below average students didn't have the wherewithal to figure out how to fix an intergalactic spaceship, even if it was a hoopty.

I wasn't an electrician. I had no mechanical knowledge of vehicles. I couldn't allow Yva to pilot an unknown ship through the galaxy on my miniscule knowledge – and I only knew one person who could help me; the same person who kept our busted ass car running when it barely started. I had to let Dad in on the secret. It was the only way to ensure Yva's safety.

But I had to find him first.

*

Frank didn't like the idea of letting Dad in on Yva's true origins one bit. In fact, he hated it; a fact he made clear over and over and over again on the walk home that day.

"You know 'e's a scumbag, right, mate?" he asked.

"Of course," I responded. "But I'm not swimmin' in people that know how to fix a carburetor, am I?"

"What about the internet of things, ay? You can learn anything on there."

"I don't think that means what you think it means."

He didn't get it. No matter how much I tried to explain it to him. He couldn't understand that I needed somebody that knew cars, at least they had a chance to move that mechanical knowledge to spaceships. But fighting him wasn't gonna help. Frank was a dear, old soul, but he wasn't the brightest bulb in the shed. All you could do with him after a while is bless his soul, smile, and nod.

"Maybe I'll look into it," I threw out. We both knew I wouldn't. By the time we got back to my house, the heaviness of our conversation lifted, and we turned to discussing the best superhero crossover special Marvel ever released.

He saw it first, the pink slip waving on the door. An eviction notice. In thirty days we had to vacate the house for non-payment of funds.

*

We sat outside all night waiting on Mom to come home. She'd taken more jobs, and more jobs on top of those jobs to fill the hours in the day. There weren't enough to sleep, or pop pills, or think. There was just time to work. Still, there wasn't money to live.

"Where you gonna go?" Frank asked.

"Where can we go?" I replied.

Mom came up the driveway and pulled down the eviction notice matter-of-factly. She'd known it was coming. We all knew it was coming. You can't not pay your mortgage and expect to stay in your house. It would be a nice thought, if banks had humanity, but they're not people. They only see dollar signs.

"Let them try to kick us out," she said. "We're not out yet, slugger. Now come to bed. We'll deal with it in the morning."

But we didn't deal with it the next morning—or the next morning – or the morning after that – or the one after that. She acted as if nothing happened. The less they worried about it, the less I worried. I should have worried, but I didn't.

Something about being a child, you always expect adults to have a plan. Always. Only later do you realize they rarely do.

*

The principal pulled me into her office later that week. "Now you're not even getting your absences excused. I'm sorry. You've just missed too many days, Samuel, for me to just let it slide. I've tried to turn the other way and the other cheek, but it comes down to the fact that a judicial review board has been convened to discuss your continued school participation. You've missed too many days by a factor of 10 and despite me reaching out to your parents, they have been uncooperative with my initiatives. Are they aware they can be fined or jailed for your truancy?"

"I don't think they could possibly care about that the way things are going."

"I will not engage the police on these matters out of a courtesy. However, your continued engagement with this school cannot be tolerated. I'm very sorry."

"I'll let them know."

"I hope you do. There will be a hearing. You will be allowed to stay in school until the review process is over."

"Whoopty doo."

"And if you see your father, let him know he's fired."

*

I tried to find Dad for weeks with no avail. I thought I'd see him around every corner. It's funny, when I wanted him gone, he wouldn't leave. Now that I needed him, he became a ghost. I wondered if he fled town. He should have fled town.

He had a bench warrant out for him, but it's not like they put together a manhunt for a low-level scumbag. It's not like the cops were on high alert for somebody who skipped out on an assault charge. He would have been wise to keep gone, but he wasn't a wise man. He wasn't much of a man at all. And eventually I found him skulking around the school again, in a new hoopty, sporting a beard, thinking himself clever for his patchy disguise.

I ran up to him. "Not much of a disguise."

"Shhh," he responded. "I'm bein' incognito."

"I need your help."

"Don't you got nothin' else to say to me? Don't you wonder where I've been, or anything?"

"I really don't care. You should be happy I'm speaking to you. Do you wanna help or not?"

"I guess that's true. Just the fact yer talkin' to me's good nuff for me, Sammy boy. Maybe we'll be alright yet."

"Don't push it, Dad."

*

By the time we reached the seventh ridge on our way to Yva's ship, Dad was out of gas. I only had to stop a half-dozen times, a personal best.

"Just a minute, buddy," he said.

"Just one more ridge, Dad."

"You said that six ridges ago!"

"But this time I mean it." I scuttled up the ridge and watched Dad do the same. It still felt weird to see Dad trying. I'd known him my entire life and never knew him to work hard for anything.

At the top, he overlooked the valley; the same one that made Frank and I believers. He watched the sun set and the blue hue rise like illuminated jellyfish.

He wasn't quite as impressed. "Not bad" was all he said.

*

He trotted down the hill with caution and without enthusiasm. "How'd this get built, champ?"

I shrugged my shoulders. "I don't know honestly. It was like this when I found it."

"So, what can I help with then?"

I pulled out the blueprint; Yva's blueprint. "I can't do this, Dad. I need you to help me get this thing operational."

"What makes you think I can?" he responded.

"I don't think. But I'm out of options. And if you tell anybody I swear you'll never see me again. I'll run away. I'll disappear. I'll die if you let anybody know about this. Okay?"

Dad nodded. He never relished trust before. He certainly didn't deserve it. But I had to trust in him, for Yva's sake: for my own sake too.

Dad examined the blueprints. "I need to know how you found that thing, Sammy. There's a lot of dangerous stuff in those blueprints. And if I'm going to keep helping you, and hide it from your mom, I need you to tell me the truth, the whole truth, and nothing but the truth. Capiche?"

"Fine," I spewed. "Follow me."

*

I trudged him through the woods behind Pop's house and up to Yva's tent. "You're late," Yva said with a smile.

Dad followed me inside the tent. "Yva, this is my dad. I showed him the ship. He's been helping me. He's a friend. But he needs to know everything if he's going to keep helping us."

Yva didn't even hesitant for a moment. She seemed all too eager to spill her story, for any company that wasn't me or the squirrels. I heard it many times before, but it always fascinated me.

"My father and mother wanted a new life. Their species—our species— raped all their planet's natural resources. They lived in terraformed terrariums that reached the sky.

"Once my mother got pregnant, they realized it wasn't a good environment to raise their children, and they made plans to leave. They bought a junker and set off across the galaxy.

"Halfway across the Milky Way, our ship blew a gasket and they crashed. They died instantly. I was three.

"I plotted my parents' course and started rebuilding their ship almost immediately. I traveled around the world finding the parts to make my ship whole again, which led me here to the final pieces."

She winced. "I'm sorry. I'm not very strong and this has taken a lot out of me. Maybe we can continue this tomorrow?"

She rolled over and fell asleep.

"I'm sorry, Dad," I said. "She's asleep and there's nothing we can do to wake her."

*

I led Dad back outside. His expression remained motionless for several seconds.

"You're not to see her anymore, Sammy. You're not to think about her or talk about her. Not one word; at all. Got me?"

"What are you talking abo—"

He pulled the blueprints from my hand and ripped them in half. "I'm serious."

"You can't do that!" I chased after him. I grabbed him, tugged on him, but he kept going. "I trusted you!"

He flung open his car door. "Not one more word about it. I don't want to even catch a glimpse of a thought of her. You got me?"

"Dad, please!" I shouted. "I need you! I trusted you!"

He stuck his bony finger up. "No! You're my son. And I'm your father. Now, read my lips. Stay away from that, whatever you think it is!"

"She's not an "it", she's a she!"

"You need help! I'm telling your mother and—"

I grabbed him. I've never grabbed him before. And pulled him, yanked him hard. "No! Dad! No!"

He spun me around and grabbed my arm. His nails dug deep. I struggled against him as he pulled me toward him.

"Don't make me say another word about it! You will respect me. I'm your father!"

That's when it happened. I wriggled and waggled. I pulled and yanked. My arm slid away and smacked him in the face.

I'd never struck anybody before, and this one reopened a partially healed wound on his lip. His eyes glowed red. "You! Ungrateful little son of a bitch!"

He hit me. I'd never been hit before. Years of his verbal abuse and I'd always been sheltered from his brutal hits. I crumpled to the ground, gasping for air. It didn't stop him. He kept hitting and hitting and hitting. I lost count after the first ten. Mom was wrong. It hurt worse after the first one.

He screamed the vile bitterness so fresh in my memory. "This will teach you some respect! And never ever talk to me like that again!"

For the second time since moving to East Willow, I blacked out.

TWENTY-FOUR

I woke up in the E.R. Yva sat by my side, hands cupped in mumbled prayer. "What are you doing here?" I asked. "You should be resting."

"Who do you think found you and ran that monster off?"

I smiled. "I'm sorry. I shouldn't have trusted him. I know better. He's just—"

"Your dad, I know. Don't worry about that now. It's okay."

Frank was next. "I shoulda known better'n ta trust that guy. Or let you trust 'em. If I see 'im again, I'll hit 'em square in the jaw."

Mom stormed in like a bull in a china shop, almost crushing Yva in the process. "Sammy! Oh my god! What happened? What did he do to you? Doctor! Doctor!! Where are you? How's my Sammy doing?"

She bolted out the room and returned a few seconds later with a doctor wrapped around her arm. "How is he? How is he, Doctor? Tell me how he is!"

"Surprisingly okay," the doctor replied. "No broken bones. No cracked ribs. No punctured lungs. A black eye and some soreness to be sure, but otherwise he took that beating like a champ."

She pulled at her hair. "I'm going kill that man. I swear I should have killed him before."

I shook my head. "He's not worth it, Mom."

Mom was worth it. Yva was worth it. Frank was worth it. Dad, though, was worthless. He suckered me in, just like he'd done to Mom so many times before, with a false sainthood persona. And I fell for it. I fell for it hook, line, and sinker.

I wanted him to change. I needed him to change: to be a bigger, better man. I needed him to be there for me. Maybe even be the man I remembered. But he couldn't. He was the man he was. That's all there was to it.

My relationship with Mom was messy to be sure, but she was always there for me. She disappointed me, sure, but she was always there for me. She didn't hit me. She barely scolded me. She didn't put me down. Somewhere in all the confusion, the drugs, and the craziness, I forgot that. I hadn't even given her a chance to understand Yva, or what was happening in my life. It shamed me.

So, I came clean. I told her everything. Every dirty, little detail. And she did something amazing. She listened to me. She didn't judge me. Her eyes welled when I wounded her with my mistrust, but she didn't break.

"I…see…" she choked out.

I swelled with pride, and joy, and shame, for trusting a monster and not an angel. Never again, I promised myself. Never again would I forget my mother's amazing spirit.

*

Dad never came to school again. They issued a second warrant for his arrest. He collected them now, like badges of dishonor or decoder rings. I filed a restraining order just to be safe, but never expected to see Dad again. The arbiter and lawyer, who until recently sided with Dad, swung their pendulum of trust toward Mom, as was the parlance of that time. Without his presence and with dad's abandonment of the negotiations, they awarded her full custody.

She'd been wonderful since I went to the hospital. She didn't even bat an eye when I brought Yva in from the cold and set her up in our basement. She even lent me a gaggle of extra blankets and pillows for the cold nights in the dank cellar.

*

Yva ceased being the ethereal, ephemeral girl and became a three-dimensional person, full of hopes and dreams, love lost, great humility and great compassion like Mom; cantankerous, gruff, no-nonsense like Pop. "Oh brothers", "come ons", and "get reals" flowed out their mouths quicker than hello.

It saddened me to think I cost Yva a family for so long with my selfishness. I should have known Mom would welcome Yva with open arms. Though she kept a stiff upper lip, in quiet moments of reflection Mom looked at me differently – wounded that I could trust my father and not her.

"I don't know why you didn't trust me, Sammy," Mom repeated.

I didn't know. I couldn't explain it. All I knew was for the first time in Yva's short life she had a home.

I taped the blueprints Dad destroyed back together and left them with Pop and Yva when I went to school. I dropped any harbored pretenses of secrecy. I wanted him to know everything now; needed him to know really.

*

When I got home, Pop read the blueprints to me as if they were the Pokey Little Puppy. He understood it like it was his native language.

"I used to be a mechanic, dumb-dumb," he said. "Who do you think fixed all the trucks at the depot, huh? And this one is a doozy. The intricacy and attention to detail – It's incredible."

It was the first time somebody recognized the complexity and beauty of the mechanics behind the ship, instead of standing slack-jawed in front of it. We'd all marveled at the coolness and prettiness, but neither Dad, nor Frank, nor I could appreciate the system's complexity.

*

Pop begged and begged and pleaded and pleaded to see the ship. So, over the next weekend, we trekked out to the site. The ship sat there untouched, which was a great relief to me. I knew Frank checked in on it from time to time, but until I saw it with my own eyes I half-expected Dad's vengeance.

"This is some piece of machinery," Pop said as he looked under the hood. He ran down the hill like a schoolboy, giddy and carefree. His physically addled body refreshed to childhood.

"Wowie zowie," he said.

Pop gave a thorough examination; a level of detail nobody else I knew could approximate. He asked questions I certainly couldn't answer. Eventually, he just went to work.

It was amazing to watch. He was like the ship whisperer…and not only because he whispered to the ship. His nimble fingers reconnected discarded wires and rehoused hanging fragments like he'd been born to do it.

Maybe he had been. Who knew?

*

I left him to work on the ship in silence while I attended to a most important matter. The principal's disciplinary review board finally came to fruition. I had to answer for my lack of enthusiasm for my education.

I can't remember how many days of school I missed between the ship, Dad, Mom, the trial, and just not giving a care, but it was significant.

I fell behind on my schoolwork too. My interim grades fell below my normal Cs, down to Ds, and finally to Fs, where they never recovered. Had there been a G or H grade, I surely would have gotten those instead.

The principal compiled a series of charges and infractions on top of my god awful grades, from disrespect of authority, to the subversion and manipulation of the principal's innocent spirit. If half of them were a quarter true, I was a monster.

I showed up to the hearing early. As much as I didn't care about school, the last thing I wanted was an expulsion on my record. It didn't matter where you went after that, expulsion tainted perceptions. As a "special needs" kid, the last thing I needed was more things going against me leading a normal life.

The room was empty when Frank and I arrived. I told Frank to stay home, that it would be insanely boring, but he insisted on being a character witness and protecting me in case Dad showed up – which would have been insane since he'd be arrested on sight.

*

It wasn't long before the room began to fill. In front of the room, in three chairs, sat plump school board members looking very dour and serious, trying to fulfill the gravitas of the situation and determined not to take any decision lightly.

A few onlookers met with a flock of looky-loos who'd been to every school board meeting in sixty years. They knew each other, and the members, and chit-chatted with them like old friends.

Eventually, the room fell silent and a cold filled the air. Shivers ran down my spine. The principal stomped toward a small table in the front of the room.

"Good evening, school board members. Let's get down to it, shall we? Samuel is a distraction to those around him. He's flaunted every rule we've put in place for his safety and the safety of our other children. He's missed seventy-three days this school year, far above the acceptable amount by a magnitude of ten. On top of that, he refuses to turn in school work, and his grades hover around 0s. There is very little we can do at this point to turn his career at East Willow Middle around, nor does he want us to. It is my recommendation he be expelled post haste, for the good of the school and his career."

The school board fired questions back at her, and she manipulated my words in one way or another for the next 30 minutes.

"He was completely uncooperative every time I tried to help him." *Lie. Scold me was more like it.*

"I provided him special attention, and he scoffed at it." *Never happened. She gave me unnecessary hurdles to overcome, though.*

"He brought a known felon onto school grounds." *Actually, she hired my dad, not I.*

She talked until she was blue in the face and then turned to me. "And what's worse, his family doesn't even seem to care about his education. Dozens of calls and letters have been disregarded or unreturned. There's truly nothing more we can do."

I couldn't argue with her. Mom and Pop were nowhere to be found; mostly because I didn't tell them about it. I hid every letter before they could find it. I redirected the CPS and the police away from our house. I fought away the truancy officer. After a spell, they all gave up. It was liberating. Now I wished I'd been more open. Mom was always open with me about her troubles.

Maybe that's why I hid this away. I couldn't worry Mom with more. She had so much, and with her trust in me already teetering on the edge, this would have thrown her off it.

I needed to handle this one thing on my own. We were still fighting for our house, and our lives. Mom still worked three jobs and Pop busied himself with the ship to keep his mind distracted.

Without them, though, I had no case. All I had was Frank and they never even called him to witness. Not that a character witness like Frank would have mattered. Even if he gave an impassioned speech filled with "um…", "errs…", and incoherent ramblings, it wouldn't be enough to change the dour expressions plastered on the women's faces, nor wipe the smile off the principal's face.

And that's why I really hated her after all these years. I've never known somebody good who enjoyed the destruction of somebody else's life. But I think about that smile sometimes and yearn to wipe it off her face with extreme prejudice.

"Would you care to plead your case, young man?" one of the members asked.

"What's the point?" I replied. "You've already made up your minds."

They were gonna do whatever they were gonna do. I didn't have to watch it though. My fate was sealed.

So, I left.

*

By the time the expulsion notice came it was too late to fight anything. The school board saw the evidence of my constant absences (even though many were excused), and bouts of "talking to myself" as reasons to jettison themselves from a toxic situation in the cleanest way possible.

They delivered the expulsion notice certified letter directly to Mom's maid service, so I couldn't keep her in blissful ignorance. When she opened the letter, she flipped out. Luckily, the old lady who hired her was out of the house or her expletive laden rant would have surely gotten her fired.

*

She lectured me for the next week. I didn't fight her. I let her yell until she was blue in the face, nap it off, and add my appeal to her insane list of responsibilities.

She demanded a meeting with the principal. "This is ridiculous. Sammy's been doing so well, hasn't he?"

"You're asking the right questions, just at the wrong time. My decision and that of the board is final."

"This is insanely unfair."

"So now you care about your son's education," the principal told her. "Little late I'm afraid."

Mom prepared briefs and doctors to testify, but they were ill-prepared and poorly planned in the sleep deprivation between shifts. It did little good; the school board was unyielding.

*

I moved on. I had more important matters to attend. Yva's ship was coming along nicely. Pop didn't like my sudden disregard for learning, but he appreciated my newfound interest in the one thing he'd ever been good at.

Once Pop got involved, the diagrams came together almost immediately. "Math is the universal language," Pop said. "I always thought that was a stupid saying, but it looks like it's true."

It **_was_** true. Three-fourths of a triple squiggly line was 1.5 feet every time. And seven smiley birds were always 3.74 inches. The measurements were always the same. They had to be; can't build an intergalactic spaceship on faulty math.

Pop was a master. Rearranging wires and remapping parts to their proper place. "Well, that doesn't go there," he said with a head shake and eye roll.

He often chuckled under his breath, grabbing one hunk of metal or another. "You think this manifold goes next to the carburetor? Who taught you spaceships?"

The answer was nobody. It was a rhetorical question of course, so I just let him work. It amazed us constantly how similar a car's design was to a spaceship's.

"Everything's gotta have an engine. Whether they call it a piston or a flip flop – there's gotta be a way to pump gas through the system."

He was right. Sure, it didn't look like the kind of pistons we knew, but he traced back the power to a huge manifold that pumped the power through the system. "Can't get very far without some sorta power, either."

Sure enough, he popped open some panel or another and found what amounted to four space pistons and a space carburetor.

*

After a month we neared completion. In two decades I couldn't have accomplished a millionth of what he did in that month.

Pop grinned ear to ear in those days. He had drifted without a purpose for a long time and this gave him a reason to get up in the morning. It was nice to see.

When we finished a buffing and wax, we ran an inventory and came up one piece short. We needed an ignition starter.

One simple piece and Yva could go home. It was a minor miracle she'd been so close, given the resources with which she had to work.

The major miracle was that by the end Pop believed aliens built it. "Ain't no 12-year-old made something that complicated. It was machine made. That thing was made on an assembly line. By pros. They may not have been great pros, but they were pros."

I was an easy mark, but turning Pop was a true test.

*

"Why don't you get a job too, Pop? Help Mom out." I asked him while we built.

"Why don't you?"

"I'm just a kid."

"I worked at your age. I worked until I couldn't work anymore. I can't work no more. If it all goes to pot, then it all goes to pot. Your mom can keep it going as long as she wants, but it always goes to pot in the end. That's the natural state of things."

"I don't like it."

"You don't have to like something for it to be true."

TWENTY-FIVE

We were forced into courthouses too many times in that year. Bailiffs, clerks, and judges alike knew us by name. Even repeat offenders recognized our faces and waved on sight. It's not the place you want to be Cheers'd. If everybody knows your name in court, you're doing life wrong.

Yet, that's where we found ourselves again, fighting for our house. We cobbled up just enough money between Pop's scratcher winnings and our meager bank account to hire a lawyer for one hearing about our eviction.

We wore our best clothes and sat across the aisle from the company trying to evict us. We already sent letters, called, and met with bank executives. At every turn they cast us aside. Once they made a decision, it was unilateral and unyielding.

Who cared about some blight on humanity like our family, anyway, in the grand scheme? People wrote us off and threw us aside since the beginning of time.

If vim, vigor, and pluck could by themselves win the day and lead to victory, we would've come out victorious. We really, really wanted to stay in Pop's home. However, our contract very clearly stated that non-payment, of even one month, could lead to eviction – what they really meant was that it would lead to eviction. It was a bad rule, and a terrible contract, but it was airtight.

"The plaintiff failed to pay on more than one occasion, and our policies are very clear. The plaintiff signed and agreed to them in triplicate," their lawyer said. "My client didn't evict them after one failure to pay though. They gave the plaintiff multiple attempts over consecutive months to meet their financial obligations. They failed at every turn. My client was magnanimous and gracious with their leniency. They cared. The plaintiff took advantage of their generosity."

Their lawyers were very good. Ours were not. They were bargain basement, like year-old Spam. We didn't have a case. We didn't have a good lawyer. We didn't have anything. The bank wiped the floor with us.

"I'm sorry," the judge declared. "You'll have thirty days to vacate the residence."

That was it. Pop's decades in that home meant nothing. It would be on the market, sold off, and repopulated. Our time there would be forgotten; our memories erased.

*

Mom went straight from that fight to the one to keep me in school. Not that it mattered much. I'd be in a different school come the following year. But Mom wasn't about to face two defeats.

"I will not abide by such strict rules," she said. "They're gonna bend or break. I don't care which."

Mom argued and pleaded (see: complained and whined) until the school board acquiesced to some of her demands. They let me play out the semester, but I would have to leave at the end of the year. They wouldn't give me an expulsion, since I "voluntarily left".

I was glad to skirt all that, and appreciated my mom's efforts, but I had bigger fish to fry. School was never my thing anyway. Why would I want to spend my few good years learning when I could be doing; when I could be helping an alien build her spaceship and get home? That was a better use of my short time left on Earth.

I didn't have a choice in the matter, though. Mom said go to school and I dutifully went, passing eyes with the principal every day. We grew tired of trying to destroy each other. With the school year winding down, she moved on to bigger and badder things than I.

The principal won, after all. She kept her job and I'd be gone before the following year, some other poor principal's problem, some other bus driver, some other janitor, some other pitiful lunch lady's.

I just wanted the sweet release of summer and promise of more time with Yva; more stories about her parents.

*

Yva's family lived poor. If there were another side of the tracks, they would have been on it, over it, above it, and through it. They bred scrappy. That's probably why Yva survived with so little for so long on her adopted planet.

They lived in a place called the Dregs. The lowest of the low. On their planet, cities rose thousands of feet tall and millions of stories high. The skyscrapers blotted out the sun and stars.

People lived according to their wealth. The most had the highest levels, the least fought over the table scraps. The lowest of the low lived in the shadows on the ground floor of the planet.

Light never fell there. Money never fell there. Rancid scraps of food rarely fell there. Nothing was certain. There was no hope. There was only one constant; there was no escape. Smart or stupid, it didn't matter. You couldn't escape the Dregs. The pull of it brought you down into the muck and the mire and there you stayed. It was easy to fall down into the Dregs, but impossible to escape.

As it was for Yva's family. Born as socialites, two bad moves and they were living in hovels, fighting over scraps and their right to live. Yva's grandfather was a scientist and her grandmother a teacher, their children grew with a love of both.

Yva's parents were instilled with a love of science and an intellect which put them above the awareness of the average inhabitant of the Dregs, a dangerous place to be; at least idiocy meant ignorance to their plight. Intelligence was a burden. It was their burden.

Their only chance to improve their lot was to get off the planet. They had one thing that aided their escape; the only valuable addition their new place in society brought - a junk yard.

A junk yard where the rich threw their old parts, blueprints, scraps of wire, and nearly anything useful in the entire world. Every day, Yva's parents chased the scrap heaps after they were discarded and before they were melted into materials the rich reused.

It took them twenty years, but by the time Yva was born, they'd built a workable shuttle to blast off into the great beyond.

*

I listened to Yva's stories all day. I lost myself in them when I walked to and fro. So much so I barely noticed a shadow following me wherever I went. I caught it from the corner of my eye for a week before I paid it any notice. A grimy, dingy, bony, little man paced the parking lot at school, cut through the trees with me toward home, watched me eat dinner. I thought it was my father. His matted brown hair and greyed skin mirrored Dad so perfectly.

When I caught his eye, he vanished into the either, but always returned, like herpes. He eyed me across the lunch line. He trailed me to the bus. He perched in trees and bushes. I recognized him after the third day. I'd seen him at the hospital with Yva, in the motel we found Mom in, and even at the court the day of my trial.

He was Creepy Gray Dude. I remembered him lurking around Yva's hospital room. He blended in with the tapestry of life that year, but there was no denying he was my stalker.

I pointed him out to Frank on our walks home. "You're bonkers, mate. There's nothin' there. Yer seein' things."

I wasn't crazy, though. I knew he wanted something from me. I knew in my gut he wanted Yva. Luckily, she was safely tucked away. I did a fine job hiding her. Mom and Pop never acknowledged her presence and they lived with her.

*

Two weeks into having my new shadow, I walked into the house and Yva squealed from the living room. "Sam! Get in here!"

I dropped my bags and ran into the living room. Yva had mapped out the entire tri county area on poster board covering the carpet. Barry's was labeled in the center. Our house on the outskirts, collected with the trash. I never realized just how far from the action our house was until then; how discarded and desolate from the hustle and bustle of the town's center. In the furthest corner, two counties and dozens of miles from Pop's house, in the mountains of East Willow, she drew an X.

Yva bounced on her knee. "I found it. I found it. I found it!"

"Found what? Found what? Found what??" I responded

"It's big. You should sit down. Never mind it's too big. Are you ready? I don't think you're ready. I found the ignition switch! I mapped the trajectory and did a bunch of boring science-y things and BAM! There it was. Aren't you proud of me?"

I smiled. "Very. Let's go get it!"

"That's going to be a problem." She pointed at the X on the map. "Because it's here."

The door creaked open. I expected the creepy man, there to take his revenge or carry out his plan; whatever that was. But it was just Pops, covered in muck and grime.

"What going on here?" he asked.

I cleared my throat and uttered the words that flew out of my mouth so often in those days. "I need your help."

"What do ya need?" he responded.

*

Pop was more into finishing Yva's ship than I, so he had no problem driving me the thousand hours across town to the base of EAST WILLOW MOUNTAIN. Joggers and hikers considered it a mild climb, easy even, but for an ancient, a hobbled alien, and a sick teen, it cut an imposing figure.

"It's about halfway up the mountain," Yva said. "On the east face. Shouldn't be too hard to spot."

We started up together, Pop and Yva barely made it 200 hundred paces before their legs gave out on them. I thought about doing the same, but my months of hiking gave me the stamina to continue.

"Go on alone," Yva said.

"What if I get in trouble?" I asked.

"How arc an old man and a cripple going to help if you get in trouble?" Yva responded.

"Come on, kid. Use your head. I'll be right here if you need me," Pop added. "Or I could just come back later. It's up to you."

I never did Boy Scouts. I never spent time in the wilderness except for the walk to and from Pop's. Dad didn't like camping. Mom didn't like the outdoors. I hated both. I tolerated it only to see the sight of Yva's ship gloriously rising into the heavens.

"No. I have to do it now," I told them. "I'll be back…soon."

*

I set off. Pluck and determination didn't help my sense of direction. I knew about following the North Star, that the sun rose in the east and set in the west, and shadows grew smaller the closer to noon it became — but I couldn't put any of it into practical use.

Couple that with my constant fear of dying alone and it was not a recipe for success. My breathing labored quickly on the incline. Images of lions, tigers, bears, and oh my flashed through my head. *If a puma leapt out and attacked me, I wouldn't have the wherewithal to escape.*

I made it four steps or so, then stopped to catch my breath, lathered, rinsed, and repeated. My heart pounded in my brain. The constant thump annoyed me terribly, but at least it meant I was alive.

*

About an hour into the hike my paranoia kicked in. I was being followed; stalked even. I didn't know if it was a bear, cougar, or lemur, but trees snapped in the background and shadows scurried by too often for my liking. The midday heat worsened the effect

After hours of hiking I reached the halfway point. "You should see it from the ledge," Yva said in my memory. "If it's not there, just keep climbing."

I glanced up at the mountain peak. There was no way I was going any further. Not in my sweaty, feeble condition. My body couldn't take any more walking. It wasn't built for physical activity. If it wasn't on that ledge, it was lost forever.

I crawled and inched and scratched forward those last inches onto the ledge. My deep breaths competed with the thumping of my accursed heart inside my head. Between moments of exhaustion and excruciating muscle cramps, I rolled over onto my stomach and scanned the ledge below me. My eyes tracked across the tree line and systematically made my way back to the ledge. Then, I threw my gaze out into the horizon and repeated.

I saw it immediately; a rusted metal box about the size of a loaf of bread. Nasty tree sap covered the ignition switch. A rusted metal cog heaped with every manner of filth resided at its center. Gnarled branches warped the once majestic piece of Yva's ship. It teetered on the ledge cradled by two, thin branches. A swift gust of wind could send it falling into eternity.

I reached out with the tips of my fingers and grazed it. I struggled for every extra inch. The rustling shadows grew closer, yet I splayed more. I latched onto a precarious rock ledge with the sole of my shoe.

One final lunge and I clutched it in my hand.

*

I wibbled and wobbled, then steadied myself with a tree branch. I pulled myself in slowly. "Not a very good spot you're in," I heard behind me. It was the shadow. I recognized it immediately. Well, semi-immediately. Once it moved out of the light, its matted hair and grayed complexion; Creepy Gray Dude.

"Give it here, kid," he said. "I don't want no trouble. I just want the switch."

I clasped it tight. "You're not getting anything. Just go away."

He chuckled. "Come on, kid. You're a cripple. I'm not askin'."

"You're welcome to try and take it," I shouted.

Try he did. And succeed he did. He grabbed it from me against my entire might. I gave it a valiant effort. I lasted longer than he thought I could. Heck, I lasted longer than I thought I could.

But eventually he won, as was inevitable. All my kicking and screaming couldn't stop that. He had the ignition switch and he was gone.

"Come back here," I shouted after him, but he was gone. He ran down the hill and left me there; defeated and alone, a failure. I collapsed exhausted and thought of my failure. *What would I tell Yva?*

I hated disappointing her, mostly because of the look of hurt on her eyes when I came up wanting; partially though, because she would shred me down to size without mercy. Pop's condemnation meant I would hear it in stereo.

*

Yva got her quick wit from her mother and intelligence from her father. But she inherited her iron will and spirit from both of them. Neither were quick with a joke nor with their affection, but once they set their mind to something, it was as good as done.

They worked steadily on their ship for years. They plodded along carefully. They never took more than they needed. They never aroused suspicion. They kept to the dumps and bided their time. It would have driven lesser aliens crazy.

When Yva's mother became pregnant with her, it all changed. Their little hobby project they worked on little by little became prevalent and necessary to finish; imperative even.

Their misdemeanors became felonies. Her father broke into factories and took parts right off assembly lines. They stole military grade machinery and vandalized the weaponized police. They worked tirelessly until Yva's mother couldn't any more.

A month before Yva's birth, it was time. Launching into space was a tedious and lengthy procedure requiring permits and bureaucracy. Yva's parents had time for neither. They wouldn't let their daughter be born into their awful lives on their terrible planet.

The night they finished tightening the last bolts on their Frankenstein ship, her father wheeled it onto the roof of their secret machine shop and blasted off into the unknown. Thousands of onlookers gasped as they rose into the night sky.

That was the kind of will Yva inherited. That was the spirit. The spirit I had no interest in denting or tarnishing. It took me longer to get down the mountain than it did to get up it. I purposely lost myself in the trees three times and dragged my feet with every step. I wasn't in any rush to recount my monumental failure in the menial task assigned to me.

TWENTY-SIX

I heard Yva's voice ringing through my head as I trudged down the mountain. "You had one job: get a stupid, little box off a stupid, little mountain."

My heart didn't ache from exhaustion, just from of failure, and my head didn't pound, except for the pounding of worry. Thoughts of running away flittered through my head with every heartbreaking step but shook out as fast as they entered.

I thought back to Frank. He'd asked if I needed a hand, but I blew him off. He couldn't climb a mountain. He was a big tub of lard. He'd only grown heavier and more out of shape in the last several months. Climbing would kill him. It nearly killed me.

"I don't know why you keep helpin' that girl, anyway," he said. The bitterness of my ignoring him came through in spades.

"Well think of it this way," I responded. "I get this piece and she's that much closer to being out of your life."

"Yours, too," he said without a smile.

I chose not to think about that part; the part about Yva leaving. She'd leave anyway, when she knew I failed her. *Did I really try my hardest? Or did my fingers slide too quickly? Did I give up too easily? Did I want myself to fail? Did I will it to happen?*

Eventually, with my head slung low, I walked out of the woods empty handed. "You're back!" Yva exclaimed. "Are you okay? Where was it?"

It didn't take long for them to read my face and drop their faces. I failed them, miserably. I knew it. They knew it. Only they were too polite to say it.

*

On the ride home Pop didn't say a word. He didn't have to; disappointment oozed out of every pore. "It's okay, kid. Can't get them all. There's another way."

Yva asked me to recount the story to her, over and over in minute detail. She asked about the man, his fingers, his hair, and his skin. When she exhausted herself, she placed her soft finger on her still tender cheek.

"Why are you asking so many questions?" I asked. "Did you know the guy or something?"

She turned to the window. Her voice cracked. "Of course, I do. He's the one that sent me to the hospital." She rubbed her face. "He – he did this to me."

*

Some days it's hard to comprehend the evil in the world. There was so much. It seems so arbitrary. How it can skip one house, and one family, and hit another so hard?

First it was my mother – then my grandfather – then the love of my life. I watched other families. I heard them laugh and play. The Brewer kids were always so happy and playful with their new clothes and bright, white smiles. Cheerleaders seemed like they've got the world by the hojoes.

Even if they dealt with the occasional misery: the sometimes sickness, the once-in-a-while death, it didn't hit them like never-ending waves. It didn't drag them into the muck and the bile over and over. Then there were people connected to me, who drew sociopaths to them like magnets. There are people like Yva, who just can't seem to catch a break.

*

I took Yva in my arms and held her the whole bumpy way back from the mountain. How could a benevolent God disproportionately screw over such a small number of people? It wouldn't. Any benevolent God would look upon the crap salad of my loved ones and back off.

People often say, "there are no atheists in a foxhole." There are no atheists in a hospital either. There are no atheists when you're watching your mother struggle to breathe, or your friends die, or your grandparents die even. God always exists in the worst of times. As humans, it's in our nature. We have to have someone to beg or plead to and eventually blame.

I prayed to a useless God more times that I cared to remember. Even when I didn't believe in him, I still prayed for his help. When the ones you love are in pain, you will do anything, risk anything, believe anything for them to get better.

"God helps those that help themselves," people said. I could have prayed that the piece of garbage who hurt Yva and stole her ship piece got his comeuppance, or I could take action and teach him a lesson.

I chose the latter.

*

It wasn't until halfway through the quadrant that the life support blew on Yva's parents' ship. The trip took well into Yva's third year. It wasn't a glamorous life, but it was hers and she loved it. Yva's mother read to her all day and night. They played games, and sung, and loved.

They intended to stay with cousins on Andromeda's third moon, but a blown gasket derailed those plans. They had to land or risk drifting through the emptiness of the cosmos; even aliens can't survive the blackness of space.

Earth was the last place they wanted to raise a child, but it was a right bit better than an excruciating death in the cold vacuum of space.

A console fire on planetary entry took her father. Internal bleeding from the crash felled her mother. She was an orphan.

The change in atmosphere and sun color – or something – caused her to grow more quickly and heal more rapidly than on her home world – or so she thought. Honestly, it could have been a skill everybody had on her planet. There wasn't an owner's manual.

Yva only knew one thing for sure – she was wholly alone. Earth technology hadn't evolved to a level where it could rebuild her ship with our parts. They couldn't help her survive extended space travel. The few parts that could help were so safely guarded trying to get them would be suicide.

So, she scraped and scratched. She traveled the world until she found enough parts from the crash to rebuild her ship. It was a lonely, lonely existence for a child.

Yva didn't talk much about those days. When she did, they were throw-away tales. Once and a while she nearly formed the words raped, beaten, starved, captured, or molested to describe those days, but she couldn't bring the words to escape her lips. I respected her wounds and her desire to keep them buried. I wanted to help her. I wanted to know everything about her, but I let her keep the fleeting dignity which came from keeping those horrors secret.

*

I wrote down everything I knew about the Creepy Gray Dude since the first time I saw him at the hospital through the court house, and right on through our mountainside encounter. He smoked Lucky Strike cigarettes and drank Dunkin Donuts coffee. A couple of times he blew his nose with a Quiznos napkin.

I biked around for days scouting every shopping mall and strip mall in East Willow. There was only one place in town that had a convenience store, a DD and a Quiznos in the same shopping center. All I had to do was stake the place out for long enough and he was sure to amble through, for convenience's sake alone.

*

It took a few days, but he eventually showed. He slurped his coffee through a tiny straw and popped donut holes in his mouth a half-dozen at a time. He strode with a confident gait that belied a lifetime of worthlessness. His unfounded bravado sickened me.

He never saw me follow him. It was ironic that I stalked a stalker without incident, especially since he'd been so bad at following me. Twenty minutes later, I stood in front of his house; three streets down from mine and two blocks north.

It made sense. My neighborhood was the perfect combination of hard-working, lower-class families and criminal dirt bags. Pop was the former, CGD was the latter.

He lived in the worst house ever. It was no more than a shack in the middle of a burnt lawn; not burnt like yellow, unkempt grass; burnt like charred to embers. Condemned signs scattered the sidewalk and eviction notices plastered the front porch.

Most homeowners in our neighborhood took pride in their houses, small as they were. Their home was a reflection of them and they mostly reflected pride. I appreciated their blue-collar work ethic. They had little but took care of what they had.

Not CGD though. His home garnered contempt in the neighborhood. Pop talked about it a time or two with his harem of neighbors. I never thought anybody could actually live in such a hovel.

Houses tended to match their owners' personality, and CGD's was no exception; a crappy house and a crappy human being.

*

For three days, I watched him enter and exit before I mustered the courage to go inside. I didn't know how much time I had, but it didn't matter. I needed that switch. I needed to send Yva home, no matter the deep cost. That was true love at its core.

CGD's house was the WORST place in the entire galaxy, including Omicron Persii 8. Shanty towns in India had more charm and Chinese dirt farms more class. There was so much mold, feces, and dirt CGD must've hired a schizophrenic, monkey, serial killer as an interior designer.

The floorboards—where there were floorboards – warped into death spirals of terror, liable to buckle under the force of a light sneeze and send you crashing into the sub-basement. There were cords snaking all over the rickety floor boards of the hovel. They all branched off of stolen lines outside the window; cable and power among others. They connected to the few appliances he had, an old rotary phone, first generation Nintendo and an old, black and white, rabbit-eared TV.

The cords were thin and frayed save for one; one single cord bore the weight of the creaky window and trailed into the house's back room. I followed it into a bedroom adorned with wall to wall pictures of spaceships and celestial maps.

It finally dead-ended in the bathroom. Inside, that bathroom held a sight marvelous to behold: another spaceship, similar to Yva's yet smaller and more poorly constructed; like a baby's head alone could fit inside. Wires shot out from all angles and tangled through the cheaply constructed engine block. The ship seemed to be salvaged from only the loosest diagram, hidden deep within an addled mind.

Rotten wood enclosed the crudely-built structure and copper wire held it together; the wiring and wood that matched the pried-up floor board and gutted walls. It didn't take Pop's mechanical genius to figure out it would burn up or fall apart before it sniffed Earth's inner atmosphere.

*

My eyes tracked to a whirring sound from the center of the console. I recognized it instantly; ignition switch. He must've cleaned it up, because the rusted cog, that had adorned the center of the box, sat at the base of the tub in a heap, ready to be discarded.

I crept slowly into the room and pulled it free. That's when I saw him standing in the doorway: CGD.

"Give that here," he squeaked with a shrill voice. "It's rightfully mine. If there's one thing this backwater planet taught me it's that possession's 9/10ths of the law."

"Well it that case, it's mine," I responded.

He inched forward. "Not for long."

I was trapped. "What are you building in there? Spaceship? You an alien?"

"Duh." He chuckled. "You didn't think your precious girlfriend was the only alien on this hick rock, didya?"

"She's not my girl—but kinda—yeah—"

He hopped over a hole in the floorboards. The wood creaked when he landed. "Ignorant child. In a universe with a billion-billion galaxies, each of which with a billion-billion stars, you are arrogant enough to believe she alone inhabited this world made of psychotic apes. How very human of you; the fatal flaw of your worthless kind."

"If you hate us so much, why don't you just leave?"

"I've tried. Believe me I've tried. Your primitive technology isn't suitable for space travel. I'd die before I reached the outer reaches of your solar system. No aliens of consequence ever come here; ever cares about you stupid humans. I waited three decades with nothing to show for it. I found no sign of intelligent life. Then your little friend fell into my lap. A friend with a nearly functional space ship. Now, I can finally go home. SO GIVE THAT BACK TO ME!"

He reached out and latched onto my arm. I pushed him back with all my strength. He stumbled on the loose floorboards and lost his balance on a rickety beam. He fell backward on his ass and crashed into the sub basement. I didn't look back. My head pounded. If I didn't move fast, I'd pass out inside the house and all would be lost.

I didn't know where he was from or who he was, but I knew one thing; time was short. I had to get Yva off the planet now.

*

I ran home as fast as my terrible lungs carried me. Even when I crumpled into myself, I walked through the piercing pain, the heaving cough, and the spewing blood. By the time I arrived I was dizzy, weak, and about to pass out. I dragged myself across the grass and finally up to the door.

Pop and Yva sat in the living room, solely focused on the TV. I couldn't speak. I needed oxygen.

"You nearly scared us half to death!" Yva shouted. "Are you okay?"

I nodded and held up a finger. Any uttered word nearly guaranteed my collapse. So, they sat, and waited, anxious, for five full minutes while I sucked a tank dry. "We—have—go now."

"Chill out, kid," Pop said. "We got time. Just squat for a minute."

"Now. We have—to go now."

They didn't ask more questions. The burning in my eyes said it all. We piled into Pop's car, the switch tucked under my arm. By the time we turned the corner CGD came into view. He stood in the middle of the street, stoic.

"Gun it!" Pop nailed his foot on the gas and sped toward CGD, who dove out of the way at the last second.

*

The trek was arduous; more arduous than any other time I remembered. I was tired, weary, and barely able to stand by the end. Bile and blood coated my throat and my mouth. Spots formed in my eyes with every passing step, but I refused to yield.

In time, we reached the ridge and looked down. It was as beautiful as ever. At the bottom of the valley, Frank sat on guard.

"It's time," I shouted down at him.

A deep smile crept across Frank's doughy face. He'd been waiting for this moment forever: Yva gone, me back, and his guard duties alleviated. "Bloody brilliant. I don't think I could've stood here another bloody moment, mate."

Pop slid under the ship. His fingers carried the nimbleness of a man decades his junior. "Shouldn't take too long to power this baby up. Get ready with the key."

I looked at Yva in horror. "The key—?"

"You do have the key, right?" Yva said. "It was inside the ignition switch."

"I have no idea what a key would even look like. The only thing on that stake was a nasty-looking, rusted, metal cog."

"Yup. That's it. A metal cog. It plugs right into the center."

I knew exactly where it was: CGD's house, somewhere I had no interest going. "I'll find it. Pop, you keep working. Frank, come with me."

*

Pop barely heard me. His mind rested on his work. In his right mind, he never would let me lift the keys from his pocket and run off into the woods with them. Not in a million years. But that's what happened.

Frank and I scrambled back to the car and I climbed wearily into the driver's seat. Starting a car was so easy even a twelve-year-old could do it – especially one that's had prior practice in high-pressure conditions.

Frank would've made a better driver than a passenger being taller and all, but he straight refused. "You think I'm getting' in trouble for drivin' without a license? Not for that bird."

"Fine!" I guided the gear shift into reverse. *Steady*, I thought to myself. *Steady*. I eased out of the space with a couple of jerked stops and starts. "Am I straight?"

"You're good," Frank responded. "Now pop the car into drive."

The car lurched forward, and we eased down the street, Frank careful to direct me away from traffic. It must've been a sight to see, big ole lug talking to himself with a driverless car.

TWENTY-SEVEN

We jerked and jeered our way, burning the clutch to the ground and smoking the transmission, until we finally stopped in front of CGD's house. Walking might've been faster, since we kept forgetting to pop the clutch into second gear. The car stalled on us at least infinity times.

Inside the house was worse than my last encounter. Somebody smashed the TV, laid it on its side and gutted it. The Nintendo had been stripped for parts; the floorboards were in even greater disrepair.

I made my way to the bathroom. The ship was smashed into a million pieces. It didn't even look like a ship. It looked like a bad cabinet project gone wrong. Somebody destroyed it in a fit of rage. There wasn't a hint of CGD anywhere either. There wasn't even a hint of the discarded, rusted cog which would be my salvation.

I hoped he wasn't dumb enough to throw it away. I checked the trash cans inside and outside the house, but no sign of it. The only other option was CGD knew exactly what that cog was and kept it with him. If he knew where they were…that would be trouble.

I had to tell Yva and Pop and find CGD as fast as possible.

*

Frank and I kept mostly silent through the whole ride, except for a couple of directions from Frank. "Right here.", "Keep straight.", "Pull over in three lights."

We parked and hoofed it back to the ship with much difficulty. I heard the sound of the engine over the final ridge. The ship whirled and whizzed to life. Pop had done it.

We popped our heads over the ridge. The lights danced off the trees and the whirling of the engine echoed through the forest.

"Pop, you did it!" I shouted from the hilltop but got no response. He and Yva were mysteriously absent.

We stumbled down the ridge to see the lights twinkling every shade under the rainbow. "How did you do it without the key?"

"Oh, I have the key." CGD revealed himself behind the ship. "Just in time," he said. "I was about to take off. Of course, this is better. Now you can witness me killing your dear, old Pop and girlfriend first hand, instead of finding their charred bodies. They both spoke very highly of you—thought you might even save them. Guess they were half right. You came, but there ain't no savin' today."

"How did you find us?"

CGD waved something in the air. "You weren't very careful, were you?" My eyes focused on it: a map, my map of the town. I kept it in my back pocket next to the blueprint.

I patted all my pockets on instinct, but of course it wasn't there. It must've fallen out during our last encounter.

Dammit. Yva marked her ship on it, and it led CGD right to her. I led him right to his way off the planet and put my loved ones in danger. *Stupid.*

"Let them go," I shouted.

"Or what? You'll kill me, little, sick baby?"

"Try me. I'll make sure you never make it home again."

"You punk!" CGD lunged forward. Behind him, Yva and Pop revealed themselves, tied to adjacent trees underneath the ship. A sharp blast from the engines would char them to bits. *I couldn't let that happen.*

I swung my book bag at his fast approaching fist, so it connected with it instead of me. The oxygen tank hissed and connected with a thud. "Anger? I know anger. I can handle anger!"

"You son of a—" He rushed me again.

"Stay off of my son!" A blue streak rushed forward and knocked over CGD. It rolled across the ground. It was Dad, coming to save me.

"Frank!" I shouted. "Stop him!"

He popped his head over the embankment. "Which one?"

"Whichever one wins!" I ran toward Yva and Pop. "Are you okay?"

Pop's eye swelled and his nose bled. "I'm fine." I untied their knots and freed them. Yva fell into my arms. "I knew you'd come help us!"

Pop patted me on the back. "Good job, kid."

"We have to get you out of here," I said. "Now."

Yva ran toward the ship. "You don't have to tell me twice!"

*

I followed Yva into the ship and closed the door behind us. I felt pangs in my stomach. Pangs of loss. My family. Dad. Pop. Who knew if I'd ever see them again? Who knew where I'd end up; definitely not in East Willow, probably not in America, likely not in our solar system, possibly not even in the Milky Way.

CGD did the heavy lifting getting the ship ready for takeoff. He'd started the ship and primed the engine. All we had to do was lift off. Of course, Yva and I hadn't gotten that far yet.

"How do we get this off the ground?!?" Yva screamed.

"I don't know! I don't know!" I screamed back, pushing every button in sight.

I peered out the window. Frank tackled Dad. Pop socked CGD in the gut.

"Now or never!" I shouted.

Yva slammed her hand down on a large, blue button in the center of the steering column. The ship jerked forward, freeing itself from the branch it had called home for so many unknown nights.

"AGAIN!" I screamed.

She slammed her hand down again and we rose off the ground. She slammed, slammed, and hit. Hit and slammed. Up. Up. And up we went. After a few seconds, I no longer saw Dad. Or Pop. Or Frank.

*

We rose higher and higher into the air. I clutched with dear life onto the back of a seat. We were nearly into the cloud cover when the ship stalled—

—If there is a scarier feeling that an intergalactic space ship stalling out, I haven't found it.

Closer and closer we fell toward Earth. Yva kicked, punched, screamed, and shouted at the controls, but nothing happened. We whizzed past the arcade – snapping off their new antenna. "There's a big red X," she yelled. "I don't know what a big red X is, but it can't be good!"

The sirens started. And the ship screamed "WARNING! WARNING! WARNING!" All we could do was brace for impact. We wrapped ourselves in each other's arms and prayed.

"Our father who art in heaven, let us live!"

*

We crashed into the dump. Right into the disgusting muck I once pulled the bumper from so many moons ago.

I'd been in one other car crash in my life. I was nine, and we were coming home late from a restaurant. Or the movies. I think it might have been dinner and a movie. I forget which movie it was, but I know I was a kid and I liked it… so it was probably some sort of Muppet movie or something. We were halfway home with Dad shaking his head the whole time.

"That movie is a farce, son. There ain't no happy endings." Dad said. "There ain't no happy ending for Sammy or me or you."

"I know," Mom said.

"What do you mean, you know? What's that supposed to mean?" Dad swerved across the road screaming about being taken seriously. It was a real crap salad. All my mother wanted to do was agree and nip an argument in the bud before it could get started, get home, guzzle a bottle of wine, and pass out.

Instead, Dad slammed head first into a truck at fifty miles an hour. It crippled our little car and crumpled our front end. Air bags deployed, police rallied to the scene, paramedics checked us out. We spent the night in the ER. It was a show. It didn't hurt nearly as bad as crashing a spaceship into the ground.

*

We finally came to a stop in the middle of the dump. The crash jostled us around, and left us bruised, but neither of us died. "That sucked!" Yva screamed. "Are you alright?"

My head pounded. My lungs burned, and the trash stench invaded my nostrils. "I'm fine. You?"

She nodded. "I'm fine. Come on. Let's get out of here and survey the damage. The dogs will be on us soon and that crash must've alerted everybody in three counties. We don't have much time."

I pulled Yva out of the ship. "What do we do?"

"There has to be something. Something to tell us what that red x was, just look for it!"

We searched for an instruction manual, but there was nothing to find. "There has to be something. Something we missed," I muttered.

"Duh! How about we don't state the obvious," she responded.

There was no manual. No instructions. No glove compartment. There was nothing. Nothing except a red X.

Then I saw it; buried in the corner of a luggage compartment: maximum capacity a crosshatched dog with four fingers, more commonly known on Earth as one hundred thirty-eight pounds.

"We're over capacity," I said.

"What does that mean?" Yva asked.

"I can't go with you."

We didn't know until that second that being together in the vastness of space was all we'd ever wanted. It didn't matter though. It could never happen now. "You have to get out of here, quickly."

 Yva grabbed my hand. "There has to be a way. I don't want to go alone."

I shook my head. "We'll stall out if we try it again. You have to go without me."

"I could stay here forever, let Creepy Gray Dude have the ship and forget about leaving."

"Is that what you want? What you really want? Because it's what I really want; to be with you."

She sighed. Her eyes met mine. "I'm going to miss you, Sam. I never thought I would miss anything about this planet."

"I brought you something," I told her. "To remember me by."

I pulled out my logbook, the one I used to track her movements so many moons ago. I'd grabbed it on my way out of the house and hid it in the back of my pants. I didn't need it anymore. I would always remember her, every day in every moment, in every tree and every shop, in Barry's and in the junkyard, in everything. But she would need something to remember me by as she flew through the sky. "Don't think too little of me when you read it. In fact, promise not to read it until you're far past our solar system."

"I promise," she said. "I got you something too."

She placed her hand on my heart. The warmth from her hand pulsed through me. And then she kissed me; a real kiss. It lingered. I felt the warmth all over. She pulled me close, and it seemed to last forever.

"You know, my name's not really Yva either."

"It was a dumb name anyway."

"I am called Kalei."

"That's even dumber."

She smiled. "This isn't goodbye, Sam. Remember me."

She kissed me softly again. I closed my eyes. When I opened them again, I was alone, and she was gone. And her ship was gone. I was alone. In the dump. And for the first time I smelled it. I really smelled it. It smelled terrible.

TWENTY-EIGHT

Mom found me bawling like a baby in the garbage dump. She wiped my nose and brought me inside. It was the end. A fitting end to a terrible year.

She was battered, bruised, and tired. She had close to 20 jobs in the year since I met Yva, she separated from her husband, moved back with her awful father, and taken every denigrating, demoralizing thing that paid any bills.

"I'm tired, kiddo," she confided in me. It reminded me of the first night at Pop's, when she made sure I wasn't gonna die of some infection. "I'm real tired."

Her eyes sunk, bagged from a long trip, blackened by the past year. I'd been so caught up in my own stuff that I didn't notice her, and she didn't notice me. "Everything's going to be alright now, kiddo."

"No, it's not."

She shook her head. "No. It's not. But it will be."

I sat up for a while after she went to bed, thinking and drifting back to Yva. I thought about the previous year. I thought about Yva's parents and the sacrifices they made. And I cried. I cried for Mom, and for Yva, and for families everywhere.

*

The next day I woke up heart-broken. My lungs felt even worse now that I had nothing to look forward to in my crappy, little life. I could have died right there.

But I didn't. That would have been too fair. Instead, I trudged out of the house and off to school. I didn't see Pop, Mom, or Frank on my way. I thought it funny that they might have disappeared into the stratosphere like Yva but knew that to be impossible. They must have been at work, or some other place.

It was my last week of school, so there was a little spring in my downtrodden step. I knew we'd be moving soon after, to another school, but I was determined to make the most out of the last few days, try to get my mind off my problems.

I wasn't given the chance. The principal's assistant steered me into her office the moment I stepped through the door. Sitting in the room was Mom and Pop. The principal stood behind her desk.

"Good morning, Sammy," she started. "I'll keep this short and sweet. Your mother came in this morning with a fantastical story. She was worried and wanted to know if I'd seen anything that could warrant a break from reality."

"I didn't quite use those words—" Mom interjected.

"Of course, you didn't, dear, but no need to beat around the bush." She walked toward me. "The truth is that I've always found you odd, a bit of a problem child and what not, but never somebody having a psychotic break."

"I'm not—" I said.

"Now, now. Don't be rude. Let me finish" She paced around me. "The truth is, though, the more she told me, the more I began picking through the pieces and made some startling discoveries."

"Oh yeah, what's that?"

"Well, I asked around, and your teachers said you talked about a kid named Frank all the time. She assumed it was somebody from home that went to a different school since she always saw you alone, but I figure you're talking about Frank Bennett, right? The fat child who bullied you earlier this year?"

"He didn't bully me. He was my friend."

"He hasn't gone here since the day he harassed you. We have a zero-tolerance policy for things like that. I believe they shipped him back to Australia soon after."

It couldn't be true. I didn't believe it. But she opened the file and there is was. He was suspended pending expulsion, and officially expelled two weeks later.

"As for this Yva character, there's never been anybody enrolled here by that name. I pride myself on knowing all my students and I've never seen anybody matching her description before."

"That's ridiculous! I know she exists. Pops. Tell her. Tell her!"

Pop looked toward the floor. "I never saw her, kiddo."

"What about the ship? The parts?"

Pop shrugged. "It looked like a cool science experiment or somethin'. I wanted to help. Those schematics were nothing. I was just making it up as I went for you. I let it go too far."

"So, none of you believe that…What about the fight? You were caught by CGD."

Pop shook his head. "Never happened, kiddo. I was home watching TV all night 'til I fell asleep."

It was no use. There was nothing I could say or do. Which is how I ended up in the loony bin.

*

I never shied away from a good poke and prod. At least the physical ones. They were tolerable. There was plenty of that in the looney bin – blood tests, and saliva tests, poop tests, pee tests, and all sorts of really gross tests – but mostly it was prodding my mind.

They asked me feeling questions, and sensing questions, and questions that quacks ask after too much schooling. *"Why do you think this happened?"*, *"How do you feel about your mother?"*, and *"What do you think that meant?"*, and other banalities I'd rather not remember.

They made me cry, they sometimes even made me laugh, but mostly they just made me angry.

Angry because they denied my life; my experiences. They told me I made it up. They thought everything I experienced in the past year was a lie – that I was a liar.

No matter how much evidence they presented to the contrary, I tried to fight it. I hated liars more than anything. I fought and fought, defending my truth, for as long as I could.

I was only supposed to be on a 72-hour hold, but my insistent stubbornness kept me there for two full weeks.

They showed me pictures of the spaceship, still pristine in its tree stump, nothing but a pile of garbage molded into a sculpture of a ship, put together by a kid having a mental breakdown.

They showed me video of Frank, admitting to not knowing me, and they showed photos of my father date and time stamped in such a way that he couldn't possibly be in the state to help me fight CGD because he was ten states away getting arrested.

They showed me condemned and empty photos of the house that housed CGD, and neighbors who testified that there was never anybody staying there even for one day in the past year. Still, I held out. For a time at least.

*

It got harder and harder to deny it over time. But it's not like their story was any less fantastical.

I couldn't believe that I'd built a junker in the woods and not remembered it. I couldn't believe that I could build a spaceship in a condemned building without even the slightest recollection. I couldn't believe I walked or stumbled home from the woods to the junkyard without even a hint or a whiff of an idea. Mostly, I couldn't believe I had the stamina to do it all without dying.

*

Eventually, my mind collapsed in upon itself. I dreamt of Heaven and Hell, cosmos and Earth, the beginning of time and the end. It was then I allowed for the possibility that I was crazy, that the year wore on me, that it was my way of coping. It was my neurotic break. Yet another diagnosis in a long string of diagnoses.

But still, in the back of my mind, still to this day, I still can't help but think it was real, just for a moment, every now and then.

*

By the time they'd released me, we'd lost the house. They scheduled an auction post haste and three months later a very nice Indian couple moved in with their two children.

Their kids now shared the same room I shared with Mom. I drove by there when I aged into a car properly. They painted the shutters blue and fixed the grass. Pop's pace marks vanished from the lawn along with any trace of him. Without a trace of any of us.

The train still ran throughout the day. Sometimes I went behind the house and left pennies on the tracks for them. I still marveled at the beauty pressure could bring.

*

Pop decided to move into a nursing home. He loathed the idea, but by going in a home with his wits about him, he got to pick a good one, instead of being stuck with one that wraps you in a diaper and throws you in front of a TV. Every Wednesday, he went to see his harem and every Thursday he came over for dinner.

He never explained what he saw in the woods. He never explained the blueprints. He never explained what he did with that ship or how he helped make it work. He only said he wanted to be with me and it seemed like the only way. I felt bad that I'd left him no option but to lie to me for my attention.

*

Mom went back to school and got her nursing degree. How did she afford it? A hefty lawsuit won from Dr. Phil for discrimination and sexual harassment. Apparently, he'd fondled Mom on more than one occasion. That's the reason his previous nurse had hated him and why she quit. She made a great character witness. The settlement was enough to clear any outstanding debt and then some. Since we didn't have the house anymore it was all ours.

She moved into an apartment across town and got a job as a school nurse in my high school. She got to keep tabs on me, which brought her endless joy.

Most kids would have been embarrassed of their mother being so close, but I liked it. Now, whenever I needed shots or something, I already knew the annoying nurse. We ate together every day. Our relationship grew. Her callouses broke and she even grew to tolerate the world.

*

High school changed me. I got all the rebellion out of my system with Yva. I didn't need to curse the system. I didn't need to fight school. Middle school didn't much matter in the grand scheme, but high school mattered plenty. I wanted to go to college. I wanted to live long enough to go to college.

*

Now I'm a freshman art major. I figure head cases are welcome in the art department. A little crazy might even be a prerequisite.

But that doesn't change the fact that I'm a sickly, neurotic mess that's still a little in love with a figment of my imagination, one I have a hard time forgetting most days. It's a lot to keep track of, especially since I'm not the smartest guy in the world.

*

So, I have to ask you one last time. Are you sure you still want to date me, even after all this time? Even after I came clean? I mean this is a lot for somebody to take in after only three months.

*

I told you before, idiot. I love you no matter what. Nothing's going to change that.

*

Oh. Oh really? Well, I love you too.

*

Just promise me you won't murder me in my sleep, okay?

*

I think I can manage that. You really have low standards, you know?

*

If you like this book, try *My Father Didn't Kill Himself,* a mystery novel told all in blog posts and set in East Willow, just like *Sorry for Existing.*

*

Now, here is a sample from *My Father Didn't Kill Himself.*

MY FATHER DIDN'T KILL HIMSELF

By:

Russell Nohelty

Edited by:
Melissa Van Natta

Additional Editing by:
Gretchen Sparkman

Proofread by:
Katrina Roets

Cover by:
Paramita Bhattacharjee

SITTING SHIVA

Posted by Delilah Clark × September 24 at 9:27 am.

Chunks of time are missing. Alex has been here, by my side, every step of the way. She's the only connection with reality I have left. She keeps pinching me to keep me awake.

That's the only way I know this isn't a dream. It's a living nightmare. Most of my time is spent staring at a wall in my living room doing something called "sitting shiva".

Basically, in Jewish tradition, immediately after a death, extended family sits in their deceased relative's house for a week and receives visitors. It's annoying and I want them all to leave. Only four more days left.

You're also supposed to bury the dead immediately, but Mom refused that little tidbit as a giant jab to grandma's side.

She had to be polite, for dad's sake. She would let them invade her house. There was nothing she could do about that, but her seething bitterness made her not schedule the funeral until after shiva was good and sat.

She hates dad's family, and they hate her.

My family's never been very religious. We've never been very family oriented, aside from the three of us. I'd never so much as spoken with a cousin on the phone until yesterday.

According to the scuttlebutt, my grandmother banished my dad from the family for marrying a Gentile or something like that.

At least that's what I've gathered from my seemingly endless conclave of previously unknown relations that have descended upon my peaceful house. The story seems to hold together because whenever my mother enters the room, my grandmother curses under her breath.

My poor mother. God love her. I don't believe she's said a word in days. She walks around in a trance—a waking daze.

Every once in a while, she'll enter the living room with a tray of food or some drinks, but otherwise she sits in the kitchen alone, smoking and drinking. I didn't know she'd ever smoked. I don't have the heart to tell her how much I hate it.

Meanwhile, I'm left glad-handing every jerk that walks through the door.

I'm as cordial as the next person, but after my dad dies, the last thing I want is to hang out with a bunch of people placating me and trying to make me feel better. So, the fact that our house has been brimming with guests for the past few days is extremely unwanted.

"His laugh was infectious," Mrs. Turnbell said. She never liked my father and frankly we never liked her either. As the head of the housing association, she cited my father for every minor infraction in the book. And now she was being nice to me? No thanks.

I told her Alex had pissed on her flowers and she stormed away in a huff. Alex overheard me and stormed off the other way. For one glorious moment, I was alone. But it didn't last long. Two seconds later a new murder of cackling crows descended upon me.

People like that came out of the woodwork—people that once had a grudge against my dad or a grudge against my family. People who thought they knew us, but all they'd done was live across the street for ten years without so much as a peep. His coworkers, some of them crying, others baking their feelings away. The fake sincerity and concern boiled my blood. By the end of the first day, I never wanted to see another living soul again. Now I'm numb to it. I just want it to be over.

Worst of all, I hate the conversations with total strangers.

"Your father was a great guy," Janie, his deskmate, said, as if that meant anything.

"He always kept his desk so neat," his boss, Edward, told me. Like that would make me feel better. As he spoke, I focused on the single piece of dandruff on his shoulder. How does one get a single piece of dandruff?

The only halfway-interesting person that came through was Jeremiah. He stopped by once, high as a kite. I think he saw the free food and thought it was a dinner party.

When he realized why we were gathered, the look of shock on his face was priceless. He ran out and returned with a gift for the house.

A parrot. A no joke parrot.

He said it helped him through his parents' death. He said he was sorry.

Jeremiah called my family "man" a lot, shook their hands one by one, and then hugged my grandmother. It was a lovely disaster. Then he left as mysteriously as he came, leaving me with a parrot.

Everything the parrot says is gibberish, except the word "death". It repeats the word death day and night.

I was already having fitful sleep, and the squawking through the night isn't helping matters.

So, I pawned it off on my cousin. Let it keep my pompous Aunt Patty up for rest of its godforsaken life.

SHIVA

Posted by Alex Dewitt × September 24 at 8:10 am.

Delilah hasn't eaten since her family came to town. It's just been a constant barrage of questions, comments, sidebars, and bitterness. I never knew people could come together for such a somber occasion and bring so much hate.

I don't have much family. I'm pretty much a lone wolf, except for the few times I see my parents when they breeze through town, and our summer trips out of the country.

Delilah's family is the only family I know. Tim was kind and funny, Kendra, caring and loving. Doting even.

Kendra and Tim told Delilah she could do anything, and they believed it. My mother never told me that. She told me I could do better, even when I won gold. "That's nice, dear," she said. "Only one?"

Kendra loves life though, really and truly. Delilah was a daddy's girl, for sure, but her mother often shopped with her, went to lunch with her, and even cuddled in bed with her while her father was away.

"You can do anything," was Kendra's motto. "Never stop believing," was Tim's motto. The best thing I could say about either of them is that they filled the world with joy.

I don't know how they did that, since they came from such cold and distant families. Families that seem to relish putting each other down.

Now everything has changed, and I have to be there for
them, like they have for me. I'm over there a lot. I sleep when
I can, but mostly I just sit around for moral support. I don't
want them going off the deep end or doing anything crazy.

DAD'S CASE

Posted by Delilah Clark × *September 25 at 7:48 pm.*

When I returned home from school today, the detective
handling my father's case was sitting at our dining room table,
filling Mom in on the latest developments.

She was crying. She was always crying.

The rest of the family watched from the corners of their eyes,
trying to be inconspicuous, but failing miserably. They're
unbearable. I can't wait 'til I can kick them to the curb.

Two more days.

I sat down next to my mother and listened to the detective. I
honestly couldn't believe the police department would let
anybody so young detect anything, let alone head up a murder
investigation.

If his badge didn't flash every time he turned the page on his
notebook, I would swear that he was one of Jenny's friends
pulling a cruel, fast one on us.

He explained to my mother that since she refused to consent
to an autopsy, some piece of Jewish law mom doggedly
agreed to for some reason, they had concluded their
investigation.

I begged her to reconsider; told her that it could help the
case, but she was unrelenting. She said she needed to "keep
the peace", and that it "wouldn't do any good". It's crap, but
I have no power. I have no power to do anything.

The detective used a lot of fancy words and police jargon, but it was all to mask a simple conclusion. Without an autopsy, they determined that my father's death was a suicide.

I flipped out. Like kirked totally and completely out.

I KNOW that is a ridiculous accusation. My dad certainly didn't die of natural causes, but in my heart of hearts, I knew he hadn't committed suicide either. There's a lot I don't know, but I'm 100% positive on that one.

My dad didn't commit suicide, for sure. If he didn't die of natural causes, he was murdered. I don't care what anybody says. I don't care about some stupid report, or the facts of the case as they stand now. I only know one thing: my dad was murdered.

Suicide wasn't in his blood. He's never been the type to cut and run. I mean, Jesus Christ! I saw him hours before his death.

He was laughing at dinner and talking about how big they made pancakes in some stupid YouTube clip he watched.

After dinner he made us watch it, twice. That pancake really was something to behold. It fed 30 people.

That's not what a suicidal guy does, you know.

I will go to my grave knowing that my dad wasn't cowardly enough to commit suicide.

And as I watched the young detective walk out the door, I made a pact with myself: if it takes 'til my dying breath, I'll make him believe my dad was murdered, too.

BLACK
Posted by Delilah Clark × September 27 at 11:01 am.

I looked at myself in the mirror last night and hated everything about myself.

I didn't feel like a blonde.

Blondes are chipper and nice. They wear pink and go to sporting events to support their friends.

They drink rape juice and flirt with boys in orange hats.

I don't want to do any of that.

Every strand of my hair belied who I was and how I felt.

So, I dyed it.

Black.

It looks great now.

I can't wait to see people's reactions.

*

If you liked this sample, make sure to pick up *My Father Didn't Kill Himself* today.

ALSO BY RUSSELL NOHELTY

NOVELS AND CHILDREN'S BOOKS

My Father Didn't Kill Himself

The Freeman Files

Katrina Hates Everything

The Little Bird and the Little Worm

Gumshoes: The Case of Madison's Father

The Katrina Series

The Lobdell Chronicles

The Vessel

The Pixie Dust Series

The Invasion Saga

The Marked Ones

Worst Thing in the Universe

GRAPHIC NOVELS AND COMIC BOOKS

Ichabod Jones: Monster Hunter

Katrina Hates the Dead

Gherkin Boy

Pixie Dust